CAVERN OF LIES

A.N. SAGE

CONTENTS

Chapter One

River

The beast roared and snapped its teeth at Savannah, causing her to shrink even further into the corpse of trees she cowered behind. I could feel warm saliva drip down its chin. My chin. It was an impossible adjustment to get used to, but as soon as I heard her scream my name, I knew what happened. My damn shifter side triggered and whatever I was seconds ago, wasn't who was standing before her. This new version of me scared my friend so much, she was actually crying, and crying was not something Savannah did well. Her gooey mascara ran down her face, making her look like a sideshow carnival extra. It wasn't a good look and if we would get out of this, I was pretty certain she'd rip me a new one for ruining her makeup.

Another roar left my mouth before I could stop it and she fell back, her eyes never leaving mine.

Panicked, I looked around and tried to force the beast to calm down, but the more I fought against it, the more adamant it became. And the more hungry. That was the part I feared the most.

Savannah's gaze darted to the left, and I knew she was looking to flee. That was a mistake. As soon as she showed any movement, the beast clenched its jaw shut and dug its disgusting paws into the ground, ready to attack.

I wanted to scream for her to stop, to not make any sudden movements, but whatever I had turned into had full control now and I was just a bystander in the entire sordid affair. Leave it to me to end up in this position. Mom did always say that I had a knack for being in the wrong place at the wrong time, and this time, I sure as shit agreed with her. My heart shivered when I thought of my mom. Even after everything she'd done to hurt me and my friends, to hurt Billie, I couldn't bring myself to hate her. Guess she was lucky I hadn't shifted back at Savannah's farm when she showed up to end Billie's life because I would have ripped her jugular off, no questions asked. Anything to save Billie.

Come on, love. Where are you? I need you back.

The air cooled around me ,and droplets of rain fell down the beast's fur from the incoming storm. It shook its hide, rattling my bones, and stomped the ground again. *Cocky asshole.*

By the look on Savannah's face, it was clear she knew she was in trouble. There was no talking to me anymore and despite myself, every part of my body wanted to tear her to pieces. I could taste her fear from where I crouched, and it brought me more joy than I cared to admit. She wasn't my best friend anymore. She was prey.

Rain plummeted on my head and its frigid wetness sent me spiraling. The beast smacked its jaw together and trained its eyes on her thin frame, kicking back its hind legs in a show of superiority. It was a pointless move, Savannah knew she had no chance here. I knew it too. She screamed and the beast took a step forward. Its muscle-stacked, fur-covered body vibrated as I struggled to hold it back from lunging, but I was too weak. Too weak and too confused about what I could do to control it. I should have listened to the other shifters in the house and let them walk me through this shift, but you know what they say about ignorance being bliss. I thought if I ignored it, it would all go away. Like I could somehow prevent what was happening to me from becoming true. Now, crouching in the middle of the woods at night with Savannah's paling face before me and that wretched red glow surrounding her body, I knew I was dead wrong.

I had the chance to change how this played out and I chose wrong. If I did anything to hurt Savannah now, I would pay for it for the rest of my life.

She let out a whimper and that was all it took.

Before I could stop myself, I lunged for her, my eyes narrowing on the red glow. Leaves and mud kicked back behind me as I ran toward her, and I could feel every taut muscle pound the ground in my wake. Savannah whirled on her heels and bolted into the forest, but there was no escaping the beast. It could see her, and the heat of her body clear as daylight. A beacon in the night. A target for its hunger.

In one swoop motion, I leaped over a fallen tree trunk and flew in the air, landing on all four of my paws with ease.

The trees were denser here and shielded me from the rain, but in the distance, I could hear thunder roar and it increased the raging energy within me. I jerked my head right and left until I spotted the glow and ran in its direction. As I neared it, I noticed Sav wasn't moving. She wasn't breathing either, or else I'd hear it rumble through the trees. I could hear everything so clearly now it was maddening. Every crunch of leaves under my paws and every owl hoot in the distance. It was like I was a part of the forest, and I reveled in its whispers as I took a few more steps to where she hid. Her body trembled with fear, and she had a hand clasped over her mouth to keep from screaming. A smart move if someone was chasing you, except this time, it wasn't just anyone on her tail. It was me and my beast, and one of us was not as easy to deflect as the other.

Savannah froze and her eyes met mine.

Run! I wanted to yell, but instead, I let out an agonizing howl and jumped.

My body soared toward her and as her eyes widened, I tried to shut my own to stop from seeing what was about to happen. What I was about to do. My paws dug into her shoulders, pinning her to the ground. Savannah's body wrestled against me, but I was so much stronger than her, it was almost laughable. The beast opened its jaw and shot for her neck, and my stomach turned.

Under me, Savannah screamed and shut her eyes tight.

Please, help me.

Something heavy knocked into my side and pushed me off her, and while the beast screamed into my head to fight back, I was relieved. I fell to the ground, paws jerking to get up as soon as my back hit the mud. My eyes snapped to the attacker, or savior in this case, and I let out a sigh. Before me, Raiden's lion towered in the woods and his broad build hid Savannah from view. I heard other voices close to us and the beast righted itself to stand as I smiled deep inside.

Its paws tensed and it clenched its teeth, growling at Raiden in the forest's darkness. If the beast attacked now,

Raiden would put it down in an instant and at that moment, I wasn't sure I would care much either way.

"Fight it, River," someone said behind the lion.

My neck swiveled to see Mel's purple head of hair pop up from behind Raiden's mane, and when she took a step in, I growled louder. Her one hand pressed against Raiden's side, and she held something buzzing with electricity in her other. *A freaking Taser? Are you guys kidding me right now?* That shit was going to hurt.

Mel's head cocked to the side and she half-smiled. "Fight it. Think of what matters."

The only thing I could think of was hunger, and I sure as hell knew that couldn't be what mattered. Inside me, the beast screamed to be set free, but the human part of my brain fought for a solution. *Think, you dumb bastard! If you attack, you're dead. Moron.* My words seemed to resonate because the beast relaxed its paws and shook its furry head. Questions lingered in my brain, but they were not my own. It was like the beast was asking me for permission to hurt them and I would not allow it.

Oh, now *you listen! But when you're about to kill my best friend, nothing.*

I steadied myself and the beast tilted its head to the side like a dog trying to understand a command. *Pay... attention...* It growled again, but I stood strong, though that didn't last long. Whatever strength and bravery I had left dissipated when the first bone cracked. My body jerked and the beast let out another howl before hitting the ground. Blazing heat tore through me, and I gritted my teeth to stay quiet. Crack by crack, each bone in my body broke and reformed until I was nothing but a mess of limbs on the ground. My skin tightened over my new form, and I shuddered as raindrops fell on me. Every drop felt like someone lit a cigarette and put it out on my flesh, and I screamed over and over as the beast left me. Convulsing, I turned to my side and hugged my legs in as though it would make anything better.

It didn't.

"Whoa!" Peyton's cheerful voice echoed over me, but my vision was too blurry to see her clearly. "Billie is one lucky girl!"

The sound of her name brought new pain and more torture. Billie was kidnapped, taken from right under our noses while we were busy with some damn party, and it was all my fault. I should have stayed glued to her freaking side instead of spending time talking to the shadowers in the resistance. Instead, I let myself relax and now, my girl was paying the price. My eyes wetted and tears flooded my already useless vision as I turned my head, stifling a sob. Digging my fingers into the dirt, I tried to level myself to rise, but my muscles were too weak to cooperate. There were footsteps somewhere in the distance, though I couldn't make out anyone's voice. Billie's face clouded my vision and I grunted as the reality of the situation sank in. She was gone and I almost killed my best friend. This was by far the worst night of my life.

"Get some clothes on him and let's get him back to the house," someone said. Raiden maybe?

The last thing I felt was rough material covering my midsection and firm hands wrapping around my chest to drag me away.

I didn't fight back, and I didn't make a sound. There was no use of it. My life was already torn to pieces.

Chapter Two

River

"And we're sure someone took her?" Peyton asked, her eyes never leaving mine. Even though it had been hours since my first shift, she still refused to stop watching me.

Billie was right, Peyton would make one hell of a leader for the shadowers, the group of supernatural creatures the witches created in some misguided attempt to form an army. Though, since I was officially a shapeshifter, I supposed that included me as well. *Wait, is Peyton my boss now?* I had a hard time wrapping my head around that fact, so instead, I shot a petty smile her way and turned to our friends.

After Raiden and Mel, the shifter leaders in the resistance group we were a part of, dragged me to the house and made sure I wasn't about to freak out and shift again, they called the witch hunters in to watch over me. I understood the logic of keeping my friends close, but I didn't need babysitters. What I needed was to find out who took Billie and to get her back and having them around to worry over me was not doing anyone any favors. I never thought I'd see the day when I was grateful that Tyler and Abigail were still in the hospital, but right now, it was four fewer eyes watching my every move and it felt like a small win. Guilt invaded my senses as soon as I thought it and I shook it off, choosing instead to focus on Savannah.

She leaned against a shadowed wall in the small room we gathered in and refused to meet eyes. *Just perfect.*

I straightened my shoulders and the soreness from the shift returned in spades. "Billie wouldn't disappear like that. Someone has her. Plus, her phone is dead, and she never turns that thing off."

"Who? Who would take her and why?" Morgan asked.

She tightened her hold on Peyton's hand and I arched an eyebrow their way, then turned to Jayden. The goofy grin on his face told me he noticed it too, and we would definitely talk about it later. I had no intention of getting in the middle of my friend's dating life, but Peyton and Morgan getting together bought happiness to Billie, which meant it mattered to me too. The girls leaned into each other and I tried to suppress my jealousy with little success. *Where are you, love?*

"What did Raiden and Mel say about it?" Savannah asked.

We all looked to her. "Why them?"

"Um, hello? Didn't that Damen moron attack you guys in a clearing and threatened to get her or some crap? Prime suspect number one, don't you think?"

She had a point. A good one at that. Raiden's cousin was one sick bastard, and he was angry enough to do something like this, but after Billie and I killed his two friends, the leaders locked him up in a cell and we heard nothing since. We also didn't get any other threats, so all of us simply assumed everyone was on board with Billie. What was it they say about assumptions? That they make an ass out of you and me? I was sure feeling like a huge ass in that moment. "He's locked up somewhere," I said, grimacing. "And last I heard, Raiden made sure it stayed that way. It couldn't have been him. But maybe he had other friends we didn't know about."

"Well, what other shifters hate the witches enough to do this?"

Everyone looked to me, and I sank in my seat. Their eyes pinned me in place and a small part of me wanted to rip them out of their sockets. The shifter part, no doubt.

"How should I know?"

I forced my gaze away from my friends and looked out the window. Night had settled over the house, and I saw shadows zoom by from the incessant patrols Lorelei set in place after we realized Billie was taken. Somehow, I knew the patrols wouldn't make a difference. Whoever took her got what they came for, and they weren't coming for us any time soon.

Peyton left Morgan's side and came to stand beside me. Her dark-lined eyes narrowed into slits as she took me in. "Can you find out?"

I nodded.

"Good. That's a good start." She smiled. "We need to get to her before..."

Her voice trailed off and emptiness filled me. We all knew what she wanted to say, something the rest of us were unwilling to admit. Whoever took Billie didn't just snatch her for a freaking tea party. She was in danger, and without knowing who the asshole was that kidnapped her, we were as useless as a canoe without a paddle.

In other words, we were screwed, and we knew it.

Bile pushed its way up my throat, and I swallowed the acidity down with a loud gulp. I would find Billie if it was the last thing I did, even if I had to tear every shifter in this house into shreds.

"I'll get Raiden to help question the shifters. Lorelei too," I whispered.

Warm fingers pressed on my shoulders, and I turned to see Jayden towering over me. "Don't stress, bruh. Billie is one badass chick, she'll be fine."

"We don't know that," I hissed.

"Dude, please! She took down the High Coven like she was swatting flies. If anyone messes with your girl, they're gonna get their asses handed to them on a platter."

Let's hope so. "So, what do we do now?"

The room grew silent, and my friends took turns looking at anything else but me. I didn't need to ask what they were thinking. Their faces said it all. There was absolutely nothing we could do now. Peyton had already tried to find anyone that might have noticed the girl that lured Billie away from the party, but no one had seen her. Whoever this kid was, she was a ghost. Most of the kids in the house didn't recognize her description and those that thought they had, raised even more questions. I shouldn't have expected much more. These were kids, after all. Kids that were too busy playing with their friends to pay attention to anything around them.

Guilt was eating me up by the second and I pushed my chair back to stand, needing to do something with my body other than slouch over the old mahogany table. As I circled the room, my gaze met Savannah's and she turned away in an instant.

Reluctantly, I approached her, and it shocked me when she didn't back away.

"Sav, listen," I started, but she cut me off.

"Don't worry about it. It wasn't you, I get it."

I frowned. "That's still no excuse. I'm really sorry. I seriously don't understand what happened and you have to know I tried to fight it. I-It wasn't me."

"It *was* you," she said with a smirk. "The new and improved River."

"HA! Improved is not exactly how it felt."

"So, how *did* it feel, wolf boy?"

Memories of her crying face and the hunger I felt flashed before me, and I closed my eyes to wipe them from view. How did it feel? What a loaded question. What was I supposed to tell her? That I wanted to kill her and that a part of me liked it? Nothing would change what happened in the woods, but I sure knew I couldn't tell her how it really felt when I was inches away from her throat and about to taste her blood on my tongue. As if in response, the beast inside me growled and disgust filled my gut. The new reality I was in was not something I wanted to deal with, at least not until we found Billie. She would know what to do, she always did, and it was one of the reasons I loved that girl so much. Jayden was right, she was strong as hell and if anyone would survive this, it was Billie.

I opened my eyes and faced Savannah. "That is not what we're calling me now."

To my surprise, she threw her head back and laughed, easing some of my tension.

"What would you prefer? Cujo?"

"So much better." I smiled. "Let's not forget you still owe me for the crap you put Billie through."

Savannah's face darkened, but she didn't speak, and I knew I won that round. It was a cheap shot but as far as I was concerned, when your best friend tries to break up your relationship, you could hold a grudge for as long as you needed. It was in the friendship handbook.

"I'll talk to Lorelei, see if we missed anyone else from the party," Peyton said. "And I'll keep pushing about the kid that was with her that night."

In seconds, Morgan was by her side with her arm on Peyton's lower back. "I'll come with you."

The two left, leaving only me, Jayden, and Savannah in the musty room. My thoughts were still jumbled from the shift, but I refused to let it bother me. Whatever issues I had with the dumb wolf that shared my body would have to wait. Finding Billie was a priority, and I wouldn't sleep until we had a trail to follow. Someone in this damn house must have seen something, and there was no doubt in my mind that the shifters were involved somehow. Whether or not I was one of them, they made a colossal mistake going after my girl.

The door creaked and we all turned to see Raiden's bald head poke through the opening. His posture was as stoic as ever, but something lurked behind his eyes that made my gut twist in agony.

"What is it?" I asked, examining the shifter leader.

Raiden's brow furrowed and he looked from me to my friends. "We found tracks in the woods, near to where you found Marcus' journal. Animal tracks."

My eyes grew in size and my teeth snapped.

"I knew shifters were involved," I bit out.

"Let's not jump to conclusions," Raiden argued. "There are plenty of tracks in that forest, it might not be related."

It only took a few short strides to reach him, and I was

pushing my way past the giant to leave. "I'll be the judge of that. I'm checking these out for myself. Join me or not, your call."

Storming past him, I tore through the house and raced outside. Whatever Raiden thought, these tracks were our first clue to finding Billie and I needed to get out there. I would find whoever took her, and this time, I wouldn't stop the beast from taking a life.

Chapter Three

Billie

*D*rip. Drip. Drip.

My eyelids fluttered and the weight of them made my head pound. Above me, the shackles groaned as I straightened my back to sit up taller. I had been in this dank place for hours, though how many, I couldn't remember. Every second blended into the next, and the pressure on my temples bore into my skull like someone was hammering my head with a nail gun. Somewhere in the distance, the sound of water dripping continued its annoying drumbeat, and I grimaced every time I heard another drop.

Whoever took me had a sick sense of humor. It was torture just being stuck in here.

Burying my feet into the cold, wet rock, I slid my back up the wall to stand. The chains that bound me were heavy enough to push me down, but I fought against them, trembling until I was upright. After hours of being in here, my eyes have adjusted to the darkness, and I could make out some details of the space.

Rock formations rose high on all sides of me, and three

tunnels seemed to stretch out from my prison. It was a cavern of some sort.

Where the hell did this bastard find a cavern in Shadowhurst? Fear gripped me as I thought about what that could mean. Perhaps I wasn't in Shadowhurst at all.

My mind raced as I tried to recall any locations around the town that might match the look of this place, but I drew a blank. If I wasn't near Shadowhurst anymore, I could have been out of it for longer than I thought. The asshat that snatched me would have needed enough time to drag me over here, chain me up, and perform whatever spell they needed to block my magic.

SHIT!

My eyes snapped open with the though. I couldn't use my magic in here, and that could only mean one thing. Witches were involved. *Damn you, Sebyl!*

If this had anything to do with the High Coven, I was in it deep. Fighting off shadowers would be hard, but taking on the coven without my magic would leave me nice and dead before I even had a chance to make a move. Still, something didn't sit right with me. There were too many unanswered questions about my kidnapping.

For starters, the girl that lured me from the party was definitely a shifter and there was no way in fresh hell those guys would side with the High Coven. Unless I was wrong to assume she was one of them. Trying to recall the night, I concentrated on the girl's features. She had the same distinct glow to her eyes that shifters possessed, which was why I assumed she was one. But something was off about her demeanor, and I couldn't remember the air feeling thicker when she was around. But if she wasn't a shifter, who was she? And who told her to get me away from the others? It couldn't have been the high priestesses. They wouldn't be ignorant enough to pull something like this so soon after we took them down in Savannah's cellar. Though Sebyl threatened to bring war on our heads, so maybe this was just step one of their sad little plans.

No, that doesn't make sense. The high priestesses were evil through and through, I knew that now, but they weren't foolish. Taking me would only anger the resistance and they were sure to attack if they thought I was dead. At least River and my friends would. The High Coven wouldn't risk that type of exposure in front of humans. Something wasn't adding up, and I hated that I didn't know what it was.

Then there was the question of my magic not working. If it was a spell, then how did the shifters know to perform it? They couldn't do it without the help of a witch and yet, here I was, useless and chained to a cavern wall like an animal. *Unless it's not a spell at all...*

Then WHAT?

I wanted to scream, but my throat was sore from the hours of screaming I'd done already, and since that yielded little results, I kept my mouth shut. The water started its melody again and I groaned.

Drip. Drip.

"Ugh, enough already. Either flood me dead or shut the hell up."

Drip.

"Awesome. Good chat."

Turning to the side, I scanned the cavern again like I had done a million times since I woke up here. The rocks were moldy and icy air filled the open space. Every once in a while, a small gust of wind blew through, but it was gone before I could figure out the direction it came from. Several times, I tried to hold my thumb out to see if I could feel it, but nothing happened and each time I did it, I felt even stupider. Did I think I was some captain of a pirate ship reading the wind to get home? So dumb. Besides, the wind could have blown from any of the three openings and if I knew something about caverns, it was that you could get lost in one forever if you took the wrong turn. Even if I could find out which tunnel led to the outside world, it still didn't help much in my current predicament.

I was still chained to the damn wall.

Rolling my foot around in my boots, I tried to feel the hidden dagger, sighing audibly when I felt nothing but wet socks. Whoever took me made sure I was left without any means of defending myself. Sure, I still had the pendants chained over my neck, but the block on my magic rendered them entirely useless. Which was exactly what I was at the moment. Useless to a fault.

A shadow swept over the opening to my left and I jerked my head in its direction. "Hello?"

Silence answered me and I squinted my eyes, trying to make out if what I saw was real or a play of the light. Not that there was much light in this place, but still. I stared for a long while before giving up and lowering down to sit. Whoever took me wasn't here now. I was alone in a cold, wet cavern and no one was coming to get me out.

This is why I don't party.

I strained a shoulder, wiping the sweat-covered hair off my face, and pressed my back into the wall. *Just keep breathing,* I urged myself. *River will find you.* My insides screamed and I battled against the vomit that rose in my throat. *Will he, though? Or does he think you're dead by now?*

In my peripheral vision, another shadow flashed over the

rocks. "Stop hiding, you coward!" I shouted. "Or are you still scared I'll kill you if you get close? Because you should be!"

The pendant River gave me rolled over my neck, hitting the side of the amethyst that dangled near it with a sharp pang. Tears flooded my vision as I thought of him, and I couldn't stop the sob that bubbled to the edges of my lips. I slunk my head back, hitting the rock with enough force to give myself a bigger headache than I already had. Black dots swarmed my vision, and I swallowed the spit that collected in my mouth. River had to find me, he just had to.

Or is he glad you're gone?

The thought felt so real, almost like a whisper, and I snapped my neck from side to side to shake it off. "SHUT... UP!"

Now he can be with Savannah... The girl he should have picked from the start...

"Shutupshutupshutup!" I shouted into the murkiness and my words echoed back to me. "Go away!"

If it wasn't for you, he'd still have his mom...

This wasn't happening. I refused to believe it. Whatever dark thoughts crept in my mind were simply a manifestation of my fears. They had to be because if they weren't, I was screwed. At least I knew enough to know that being afraid meant I was still alive, and that was the only thing I had to keep me going at that moment. I may have been going batshit crazy, but I was alive.

I tugged at the chains again and let the burning pain the shackles left behind calm my mind. At this point, I welcomed physical pain like one welcomed a cold shower on a hot day. It left me paralyzed, but at least it made my mind stop racing and kept those damn thoughts at bay. I pulled the chains again and winced as the sting of the metal collided with my skin. My fingers were swollen from the pressure, and I could sense the silver of my moonstone ring press into my flesh. My muscles strained as I closed my eyes and attempted to connect to my magic for the hundredth time. As always, I could feel it deep inside, but as soon as I made contact, it knocked me back on my ass like someone punched me in the gut. Slithering in my restraints, I dropped my hold on the magic and fell into the wall, my breathing ragged and hard.

There was a shuffle of feet down a tunnel and my gaze snapped to attention. *Someone is coming!*

Carefully, I peeled myself off the floor and wrapped my fingers around the chains to keep them from making noise as I stood. If the person who took me was returning, they probably expected to find me in a pool of tears and hopelessness when they arrived. I would not give them the satisfaction. *Come at me, asshole!*

The footsteps grew closer, and an ominous shadow appeared from the tunnel on my right. It grew as the figure neared, closer and closer until I could see every detail of their face. My eyes widened and my jaw hit the floor.

"You?"

Chapter Four

River

I paced between two large trees like a madman, pounding my sneakers into the dirt until it flattened under my feet. The tracks Raiden and Mel found were definitely shifter prints. They were larger in size than your average forest animal and their positioning implied calculated steps that circled in one area only to disappear from sight around the perimeter. Wild animals didn't cover their tracks in this way. There were shifters here the night Billie was taken. Unfortunately, I had no way to follow the direction they took her since the tracks began and ended in the area I now stomped through. It was like they flew off with Billie in tow. The thought was ludicrous. Billie was taken out of this forest somehow and it wasn't by air. The damn bastards that grabbed knew we'd look for prints and made sure to stomp them out so we could not follow.

Looking over the dense trees, my heart sank. I could sense the wolf twist and turn inside me, begging me to set it loose, but I pushed it out of my mind. There was still little I knew about how to control my shifts, but so far, not thinking about it seemed to do the trick. It was a Band-Aid solution at best, but if it worked to keep me in human form and not trying to kill any more of my friends, I was all for it.

I walked the length between the trees again and paused. Above me, the sky was brightening as the sun rose, though my mood remained as black as night. It had been almost twelve hours since Billie got snatched and we still had nothing on the person who took her. I knew she was alive. How, I had no clue, but I could feel it deep inside. I only hoped that she wasn't hurt wherever she was.

Fists formed at my sides when I thought of any pain she might be enduring, and I pounded the bark of a small tree with enough force to crack it. A sharp pain shot up my arm and I winced before delivering another blow. Tears threatened to pool, and my jaw ticked as I pummeled the wood repeatedly.

Where the hell are you, babe?

"What'd the tree ever do to you?"

I turned, wild-eyed, to see Raiden and Mel glare at me. Their bodies were touching, as they usually were, and the mate marks on both their chests were showing today. Jealousy crept to the surface as I studied the swirling spirals of their marks, and my thoughts landed back on Billie. We could never have what they had, not when Billie wasn't a shifter. That should have been the least of my worries, but I couldn't help thinking about it. Now that the wolf was awake, my need to have someone by my side intensified and it tore me up that it couldn't be Billie. *Screw the damn bond! I choose her!* My brow creased and the veins in my neck popped. I would tear the wolf apart if it ever chose someone other than her. *Reign it in, cowboy. Find her first, then worry about the rest of it.*

Peeling my fist off the trunk, I met Raiden's gaze. "These lead us nowhere. Did you find anything new?"

"Not since we talked to the shifters," Raiden said. "No one knows anything."

"What about Damen?"

The lion shifter's back froze when I mentioned his cousin and he peered warily from me to Mel. "He doesn't know anything."

"So, that's it? The damn shifters say they know nothing, and we just believe them? What about these tracks? These mean something!"

"That's not what's happening here. We've got people asking around to see if anyone might have seen someone out of place at the party except that kid, and Daria and some of her friends are checking the alibis of every shifter that has stepped foot in this house in the last few months. We'll figure this out."

My entire body vibrated at their incompetence. "Who the fuck is Daria?"

"Fox shifter. Smart kid, and has a lot of sway in the resistance. If anyone can get people to talk, it's her," Mel said assuringly.

Unlike her, I wasn't sure of any of it in the least.

"I'm pretty certain getting a shifter to question people is a horrible idea. Those animals are going to stick together, so you better think of some other plan to get the assholes to talk," I bit out.

"I would watch how you talk about them," Raiden warned. "You're one of us now."

"I don't give a shit."

"You should."

Inside me, the wolf stirred and I buried my feet into the

porch. *Don't even try it, you moron. One move and I swear I will kill myself just to end you.*

The tress on the horizon lightened as the first of the sun's rays hit them, and I had to shield my eyes from the light. I haven't slept all night and I could feel the onset of a major headache form behind my temples each time I blinked. Though I knew I couldn't sleep, even if I wanted to. I wouldn't be resting until we found Billie and I feared to think of what that could mean. I should have listened to Savannah and taken a nap, but it seemed like a moronic idea. Only a coward could relax while the girl he loved was missing.

My mind was still racing when Mel crossed the porch to stand by my side. Her lean arm reached for mine, and I tensed when she squeezed my bicep. "We think it might be a good idea for you to meet the wolf pack."

What the hell is wrong with these people? "Are you kidding me right now?" I shouted. "Billie is missing, and you want me to what? Make friends with other wolves? No, thank you! I want nothing to do with them. For all we know, they're the ones that took her."

Mel and Raiden exchanged knowing looks and my stomach turned. I was growing tired of their secret communications, and not just because it was something they were able to do because of their mating bond. The reason I hated it so much was that it seemed like they were always keeping things from the rest of us. As though being the leaders meant they should protect us from secrets. It was something Billie hated about the High Coven, and for once, I understood exactly how she felt. Even Peyton started to speak in code, and I wondered if she would get worse as time passed and she spent more time with the other leaders.

"If you have something to say, spill it," I bit out.

"Look, kid," Raiden said, and I cringed. I wasn't anyone's freaking kid, but I had to admit, it was a step up from being called a cub ,so I let it slide. "I know you're confused right now. Everyone is after their first shift, but you can't keep denying who you are forever. Every shifter has a pack, others like them, same animal and all. The beasts inside us need the camaraderie. Wolves more than others. Having the pack around will make the transition easier for you. Trust me."

"Like you trusted your cousin?"

It was a low blow, and I knew it. The destroyed look on Raiden's face made me even more aware of how unfair my comment was, but I didn't much care at that moment. The thought of having to make nice with other wolves was the last thing on my mind. I had no intention of ever being a part of whatever pack Raiden was talking about and I sure as hell wasn't looking for some weird animal family. I already had a family, and a big part of that family was missing.

"Just think about it," Mel whispered, her hand still on my arm. "Raiden is right, having a pack will help. Even if you don't want to admit it right now."

My teeth gritted against each other, and my eyes beaded her way. "I... don't...need...a pack."

"Every shifter needs a pack, kid," Raiden said with a cocky smile. "Even you."

"And if I don't want to be a shifter at all? What then?"

His booming laugh filled the porch and my blood boiled in my veins.

"I have news for you. You're a shifter whether or not you want to be. The question now is how you're going to live your life. Alone or with others like you? Take my word for it. Alone is never the answer."

"Easy for you to say," I said and gestured to the spiral on his bare chest. "You're never alone, are you?"

On my arm, Mel's fingers tensed, and her lips parted, but she stayed silent. They both knew what was eating me up, and I could tell neither wanted to press the issue further. If I met the other wolves, there was a chance the dumb animal inside me would be drawn to one of them. I couldn't risk that happening. Billie was the only one I wanted and if that meant that I would be a lone wolf until I die, then that's what I would be.

I made a promise to Billie, one I intended to keep. There was no one else for me but her, and I had to spend the rest of my life proving it if only to see that smile of hers one more time.

Raiden lowered his gaze to the floor and closed the distance between us. His arm raised, and I thought he was about to punch my teeth in, surprised when he wrapped it around my shoulders instead. His thick lips curled up and he pulled me into his side, grinning the entire time. I tried to wrestle away, but the grip he had on me was strong. I mean, the guy *was* a lion. My body stilled and I let him keep me at his side in the vice of his muscled arm.

"We'll find her, kid," he said, and for once, I didn't hate that he called me that. "In the meantime, do us all a favor and consider making some friends. Your stank attitude is making everyone in the house uncomfortable."

"Fine, okay, whatever. I won't be such an asshole if it gets you off my back."

Raiden loosened his hold and I pulled away from him, taking a few steps to put some distance back between us. *Freaking spider monkey.*

"Oh, before I forget," Mel said. "Jayden told us Tyler got

released. Abigail and he are stopping by later today. Apparently, your friends are way excited to see your wolf side."

Great. Just damn brilliant.

"What about the kid from the party? Peyton said she was looking into it some more." The shifters glanced at each then looked away, crushing any hope I may have felt. "She got nowhere, didn't she?"

"Dead end," Raiden grumbled. "Whoever this kid was, she wasn't from the house. I talked to Morgan again to go over what she saw in detail and the more I learn, the more I'm starting to think she wasn't a shifter at all."

"What the hell does that mean?"

Mel stepped around Raiden as though to shield him from my rising anger. "It doesn't add up. Shifter kids stick together and for no one to know her is uncanny."

"Maybe she's new?"

"We would know if she was. Anyone underage that joins the resistance does not go unnoticed. She would have had parents around or friends even. It doesn't make sense for her to be at the party on her own."

"So, where does that leave us?"

The shifter's brow furrowed, and she rested a hand on my shoulder. "We'll keep looking for her, but we should explore other options."

"Like what?"

"Perhaps it wasn't the shifters that took Billie," Raiden said.

As much as he wanted to believe that, I couldn't agree. Between these tracks and my gut feeling, I was convinced Raiden was wrong. Those furry bastards had something to do with it and I was going to prove it. I had to. It was our only lead.

Chapter Five

Billie

"**What** the hell are you doing here?" I yelled and yanked on the chains.

The girl stepped into the thin ray of light that hung low across the cavern, and I recognized her immediately. It was the fox shifter I trained recently, the cocky brunette with the stupid tree tattoo on her ribs. I couldn't believe some teen with anger management issues outsmarted me, but the girl's expression told me I should have been warier of her from the start. Something about the sinister look in her golden eyes made me buckle back.

This chick meant business.

She looked me over in disgust and turned her pointed nose upward, smelling the air. "Expected someone else? Your precious wolf-boy, maybe?" She grinned. "I got news for you, witch. He's not coming."

Wolf-boy? What the hell does that even mean?

"Why did you bring me here?" I asked, mustering as much confidence as I could. "Whatever idiotic plan you have, it won't work. My friends will find me."

Her evil laugh echoed down the tunnels behind us, and my blood boiled at the sound.

"You know, you're not as tough as you think you are. I mean, come on! Do you know how easy it was to get you over here?"

Flipping her shoulder-length waves, she inched closer to me, and I shrank back into the wet stone behind me. Her steps were slow and calculated like she was stalking chickens in a coop. As she crept closer, I tightened my grip on the chains to keep upright, but my knees shook despite my urging them to keep their shit together. The fox glanced at my traitorous body and laughed again. "What a serious waste of space." She smirked. "I don't see what Marcus and the others saw in you. You're no savior, and any shadower to side with you has to be an idiot. We should have killed you long ago, but this?" She gestured around the cavern. "This is so much better!"

We? Interesting. "You think you can take me on? With what army?"

"Oh, it's not just me, idiot."

"Who's helping you? Is it the High Coven?"

The fox stopped in her tracks and narrowed her eyes in my direction. "Are you seriously that slow? Or is this some act? Because I'm not buying it."

Okay, not the witches then. "So, who? Who's in this big bad army that you're planning to unleash on me? While I'm chained and powerless, by the way. Real brave."

"You'll find out soon enough. And trust me, you'll wish you hadn't."

The circles she was talking around me were making my head spin and I was tired of chasing down answers from someone that didn't seem to have any. If this tool had help, something I highly doubted was true, she wouldn't tell me who it was. Still, I needed to get a better idea of where I was, and asking questions was not looking like the best approach. I wrinkled my nose and squared my shoulders, fixing my gaze on her slender form. "You're kinda tiny, huh?"

"Excuse me?"

"Just saying, you're small. Not a lot of muscle on that body. I noticed it when I was training you, and it's even more clear now. I mean, sure, you have a big mouth and know how to use it, but I doubt you can do much more than that. Which is why I'm wondering how you got me here?" I scoffed. "Those skinny arms don't look like they're good for lifting."

Before I could berate her further, the fox was in my face and her hand ran across my cheek in a harsh slap. My skin burned from the hit and my head swung to the side, hitting the wall with a thud. I ran my tongue on the inside of my cheek and the taste of iron filled my mouth. *If this asshole broke a tooth, I swear...*

"Not so tiny now, am I?" The fox smirked and raised her hand again. "Keep talking that garbage and I'll finish you off before they get started."

"They?"

Large eyes blinked up at me and she took a step back. Fear soaked her as if she'd seen a ghost, and I had to look around the room to make sure we were still alone. The cavern was as empty as before, and my stomach growled as more questions rose to the surface. Who was this kid so afraid of? Whoever it was, I did not want to find out.

"Fine, don't tell me who you're working with," I said. "It won't matter anyway. I will get out of here and when I do, you're done for."

The shifter laughed again. "Big words for someone chained to a wall."

"Take the chains off and we'll see how good you really are..."

She squinted and creased her brow like she was considering my request before shaking her head 'no'.

DAMN IT!

"Cool story. So, what now? You're going to keep me locked up here and talk me to death?"

So far, the interaction with the fox led me nowhere, and all I knew was that she wasn't working alone. I was certain other shifters were involved, probably the same ones responsible for the attack on River and me on the trails, but with everything happening with the High Coven, we abandoned the search to find the bastards responsible. Hopefully, River and the others were one step closer to finding them while I was stuck in here. In the meantime, my best bet was to keep the fox talking so she couldn't go back to her pathetic team and tell them I'm awake. Despite not knowing who her accomplices were, I had the good sense to understand that if she called for them, I'd regret it. If I was even left alive, of course.

I tugged at the chains again to get her attention and leaned my boot against the wall. "Please, tell me you idiots actually thought of a plan before bringing me here. I know shifters aren't the brightest, but this can't be the extent of your brilliant plan?"

The fox's neck reddened, and I could see anger boil inside her. As she neared me, I tried to recall her name from the training but drew a blank. *You should have let me give them name tags like I asked, Marcus.* I groaned, but before I could look back to the shifter, her palm was on my face again and my cheek was on fire. *Enough with the damn slapping!*

"Watch your mouth, witch!" she hissed. "I wonder what your precious wolf will think when I tell him what you think of him."

"Wolf? You know what, never mind," I bit back. I was done with her games and if she couldn't give me anything to go by, she might as well get out of my face. "Tell River what I said. Break us up and see if I care."

She tsked and cocked her head to the side. "Your boyfriend doesn't know where you are. No one does. And your witch tricks won't work on me."

"Daria!" I yelled out as her name popped into my head.

The paleness of her face told me I hit the nail on the head and my lips curled into a satisfied smile.

"That's your name, right?" I asked. "Daria. Daria, the fox with the tree tat on her ribs."

Brows kissing, she turned to face me. "So, you know my name. Big deal."

"You know what the big deal is, DARIA? That if I know your name, my friends do too, and I can bet you anything that right now, they're searching the house to see who's missing. How long do you think it'll be before they find out it was you who took me? A couple of hours? Half a day? Do you and your little shifter friends have that kind of time?"

Got you now, sucker!

"My shifter friends are the least of your problems, witch," Daria said with a smirk. The coolness in her voice gave me pause, like she wasn't phased in the least with my comments. "The ones that helped us will end you. All of you. And if your dumb friends want to take us on, they'll die trying. I can promise you that."

Yeah, that's not good. "What's with all the vagueness, DARIA? Too scared to tell me who helped you out? Let me guess, you're totally useless on your own, so you crawled to the coven to help you do your bidding like the weak animal you are?"

A blazing fire rushed my face as she delivered another blow to my cheek. "I already told you, we don't make deals with your kind. We will kill all the witches. Starting with you."

I was getting a rise out of her, and I loved it. Even if it didn't get me any closer to finding out who took me or where I was, seeing her squirm and get bent out of shape was bringing the first sliver of joy I've had since I got here. Besides, I meant what I said to the fox. While she was wasting time talking to me, River was definitely tearing the house apart looking for her and her friends. I just had to buy him some time.

Ready to insult her again, I opened my mouth but before words could pour out of me, a numbing pain rushed my body. My knees buckled and I sunk, held up by my wrists as the chains strained to carry my weight. Limbs seizing, I shook as the magic inside boiled and bubbled, threatening to explode. Whatever spell was holding it contained pressed into my skin and I felt like I was being pulled apart at the seams. Glittering lights swarmed my vision as the magic attempted to escape, but each time it reached the surface, the spell knocked it back into me with so much force that it sent me flying back into the wall. Every part of my body went numb ,and I lost control of my limbs.

In front of me, Daria's smile spread wide as she watched me writhe in misery.

"Time to begin," she said and whirled on her heels to leave just seconds before the second wave of pain took me.

Chapter Six

Billie

My screams lasted for hours as the spell worked to tear me apart. Each time I thought the torture ended, another wave took its place, harsher and crueler than the first. And each one left me weaker. After the last bout, I couldn't even stand and my body hung like a heap of dung off the chains, swaying from side to side as my feet tried to right themselves on the cold stone below. The metal of the shackles tore into my skin, and I could feel blood drip down as they burrowed into my wrists. My hair was soaked with sweat, as were my clothes, and drool dripped down my chin as I gritted my teeth against each other.

One thing was certain. I had never hated my magic more.

It swarmed inside me, and I clenched my jaw, ready for another attack. This one was faster than the rest and by the time it was done turning me inside out, I couldn't see. My vision swam and when I looked up, I saw six tunnels instead of three. *What a freaking disaster.*

At this point, I would have been grateful for Daria's annoying conversation. Anything other than this.

Goddess, River, I hope you're close to finding me.

Needles ran down my thighs and my head pounded like a drum against my temples. My brain felt too big for my skull and if I could move, I would have banged it against the wall repeatedly. Somewhere in my peripheral vision, a shadow flashed by, and I snapped my head up only to see a bunch of blurry nothings once again. The cavern was darker now, and the buzzing in my ears made it hard to hear the water dripping in the distance. *Small miracles.*

Another shadow zoomed by, and I ignored it. There was no point wasting my energy chasing figments of imagination, not when another bout of pain was about to begin.

The tortures came in regular intervals, and I fought to breathe through them like I was practicing in a Lamaze class. Nothing worked, and each time my magic exploded inside me, the spell grew stronger and the pain that followed worsened. I begged my magic to stay still, but it was no longer in my control. Something else was calling it forward, and I was simply a vessel for its demands.

Wind rushed by me, and I roared as blood boiled in my veins.

Do you want to make it stop?

"W-What?" I asked, looking around, bewildered. "Who said that?"

Do you want to make it stop? the whisper asked again.

I shook my head. "Show yourself! Who the hell is this? DARIA!"

Gusts of wind answered my questions and I swayed against the wall as it hit my sides. The wind increased, pushing me around like a rag doll, and forcing me to cry out in pain each time it locked on my body. The metal cuffs ripped my wrists to pieces and blood caked my arms from the holes they tore into the soft skin. "YES!" I screamed into the empty cavern. "Yes! Make it stop!"

All you have to do is watch...

My eyes grew as golden, glittery light filled the gloom before me and my jaw slacked. *What in the actual fresh hell is this now?* The glow of the light intensified, swimming and swirling in front of me until it was all I could see. It tightened into a ball, then burst outward, caking the entire cavern in its gilded shine. As I watched, shapes formed in the light, like a memory coming into focus. A gasp escaped my lips when the shapes solidified and River's face came into view. His beautiful green eyes stared directly at me, and I yanked at the chain, desperate to reach for him. The metal pulled me back, forcing me to stand still.

"What is this?"

Watch, the whisper urged and I obliged.

River's lips parted and curled into a wide smile, and my soul screamed for him. "River! River, I'm here! I'm here!" I yelled, but he showed no recognition. The light expanded, revealing more of him inch by inch. Tears flooded my vision at the sight. I shook them off, refusing not to see the boy I was aching to be with again.

Air rent and as the golden light spread, I watched him lean on the bed he was sitting on. I recognized it immediately, my heart jumping into my throat. He was in his room, in the small attic of his house, and he looked so happy that it made me want to leap through the vision to lie next to him. His stunning smile widened, and when he looked up at me through those thick lashes, I all but fainted on the spot.

Every cell in my body vibrated with the relief of seeing

him again, and I couldn't believe the small glimpse of hope I was receiving. If I could see River this way forever, I could endure whatever tortures the damn shifters had in store for me.

A shadow crept over the base of the bed, towering over him, and I cocked my head to the side to see clearer. He wasn't alone. *Why the hell is he not alone? Who is there with him?*

The golden light fizzed, blocking him from my view.

"No!" I yelled. "What happened? Where is he?"

The light glimmered again, but River did not come back into focus. *Do you wish to see more?*

"YES! YES! Show me more!"

Obeying my desperate pleas, the light spread over the cavern, and I breathed in relief as River's eyes met mine. The shadowy figure crept closer to the edge of the bed, and his eyes widened. Horror set across his face, making him jump from the bed to face his attacker.

Step by step, Sebyl's slim body slithered over to River. Her long fingers danced, and bursts of magic flew from them like lightning. River dodged the first hit, but he was too slow, and the second bolt knocked him back. He bounced off the mattress and fell to the side, crab walking away from Sebyl's relentless hits. She threw her arms out and fire burst from her fingers and into his chest. Tears ran down River's face and he swatted at the flames, rolling around on the floor as the fire consumed him. His eyes pleaded with me to make the torture stop, but I was useless in my chains.

River screamed and I died inside.

"NONONO!" I shouted, thrashing in the chains.

Do you wish to see more?

"Are you freaking kidding me? Hell no! No, I do not wish to see more, you asshole!"

The light flickered like a broken film reel and flashed out of existence, leaving the dank cavern coated in darkness once again. Tears burnt behind my lids, and I blinked them away, trying to keep my cool without success. My heartbeat pounded at my chest and my breaths were quick and heavy as I tried to understand what I just saw. What kind of spell could do this? Nothing I've seen before, for sure. The closest thing I could think of was a mind reaper attack, but my brain didn't feel like mashed potatoes, so that couldn't have been it. That vision, or whatever it was, felt real somehow. Like it was happening at that moment, and I was watching from the sidelines. Did the shifters plant a camera in River's room, and he didn't know it?

My body shook with rage, and I saw red.

Here I was, trapped in this disgusting cavern and being tortured with my own magic, and my boyfriend was out there getting his ass handed to him by the coven. This couldn't be happening. How could the others let this happen? Or were they under attack much like River was? Pain shot through me as I imagined the remainder of my friends suffering the same fate River had been. This couldn't be real. The coven wouldn't attack in this manner and Sebyl would not have come alone. It must be a trick. It had to be.

But it felt so real...

My head slumped and I loosened my grip on the chains to lower to my knees. One way or another, this cavern would kill me and if it didn't, I would drive myself insane worrying over River and my friends.

Chapter Seven

River

"Look, I know you don't want to hear this," Savannah said, "but they might have a point. Meeting the pack can't be the worst idea."

Was she serious? "Are you serious? Whose side are you on here, Sav?"

My hands were jittery, and I took a sip of what was probably my tenth coffee that morning, swallowing the warm liquid with little satisfaction. I've never been one for the drink, unlike Billie, who was basically ninety percent coffee, but I needed to keep from passing out. The caffeine didn't help, and I returned to yawning in no time.

When I finally closed my mouth, Savannah's eyes were on me. "And did you take a nap like I said?"

"No, Mom," I scoffed. "I'm fine. Let's just figure all this out."

Beside her, Tyler and Abigail watched us get into it in the same manner one watches a tennis match. Their heads spun from me to Savannah and their jaws dragged the floor as we continued to argue. It'd been about a half-hour of this,

43

and I was over it. I was even more over Tyler's idiotic questions about my wolf. If that kid was going to ask me if I could smell the moon one more time, I'd lose it.

Muscles twitched in my jaw and my lips crashed into a thin line as I fixed Savannah with yet another 'I don't want to talk about it' glare before changing the subject. "Did Jayden have any luck tracking her phone?"

Savannah shook her head.

"Awesome. Another dead end." I slumped my head and cursed under my breath. "And nothing at her place?"

"Nope," Tyler said. "Peyton gave Silas the cover story about Billie staying with her for a while and he seemed to buy it. At least I thought he did. We're lucky the Chandlers are away on vacation. One less thing to worry about."

"Good, good, good." *It's not good. Nothing is actually good.*

Around the room, the tension was thick enough to slice through and when Savannah pulled the sleeve of my shirt, I almost fell off the chair in surprise. "What about that fox shifter girl?" she asked, face full of hope. "She get anything from the rest of them?"

"Nope," I said. "Raiden said Daria checked in with them already and she had no leads to give us. Said everyone is accounted for and those that weren't at the party had solid alibis. She told him she'll keep looking around, but as far as she can tell, no one from the house is to blame for this."

"And we trust her?"

I shrugged. "I guess. Mel and Raiden vouch for this girl and she's a pretty solid member of the resistance. It's one more helping hand, so I'm willing to see how it plays out. If she still has nothing, we'll go from there."

"What other leads do we have?" Abigail asked.

I tried to think of an answer, yet nothing came to mind. We'd been over the same ideas a million times, and no one had anything new to add. Billie was still gone, and we weren't even one step closer to finding her. With Daria and her friends hitting a wall, we were nowhere closer to finding Billie than we have been the night she disappeared. It was an exasperating position to be in. A thought gnawed at the rear of my brain, and I attempted to push it away from fear it might be true.

"Guys," I whispered. "What if it's the coven?"

My friends went still, and silence filled the small kitchen we sat in. Everyone's eyes darted across the room, and I could see they were thinking the same thing I was. If the High Coven took Billie, we wouldn't get her back without a fight. Going against the witches on a good day would have been suicide, but now, it was damn impossible. After we took them down in the cellar, there was no way they'd leave anything to chance. The townhouse was likely guarded to the brim and as much as I wanted to think we'd stand a shot, I knew we'd be dead in seconds without Billie's help.

It didn't matter. That was the only place we haven't checked yet, and it stood to reason she might be there.

Resting my chin in my hands, I slumped over the dining table. "We should send someone to check it out. Just in case."

"We'll do it," Abigail offered.

"You sure? You guys literally just got out of the hospital, and it might not be safe."

She nodded and planted a kiss on Tyler's cheek. "Trust me, we could use something to do. Being stuck in that hell-hole was boring AF. Right, babe?"

"Back to Stamwick it is," Tyler agreed.

My shoulders relaxed as the first hint of relief washed

over me. "Thanks, guys. I still think it shifters were involved and not the High Coven, but better safe than sorry."

"Why are you so sure it was them?" Abigail asked.

Biting my lower lip, I faced her. "I don't know. A gut feeling, I guess. Something doesn't add up. If it was the witches, why take her at all? She was one of them."

"It's still worth checking out, the witches were pretty pissed with her."

"Then how do you explain the shifter tracks we found? Or the girl Morgan saw? It doesn't make sense."

Tyler ran a finger through Abigail's long hair and the gesture seemed to relax her. At least enough that she stopped arguing with me, so I was grateful for the interruption. His eyes met mine and he half-smiled before speaking. "We'll check out the townhouse and if it looks like they might be involved, we'll call you."

"Thanks," I said, relaxing my shoulders.

"No worries. So, about the moon..."

I'm going to kill him. Shooting my hand up to stop Tyler from speaking seemed to do the trick, and he huffed in disappointment. His broad frame hunched and though he was silent, I could see there would be many more stupid questions in the days to come. A part of me wished I was as enthused about my wolf as my friends were, but a bigger part of me still hated the damn beast. Even as I sat there, I could feel it crawling inside me, slithering like a snake in a field. It was disgusting and infuriating, and I wanted it out of me.

Savannah poured herself another cup of coffee and sat down across me. Her hazel eyes glued to mine the entire time as she sipped, and I could sense her need to push me to my limit again. "So, are you going to meet the pack or what?"

"I already said n—"

Words caught in my throat as a throbbing pain hit me and I bent over the table, struggling to breathe. My heartbeat raced and I rubbed my hand over my chest to ease the torment, but it only continued to increase. *What is happening?* I wanted to scream and kick, but all I could do was hunch further down and bite my tongue. My mind raced, trying to understand if this was a side effect of a shift, but the wolf was quiet. Whatever was happening to me, it had nothing to do with shifting. Tears burnt my lids, and I squeezed my eyes shut, breathing through the torturous jolts of pain. It felt like my heart was breaking. Like someone was squeezing it tight in my chest.

Panic flared when Billie's tear-stained face appeared in my view and my entire body jerked.

This isn't my pain. It's hers!

"Who's doing this to you? Tell me, babe! Where are you?" I screamed, but she didn't answer. Her face blurred in my vision and little by little, the heartache dissipated, leaving me in a pile of pain on the table.

Around me, my friends rushed to my side, shaking me into awareness. I couldn't hear them, and I couldn't see them. My mind was only on Billie. Only on her and the pain she was in. Whoever had her was tearing her apart, and I could feel her emotions as though they were my own. Under my shirt, my chest burnt and throbbed and I continued to swat at it with no relief. When I thought I couldn't take any more, it stopped, only to be replaced by something else.

Something primal.

I gripped the table, nails digging into the wood and clawing at the edges until I could see the marks they left behind. My fingers snapped one by one, and a wild roar escaped me as I fell, shattering the chair I sat in. Above me,

Tyler grabbed my shoulders to hold me down, but I shoved him off.

"GET BACK!" I roared just as the bones in my legs shattered. *Not now. Please, not now.*

The wolf howled and I cursed at him to stop. He was so strong that my pathetic attempts did nothing to prevent the shift and in moments, I was on all fours in the kitchen with my three friends huddling at the opposite wall.

Fear coated Abigail's face and Tyler stepped forward to shield her from me. My own friends were afraid of what I'd do, and I wasn't sure which part rattled me more. That they were afraid, or that I was afraid for them.

The wolf's talons dug into the parquet flooring and its warm breath spread before me. He was pissed and he was hungry, and I couldn't do anything to stop him from attacking. Tyler screamed for me to back off, but that only riled the wolf more and I pushed off the floor to barrel toward him. I landed on the table, face to face with Tyler, and growled.

"River, stop this shit right now!" he screamed. "I'm warning you."

I swear I could hear the wolf laugh at him. An actual freaking laugh. It shook me to the core because I knew Tyler didn't stand a chance against the damn beast and his threats would only make things worse. This was a game to the wolf, one that only it knew the rules to.

Long fingers wrapped around Tyler's waist to pull him aside, and it shocked me to see Savannah step forward. Her curly hair clung to her forehead and her heavy breathing buzzed in my ears as she neared me. I sniffed the air, disgusted with myself, and buckled back when I realized there wasn't a hint of fear in her. How was this girl not afraid after I almost killed her in the woods? What was she playing at?

Savannah's hand outstretched until it was just inches from my wet nose, and she grinned. "Let's not do something we'll regret later," she said in the same tone one uses to calm a tempered child. "No one wants to hurt you here, and I know you don't want to hurt any of us."

I don't. I really, really don't.

Inside me, the wolf growled, but its anger subsided. It was as though, for once, it felt what I felt. Is this what Raiden meant when he told me to control the beast? I wasn't sure, but if I was going to listen to the man, now was the time. As calmly as I could manage, I pushed my thoughts out to the wolf, forcing it to listen. I wanted to beg with it to shift back, but that was the wrong approach. The last time I begged, the beast almost ate Savannah. *Listen up, moron!* I hissed at it. *We're going to do this my way from now on and if you don't play ball, I'll end both of us!*

The wolf wriggled and I could hear its loud yelp in my head. It was over my shit, but that didn't stop it from listening. I pushed myself backward on the table, struggling against its hold until I was enough away from Savannah and our friends. Little by little, I forced the wolf to simmer and when I had it under control, I closed my eyes and barked my next command.

SHIFT THE HELL BACK!

With another annoyed yelp, the wolf obeyed. Bone by bone, my body reformed and though the pain was still the most intense thing I've felt, it was almost bearable this time. Something about the new understanding we had made it better. When I was in my own body again, I crawled to the counter and snatched a tea towel to cover the important bits.

It was already awkward enough that my friends saw me go through the worst thing I've ever experienced, I didn't need to scar them for life on top of it. Besides, if Billie found out that Savannah saw me naked, she'd lose it.

Sapphire eyes flashed before me and I squared my jaw, rising to stand while clutching the unfairly small tea towel to my body. My head pounded, but I also felt stronger somehow. It was almost as if gaining some control over the wolf filled me with energy, a power booster of sorts. The animal in me was formidable, and I couldn't deny the damage it could do if I could only get it to follow me. I had to figure this out before it was too late, and my head couldn't focus on finding Billie if I was constantly trying to prevent myself from shifting. Besides, if we were to go against the coven, we would need all the help we could get, and right now, that included the angry beast living inside my body. I had to gain control of it and use it as a weapon and not the other way around.

Turning my attention to Savannah, I nodded once, and she smiled in understanding. "I'll meet the pack, see if they can help. With this," I waved a hand over my body, "and everything else. In the meantime, think you can look into the background on the shifters that were in the party?"

"What are you thinking?" Savannah asked, one eyebrow raised.

"I'm not sure yet," I answered. "Just see if you can find something that stands out. Red flags of some sort."

My best friend smiled, though her gesture did not offer me much comfort. Meeting the pack was the last thing on my mind. Still, if it helped in even the smallest way, I was willing to do it. I would meet the pack and go from there, but there was something else I had to take care of first.

Chapter Eight

Billie

When I was only four years old, Beatrix took me on my first patrol. She thought it would help me grow stronger as a witch to see her vanquish a shadower, but as I learned later down the line, Beatrix was never a candidate for the *Mother of the Year* award. Seeing her stab the woman, who I later learned was a soul sucker, in the chest haunted me for months. I would wake up screaming and covered in sweat, and when Beatrix showed up in my room to calm me, I wouldn't let her. I wasn't afraid of the night terrors, what I truly feared those days was her. Seeing your mom rip through another person's ribcage would do that to a person.

I didn't know why, but that memory continued to play on a loop in my mind every time that vile golden light returned to show me more of the High Coven's attacks. It had shown the horrifying images to me so many times, and from so many angles, that they were all but burnt into my brain. At this stage, I couldn't even count the number of tortures the coven inflicted on River. The last glimpse I got had him tied to a chair in Sebyl's basement while witches delivered blow after blow to his ragged body. His eyes were swollen shut and blood caked his hair and face, making me gag in my mouth when I saw it.

Yet, whether I cried or screamed or begged, the visions still returned. Each one was slightly different; and all were just as awful as the first. In the beginning, I didn't believe my eyes, convinced it was just my deteriorating mind playing tricks on me, but when the cavern showed me Peyton and the leaders searching for River, I knew it was all true.

At least they were trying to find him.

Across my neck, the necklace River gave me hung in constant reminder of what I couldn't protect, and I struggled to rip it off with my teeth several times. All of the attempts ended with me sobbing like an idiot with the chain still dangling across my chest. After a while, I gave up any hope of being free of it and concentrated on other things. Like Beatrix's creepy lullabies when she tried to sing me back to sleep in those horrid days.

I didn't care that no one was looking for me. All I cared about was that they found River and saved him from the coven before he took his last breath.

The cavern had grown colder since I first got here, and I spent hours jumping in one spot to get my body temperature up and the circulation back into my legs. It was a poor exercise, but the closest I could get to movement in the chains, so I made do with what I had.

Twice a day, Daria, the idiot, returned to shove tasteless bread into my mouth and wash it down with water. She even let me use the bathroom, which in my case involved being thrown into a metal collar and dragged down a tunnel to a spot further from where I was held. The first time she unchained me to let me pee, I fought her tooth and nail, but my body had grown weak from the tortures and my attempts didn't accomplish anything. Daria only laughed and kicked me in the gut a few times for good measure. I stopped trying to fight her after that.

Today, she barely pulled on my collar as we walked and instead, grinned like a moron as though she'd won some battle. In a way, I supposed she did.

We rounded a corner and she pushed me into the shadows to do my business, not bothering to look away. If I took too long, she'd throw rocks at me, so I hurried my ass up this time.

"Finally," she hissed. "Let's go."

The return to where my chains awaited was always the most brutal. Every step felt like a defeat, and it boomed through me with its taunts. *You're weak. Pathetic. A worthless loser.* I wasn't certain who was berating me anymore, the cavern or my own damn self. Whoever it was, they weren't wrong. Until that point, I hadn't realized how much I relied on my magic to save me and without it, I was nothing. A shell of a girl too weak to fight back.

Daria walked a few feet ahead of me and the chain attached to my collar dragged across the stone. The screech of metal on rock sent shivers down my legs and I gritted my teeth to keep from screaming. By now, I had learned that like fighting, screaming did not do me any good.

As we turned the same corner, something caught my eye in the distance, and I slowed my stride to make it out. Somewhere down the tunnel, another opening emerged, one I hadn't noticed before. My eyes bulged and I held back a gasp as the shadow of a woman appeared. Her face was ashen, covered in dirt and debris. Deep black hair fell over her face in matted waves and her arms were tied above her, held in the same shackles that held me.

I shook my head, unable to believe there was someone else in the cavern with me, so it shocked me when I looked up again to see she was still there. I wanted to yell for her, but Daria was too close, and I couldn't risk her hearing me. Slowing further, I found a loose rock with my foot and kicked it into the dark toward the woman. Groggily, she raised her head and her clouded eyes met mine. Hope soared inside me, though in seconds, it was replaced with fear. The pricks took someone else and whoever this woman was, she was in even more trouble than I was. From the looks of it, she couldn't even move.

Her gaze traveled over me, and she opened her mouth to speak, but no words came out.

"Hello?" I whispered, jerking my gaze to Daria to make sure she didn't hear. "Who are you?"

The woman said something so quietly I couldn't understand her.

"I can't hear you. I can't—"

The collar on my neck yanked forward and I nearly lost my balance as Daria dragged me from the opening. My feet skidded over the ground, and I tried to pull away, but she tugged the chain again and I stumbled in her direction.

"Hurry up!" she roared. "I don't have all day!"

Pulling the chain, she carried me behind her, and piercing agony flooded my body. I didn't want to leave the woman, but more than that, I didn't want to return to my prison. Every step took me closer to more visions of River's tortures, and I wasn't sure if I could handle it for much longer. In fact, I knew I couldn't.

When we reached the wall I was to be chained to, Daria

pushed me down and kicked my lower back until I turned to face her. Her evil grin spread as she buckled the shackles over my wrists and locked me up again before turning on her heels to storm out. "Have fun," she bit out over her shoulder and was gone in an instant.

Bitch. Seriously.

I looped my fingers over the chains and brought myself to stand, my sweaty back scraping over the rough surface of the wall. I'd been up and down the damn thing so much, my shirt's back was shredded by now. My legs shook to hold me up and I struggled against the pain until I was upright.

Facing the tunnel that led to the bathroom, I cleared my throat before speaking. "Hello?" I yelled out and my words echoed in the darkness. "Are you there? Who are you?"

Silence met me and it only added to my resolve.

"My name is Billie. Shifters from Shadowhurst took me. Is that what happened to you?"

Nothing.

"Hello? Please, answer!"

When I heard nothing back, I slumped my shoulders and lowered down. There was no point in wasting all my energy talking to someone who couldn't even hear me. I had to think of another way to reach the woman. Maybe the next time Daria came, I could fake an injury? Get her to take the chains off and make a run for it or something. It likely wouldn't work, but it was worth a shot. Waiting to die when I thought I was here alone was one thing, but I couldn't leave someone else to suffer, not when I still had strength left to save her.

I slumped my head, taking a deep breath as I thought over options to get us both out of this place. "Please, talk to me," I whispered. "Please."

A light wind blew by me, and I inhaled it hungrily, relieved as the coolness spread over my body. When the wind died down and the cavern was still again, I sat up straight and stared at the tunnel.

"Are you there?"

A low shuffle echoed through the cavern and my heart jumped up to my throat. My ears perked and I leaned in, waiting for some response. I had all but given up when the woman's voice finally sounded on the other side of the tunnel.

"My name is Naomi. Please, help me."

Chapter Nine

River

*D*espite Raiden's insistence to stay at the house, I was glad to be out of there. The cool air nipped at my skin as I stomped the grass surrounding Savannah's farmhouse with my heavy steps.

All around me, a score of shifters crowded the open field, and their gazes held my attention.

We had persuaded almost twenty people to join us today under the guise of requiring their help. I, of course, knew better. I didn't need their help with anything, what I needed was for someone to make a mistake when we questioned them, so I knew who to tear apart.

My teeth chattered as I ran my eyes over the group. None of them seemed to be up to the task, and there were a few here I had grown to trust since my time spent with the resistance. Still, I didn't let myself get carried away with naïve tendencies.

One of these assholes took Billie. I was going to find out who.

Keeping my fists in my jacket pocket, I tried to spot a

wolf shifter in their midst but got nothing. I wasn't sure who I was trying to kid here. I've shifted all of two times and it didn't exactly turn me into some supernatural gumshoe who could sniff out wolves. The only way I would recognize the animal the shapeshifters connected to was if everyone here shifted at once, and that was definitely something I wanted to avoid.

I squared my shoulders and looked through the crowd.

"Thanks for coming," I said, keeping the disdain in my voice hidden.

Not far from me, Raiden murmured something under his breath, and I chose to ignore it. He made his opinion quite clear about us being here, and I could sense his disappointment from where I stood. I didn't care. The big oaf needed to deal with his issues. This was important.

"I'm sorry to drag you out," I continued. I wasn't sorry at all. "I'm sure everyone heard that Billie got kidnapped at the party. I was hoping you might have seen something out of the ordinary that night."

"We already told Raiden everything we know!" someone shouted from the back.

My eyes narrowed on the middle-aged woman who sat huddled next to two young girls. Her strawberry blonde hair blazed in the sunlight and her features were so sharp, I could feel them stab me in the chest. If I had to guess, I'd say she was a coyote, but again, I had no real clue.

The woman glanced at Raiden. "It wasn't anyone in the resistance. We don't kidnap our own."

"She wasn't your own, though, was she?" I asked, arching an eyebrow. "She was a witch, and from my experience, some of you didn't want her around."

The field grew silent. After a few anxious moments, I

watched a young man rise to face me. His long, curly hair whipped in the wind, and his thick form towered over the rest. "Look, man," he said with so much strength, I buckled back. "Billie may have been a witch, but she did a lot for this resistance. No one here wanted to hurt her. That's the damn truth."

"I doubt that's actually true," I said.

"Well, that's your problem. You won't get anything from us because there's nothing else we have to say. We didn't do it!"

His voice echoed down to me, and I noticed the crowd rustle. They were getting pissed, which was what I was hoping for. Angry people let information slip out.

I dug my feet into the grass and tore my gaze from the young shifter.

"So, you're telling me none of you saw anything? I find that hard to believe. You were all there. Someone must have noticed her leave with that girl."

"You were there," the maybe-coyote retorted, "and you saw nothing. Maybe you took her."

My brow creased. "How does that even make sense? Why would I KIDNAP my own girlfriend?"

"I don't know, but it's convenient no one from the wolf pack is here, isn't it?"

So, they didn't show up. Interesting.

"The wolves are searching the woods to get a lead on her trail," Raiden offered. His gaze was trained on me with a look that told me I was wrong to think the wolves were involved in Billie's kidnapping. "I asked them for help this morning and they're doing everything they can."

"I'm good with them not being here," a soft female voice said. "Pretentious pricks."

Okay, this is new. Did the other shifters hate the wolves, or did they fear them? I banked the information to dissect at a later time and returned my attention to the lot in front of me.

"I'm sorry you have to be here. But we need help. No one knows anything, and we have nowhere to begin a search. Please," I begged, hating myself for it, "if you know anyone that might have done this, you have to tell us."

"We don't have to do anything," a stocky old man said. "This is bullshit and we all know it. I'm out of here." He turned to the slender woman at his side. "Let's go, Sam."

As they stood, I had half the mind to stop them, but one glance at Raiden told me to step aside. This was getting us nowhere. If the shifters took her as I thought, no one here was going to talk. I hated every second of it.

Watching the shifters leave one by one without a second look my way made my skin crawl. Someone here was responsible for what happened to Billie, and I was powerless to do anything about it. Whatever politics the resistance had in place were none of my concern, and I despised having to play along. If it was up to me, I'd be laying down a serious beat down on these tools until one of them spilled, but it wasn't up to me. Raiden would never allow it, and neither would the other leaders. As much as I didn't want to accept this, I was on their turf, and I had to play by the rules.

It was infuriating.

When the young girl who spoke before rose to leave, a thought jabbed at my mind. These shifters didn't like the wolf pack for some reason, and while I didn't care what that reason was, it could be useful.

If I could persuade the wolves to let me join, I would be the person the other shifters feared. It would grant me enough power in the resistance to get closer to the bastards I wanted to kill. When I turned my back on the departing crowd and faced Raiden, a new sense of hope washed over me.

"Let's go meet the pack," I said. "Get this crap over with."

Chapter Ten

River

Staying close to the doorway, I studied the wolf pack, trying to keep the disgust on my face to a bare minimum. There were twelve of them in total, nine men and three women, and each one was more intimidating than the first. The entire scene felt like a quick draw from a Wild West movie. All we were missing were saloon doors and tumbleweeds blowing through. Next to me, Raiden towered over us with Mel by his side and their stoic glares seemed to put some distance between me and the other wolves. At least these beasts had the good sense to fear the leaders, and having Raiden and Mel on my side was valuable, to say the least.

The men in the pack were all built much like Raiden, although none of them were quite as tall and menacing. A couple sniffed the air around me as though to make sure I belonged, and when they relaxed, unease filtered through my bloodstream. As much as I wished to deny it, Raiden was right. I was one of them now, and it bothered the crap out of me.

A tall, muscular man with thick eyebrows and an obnoxious wolf tattoo on his shoulder stepped forward, a curvy blonde at his side. Her presence in the room commandeered the other women and they looked to her with the intense attention of soldiers at command. I noticed the men do the same when the man passed by and wondered if these two were the alphas of the pack. It was still hard to wrap my head around the idea of a pack, though from what I knew of the shapeshifter species, packs always had alphas, and this guy was definitely it.

The man leaned over his partner and whispered something in her ear. At his words, she growled but took a few steps back to join the group opposite us. *So, you're the big bad of this little team. Good to know.*

He crossed his arms over his chest and looked me up and down. "I see the pup finally came to his senses."

"Who are you calling a pup?" Savannah sniped next to me.

She had been so quiet the entire time, I forgot she was even there. As soon as she spoke, I turned to face her, scowling when my gaze landed on the muscular guy standing behind her. I remembered him from the training sessions Billie ran, Logan something or other. A mind reaper. I had no clue why Savannah brought him along, but he was here now, and I wasn't about to turn down an extra set of helping hands. One wrong move and we would have ourselves a confrontation, and judging by the looks the wolves were throwing my way, I could use the help if it came down to that.

I nodded to Savannah and shot a smile Logan's way in thanks before turning back to the wolf alpha. "Let's keep this as friendly as possible."

"Ha!" He cackled and looked back to his girl. "The pup needs some friends. Wrong place to find them, kid."

"Give it a rest, Isaac," Raiden said. "He's here because he needs a pack. As I recall, you needed one yourself not long ago."

Isaac frowned, but didn't say anything.

"I think we started on the wrong foot," I said calmly.

"Wrong paw," Savannah whispered under her breath.

She and Logan exchanged laughs and I elbowed her in the ribs. Now was not the time for Savannah's antics.

Training my gaze on Isaac, I sucked in a breath. "Look, I don't want any trouble here. I'm sure you've heard what happened with Billie and I was hoping we could work together to bring her back. I know you've been looking for her trail, but I think there's more we can do here."

"That witch and her coven have been nothing but a pain in our asses. We only helped out of respect for Raiden and the leaders."

Blood boiled in my veins, and I could feel the wolf's possessiveness creep to the surface. Alpha or not, this guy was stepping over a line and if he didn't rein it in, we were going to have a problem. My hands fisted and I blew out a fiery breath, legs tensing and ready for a fight. A hand wrapped around my arm, and I turned to see Mel's eyes on me. *Back the hell down,* she seemed to say, so I listened. My wolf wasn't happy about it but for once, I was in control.

Reluctantly, I uncurled my fingers and relaxed my shoulders. "Billie did a lot for this resistance. I hope you remember that part."

Isaac's brows kissed and he was about to speak when his girl talked over him.

"Anyone that goes against the High Coven is fine in our

books," she said. "My name is Simone. That sad bunch back there is our pack. They're a good group and we're glad to have another."

The alpha was not pleased with her words, but he kept his shit together. Guess he knew better than to argue with his girl, and I had to give him credit for it. Whenever Billie and I disagreed, no matter how much I tried to bury my feet in, she always won the fight. I was a sap and I knew it. Seemed that Isaac had the same situation on his hands with Simone. At least we had something in common.

"It's good to meet you," I said with a nod. "All of you."

Isaac's eyes caught mine and it was clear he was not on board with me sticking around, but I would have to worry about it later. As deeply as I wanted to beat information out of him and his pack, that wasn't a smart move right now. I worked to think of what Billie would do if she was here and came up blank. My witch always knew how to talk her way out of a tough situation and if she couldn't, she sure knew how to fight her way through. I had a pretty good inkling that if she was here, the wolves would be on the floor, licking their wounds already. God, I missed her.

"Did any of you know Damen?"

The question rolled off my lips before I could stop myself and I could sense Raiden tense at my back. I didn't really care though. Just because he was convinced his cousin was innocent didn't mean I had to be.

Simone looked over the shifters and turned her attention back on me. "We didn't know him well," she said, shattering my hopes. "But we heard about what he and his friends tried to do to you and Billie. Everyone here thought that was bull-shit, if that helps."

It sure as shit didn't. I frowned. "Thanks anyway," I

said in almost a whisper. At least we could rule the wolves out from our list of suspects. It still left the rest of the shifters in the house, but I was willing to accept the small victory. "If you guys can think of anyone else, I'd really appreciate the help. And thank you for checking the woods."

"Any time," she said with a smile. "Sorry we couldn't find much though."

Not as sorry as I am.

"Who are your friends?" Isaac asked, interrupting. He eyed Savannah and Logan like he was about to eat them for lunch. "This is wolf business."

Savannah took a defiant step forward and I cringed, worried about what would come out of her mouth. To my surprise, she kept the attitude in check when she faced down the alpha. "Name's Savannah. I'm a hunter and River's friend, so you'll have no trouble from me. And this is Logan. He's—" She paused long enough to raise questions. "Helping out. So he's cool."

Since when is Logan helping out? What the hell, Sav? I banked my confusion for a later discussion.

Opposite us, the pack exchanged looks and sniffed again. It was messed up the way they did that, and I promised myself I would never be the type of asshole to go around smelling people. It was freaking weird and creepy. *Wolves are actually the worst.*

"So, how was your first shift?" Simone asked.

I struggled to ignore Raiden's chuckle at my side. "It was... different."

"Let me guess, you freaked out?"

"That's putting it mildly." I frowned. "Is it always that bad?"

She looked from Isaac to the rest of the wolves. "Nah. It'll get better. You just have to control it. We'll teach you."

"Thanks," I said. I meant it. Shockingly.

"No problem." Simone smiled and I could smell her kindness in the air. *Ew, what? Why is this a thing now?* I seriously despised what was happening to me.

My gaze drifted around the room, taking in the people that were supposedly just like me. I couldn't relate to any of them, and I wasn't sure if it was because we just met, or because we truly had nothing in common. I noticed one guy, a stocky, fridge-sized dude with a thick beard, inch closer to a slender redhead, and my eyes immediately snapped to the mate mark on his chest. It looked similar to Raiden and Mel's, though his was more triangular, with jotting lines sprouting from the center. Though I couldn't see the mark on the redhead, I assumed she had one to match. My heart contracted to look at them and my thoughts went straight to Billie.

I needed the pack's help to get a hold on my shifts and I needed it yesterday.

"You think you can teach me?" I asked. "How to control it, I mean."

Before she could answer, Isaac crossed the room to stand in front of me. His breath filled the space between us, and I could taste his rage as if it was my own. "We teach pack members only."

"So how does he get in?" Savannah asked. "Is there like an application or..."

Logan snickered again but one look from me shut him up. *Why was this guy here again?*

"Look, man. I need your help. Either offer it or we have nothing else to talk about. I don't want to be here any more than you want me here, but I need to figure this shit out before I hurt someone."

Darkness flashed over his features, and I wondered if I hit a nerve. Before my first shift, Raiden told me that most shapeshifters went through the change when they were young, and those that didn't had complications. I wondered if Isaac was one of those complications and if he was who it was that he hurt. Before I could press for information, the alpha turned tail and stormed away from me.

"Meet us in the woods out back tomorrow," he said over his shoulder. "Seven sharp or we start without you."

"Start what?"

Isaac's grin was so wide, I could see it even with his head turned away from me. "Your initiation, pup. Time to see what you got."

Chapter Eleven

Billie

atch... the cavern whispered as the vision of River's fingers being broken swirled before me. I shut my eyes, but his screams brought me back, forcing me to witness the grueling tortures of the High Coven. His head slumped over his chest and drips of blood pounded at the wooden floor beneath him, mimicking the sounds of the water that taunted my waking hours.

Close to his destroyed body, Sebyl's menacing laugh echoed and my pulse raced.

"Cut it out! Now!" I roared, but the cavern didn't listen.

Sebyl's fingers danced and magic flowed from her to River's body. When the purple haze reached him, his muscles tensed, and his chest jerked up. His eyes were wild and full of fear, a look I've never seen on River, and it made the panic inside me explode to the surface. "MAKE IT STOP!"

The golden light flickered, erasing the image of River from my vision, and I slumped down, dragging my legs into my chest.

I didn't know how many of these scenes I've seen, but as far as I was concerned, one was one too many. In all my life, I had never felt more useless. My legs shivered and I rubbed the tears off with my arm, awkwardly shifting my chained hands to dry my face. The metal clanged above me, and the sounds vibrated through the cavern, echoing down the tunnels.

"Naomi? Are you there?"

It took a few moments for her to respond, and by now, I was used to the delay. The woman chained here with me was in much worse shape than I was, and every time she spoke, I could hear she was fading. Fast. I still had no idea who she was or how she got here, but it wasn't the shifters who took her. Of that, I was certain. Something about the way she spoke told me she wasn't from Shadowhurst, and whenever I pressed her about it, she only became more confused. As much as I wanted to get information out of her, I kept my questions to myself, worried I'd drive her insane before the cavern did.

A light rustle sounded down the tunnel as Naomi rearranged herself to talk to me. "What was it today?"

"Same thing," I answered. "He's getting worse. I don't know how long he'll last if they keep beating him like this."

"Don't let it break you. You told me he's strong, right?"

"Yeah. Strong and stubborn as hell."

"Well, then he'll make it." She sounded so certain of it, I almost believed her. "And I'm sure your friends will find him soon."

My heart eased at her words. Naomi was right—my friends would find River and they would save him. I had to hold on to that. If anyone was going to make it through this, it was that annoyingly headstrong boy I loved, and I needed to keep that at the forefront of my mind. I kept the thought right next to my plans for revenge when I made it out of this damn place. If I could ever escape, the first thing I would do was pay a visit to the High Coven and tear their limbs off their bodies. I didn't care that the high priestesses accepted me when no one else would. They were going to pay for what they did to River. And I would be the one to deliver the punishment.

Resting my head on the wet stone behind me, I slumped into the wall and looked down the dark tunnel. "Can I ask you something? And, please, be honest."

"Always."

"You think we'll die down here?"

There was a long silence, and I closed my eyes while I waited for her response. When she finally spoke again, I wished she hadn't.

"Probably."

Oh, goodie. Thank the Goddess I had this positive cheerleader to talk to. I exhaled the breath I was holding and crossed my legs. "Awesome."

Naomi stayed quiet for the rest of the day, or night, I had no clue, while I spiraled out of control. My mind replayed the night the shifters took me over and over, each time thinking of ways I could have escaped the fate that held me now. If I only waited for River to look over so he saw me leave with that girl... But I didn't. I was an idiot, as always, and now, I was paying the price for it. I mean, seriously, that kid might as well have pulled up in a van and told me she had puppies in the back.

What a dumbass.

The cavern's watery melody started again, and I knew it wouldn't be long before the visions returned. No matter what I did, I was torn between watching River suffer or suffering myself. It was either the visions or my magic ripping me a new one. There was no in-between. I wondered how much a body could take before it gave out on you, and judging by the state I was in, it wasn't much at all. My arms felt like spaghetti and my legs barely worked anymore, though I had the sense that being stuck in one position had a lot to do with it. I missed everything and everyone back in Shadowhurst, but more than that, I missed my damn shadows. I couldn't feel their presence anymore, and it was as if an entire part of me had ripped away. When I first discovered the new powers I commanded, I feared them. But now, I would kill to have control over them again.

Straining, I twisted the moonstone ring on my finger and pressed the small crystal into the soft flesh of my palm. My eyelashes fluttered while I tried to connect to the shadows, but it was pointless. This time, I couldn't even feel them enough to cause the pain of the spell as it kicked back, and I wasn't sure what was worse, being in pain after connecting to my magic or having none of it left at all. The latter. Definitely the latter.

A light flickered in my line of sight and I groaned as it grew before me. My body tensed, and I got ready for what came next. My eyes bulged, terror gripping me as a vision of Peyton's house came into view. "NO! NO! NO!" I screamed, tearing at the chains as the vision expanded. "Not her!"

The golden glow blew outward, revealing the house in full, and my eyes snapped to the shadowy figures creeping in Peyton's backyard. They inched closer to the door, coming into focus while I fought the sobs trapped in my throat. Five head witches emerged from the dense foliage that surrounded Peyton's house, each one with magic at the ready. Their sinister faces locked on the tiny figure in the yard and sharp pains ripped through my stomach. Kai, Peyton's younger brother, played with toy trucks next to the pool. His face was bright with cheer as he slammed the little vehicles into each other, mimicking crashing noises with his kiddish voice.

My body jerked in the chains. "Run, Kai! Get out!" But he couldn't hear me.

The witches inched toward him, each one more evil than the next, and hatred bubbled over me. These were the women I used to admire, these monsters. I was disgusted with myself almost as much as I was with them.

Kai's bright eyes snapped up when they neared and he opened his mouth to scream, but a burst of magic flooded the vision. I couldn't see what was happening. Everything was overcome with magic.

My pulse beat like a drum and my breaths quickened as I yanked at the chains, trying to reposition myself to see better. Every part of me felt like it was on fire, and I thrashed against the rock, beating my head into it over and over. Sweat streamed down my brow, falling into my eyes. The sting of it left an agonizing blurriness in my line of sight, and I tried to blink away the spotty vision with no luck. My chest constricted as I attempted to breathe, but my body wouldn't cooperate.

One by one, my legs dropped to the ground, too weak to keep fighting. My head fell forward, and hair slumped over my face, shielding me from the horrors that unfolded.

All I heard was Kai's scream before my eyes rolled back into my head and darkness swallowed me whole.

Chapter Twelve

Billie

Long fingers twisted through my hair, yanking my head back and knocking it into the rock wall. A throbbing ache shot through me, and black dots formed in my vision when I struggled to bring my eyes into focus. Before me, the cavern swam, and nausea filled my throat.

"Time to wake up, witch," Daria hissed, her fingers still laced in my dirty locks. "Nap time's over."

I blinked, pulling away from her, and she loosened her grip to set me free. My brain felt swollen, and the pain dulled into something resembling a low hum in the back of my head.

"What day is it?" I asked when I could speak again.

Daria pulled her lips into a tight smile. "Does it matter?"

Guess not, asshole.

I needed to ask her about Naomi but didn't want to give away any of my secrets. The less the wicked fox that visited me was privy to, the better. Letting her in on the fact that I knew I wasn't alone in this place might have put Naomi in even more danger, and I wasn't about to make that mistake. In the past, my quick draw actions have not turned out that great and I couldn't risk it. Naomi was the only friend I had here, and her safety mattered to me. More than my own, even.

The black dots wavered, leaving behind a sticky mass that refused to budge, and I accepted it as my fate for the moment. Besides, seeing less of Daria's cocky stare was a blessing and I was grateful for it. I seriously wanted to tear her lips off every time she smiled, something she did a lot when I was in pain. Daria was vicious and cold. In fact, she was so awful that she made Savannah look like a freaking saint. Goddess, it would have been nice to have Savannah down here right about now. I was willing to bet the hunter would tear Daria a new one, and I'd have loved to see that.

Maybe I'll let her deal with the fox if I got out of this place.

Daria's knuckles reached for my forehead and she tapped it, bringing fresh pain to my skull. "Hello? Anyone in there?"

"What the hell do you want today?" I bit out. "Came to smack me around some more?"

"Looks like that job is taken."

With a sly grin, she gestured over my beaten down body before bursting into a fit of laughter. Her head shot back, revealing the soft flesh of her skin, and I pictured what it would feel like to stab her in it. Pretty damn good, I'd wager.

When she was finally done entertaining herself with my misery, she crouched down to face me. "Our friends have a deal for you."

"Your friends? Who are they again?" I raised an eyebrow.

"Nice try, witch." Daria grinned and I frowned. *Worth a shot.* "They'll get your boy toy out if you give them what they want. Pretty good deal, if you ask me."

No one asked you, Daria. "And what do they want?"

She ran an index finger along my leg. "The book."

My ears rang and my skin crawled at her touch. Whoever was helping her wanted the Book of Darkness. But why? My assumption that the coven took me was back in full mode and anger flashed through my mind as I thought it over. Was I wrong to drop the theory so quickly, and could this all have been some ploy to get the book back? The reasoning lined up, but something still didn't sit right. The spell holding my powers in check was not one the coven knew how to use. It was too dangerous, and if it was around, the rest of the witches would have been privy to the information. The high priestesses were first-grade tools, but they would never keep that spell hidden. Not when it could hurt other witches if it got into the wrong hands. The High Coven's entire mission was to protect our kind. Even the blocking spells they used to keep the magical prison operational did not destroy the witches held within. It only stripped them of their magic, not used it against them. At least as far as I knew.

Then again, there were a lot of secrets I uncovered in the last little while I never imagined could be true. For all I knew, the witches in the prison were suffering the same fate as me and I was too brainwashed to see it.

My heart ached as I pictured Beatrix and Evanora chained to a wall in their cells and getting tormented daily.

No, that couldn't be it.

The magic I felt in the cavern wasn't witch magic. It was different and grim.

"Why do they need the book?"

The useless idiot shrugged. Of course, she had no idea. Whoever she was working for was clearly using her and her shifter friends as a pawn for their own gain. I almost felt sorry for her. Almost.

I ousted an exasperated breath and looked up at her. "Not sure if you noticed, but I don't have the book. Forgot to pack it for this fun vacation."

"No shit, smartass," Daria hissed. "They want to know where it is."

"Can't help you there."

I wasn't lying. The Book of Darkness was with the resistance, and I did not doubt that after I was grabbed, they put it somewhere no one could access it. That thing was the only leg up we had on the High Coven, and they'd be dumb not to keep it under close watch. One thing I learned about the shadowers in the resistance since I met them was that they were far from stupid. They were organized and detail-oriented to a tee. Hiding the book would have been the first thing they did, and right now, it relieved me to believe that.

Daria scowled and veins popped out on her forehead. "Can't or won't?"

"I don't know where the book is. That's the truth."

"Suit yourself," she said, kicking my leg. "I did my part and asked you nicely. Looks like you'll be here for a while."

Goddess, that was nice? I'd hate to think what the other option looked like for Daria.

The fox grabbed something from the floor and walked over to me, tilting my head back to pour water down my throat. I choked as the liquid made its way down, but refused to spit it out. Who knew when Daria would come back with more and thirst overcame me every minute of the day in this place. When the bottle she held over me emptied, Daria shot me a look of disgust and disappeared down a tunnel.

Her steps lightened and I listened in to see if she was visiting Naomi, but the cavern was a silent void. For now, my friend was safe from Daria's bullshit, and I breathed out a long sigh.

Shockingly, the light of the visions did not return when the fox left my side. I took the chance to gather my thoughts before they got torn away again. Somewhere in the distance, drops of water beat down the rock, intensifying in their melody. When the sound reached me, I wanted to scream, but before I could, a thought pulled at my brain. It was so brief that I almost missed it, but now that I had, happiness filled my gut.

Water! Of course!

The drops sped up and my mind raced with them. Where there were drops, there was a water flow. Water I could follow if I could manage to get free. I couldn't have been kept that far deep in the cavern since I doubt Daria would make the trek every day, so it stood to reason that I was being held somewhere that was close enough to the surface to make it easy for her to visit often. If I could find the source of those damn drops, I could follow the water flow out. I just needed to figure out where they were coming from.

Every time I heard them, they sounded like they were all around me, but that couldn't be the case. It was just the cavern amplifying the sound.

I knew the direction Daria came and went every day by now, so that would be my first move. Follow it until I found the water and take it from there.

For the first time since I woke up in this place, hope

emerged, and I clung to it with all my might. I needed to get free of the chains that held me. It was the only way to test my theory and get Naomi and me out of here. Doubt clouded my thoughts, but I pushed it away. I'd get out of this wretched place, both of us would.

My fingers tightened on the metal chains, and I gritted my teeth as I dug deep down to connect to my magic. One way or another, we were leaving, but I knew there was one thing I could do to help speed up the process.

Excruciating pain coursed through my veins as I forced my magic outward, willing for it to find me. The spell tightened over my chest and beat me down until I was sweaty and breathless again. I didn't stop. Pushing harder and harder, I fought against it, casting about for the shadows in the hidden recesses of myself. If it was the last thing I did, I would have my magic back.

I was going to save us both.

Chapter Thirteen

River

If you told me that there would be a point in my life that I would find myself in the woods with twelve wolf shifters surrounding me, I would have laughed in your face. Unfortunately for me, life's idea of a good time was kicking me in the balls on the daily, so here I was; in the forest's midst at the break of dawn, about to get my ass handed to me by Isaac and his buddies.

The wolves formed a circle around me as soon as I approached, and I regretted not taking Raiden up on his offer to join. Having the massive lion shifter here for backup would have been blissful, but I knew Isaac wouldn't approve. Much as I hated bowing down to the alpha, it went against everything I stood for, I understood that getting on his good side meant having the pack's approval I desperately needed that.

They were the only ones who could teach me to control the beast inside, and my friends needed me at a hundred percent so we can save Billie.

Just thinking of her made my head pound with worry,

but I shoved the thoughts away, concentrating instead on Isaac's angry glare as he entered the circle.

"Shift," he said as soon as his gaze met mine.

My pulse thundered. *Damn it.*

Cringing at my own incompetence, I widened my stance. "I-I can't. I don't know how. The last two times it just sort of happened on its own."

"What caused it? Repeat that."

Remnants of Billie's heartache gripped my chest, and I shook my head. *Yeah, that's not going to happen.* My jaw snapped and anger bubbled to the surface. "Not an option. You got anything else, wise one?"

Shit, that was a bad move.

Before I could blink, Isaac was in my face, his heavy hand wrapped around my throat. He tightened his grip and my breath caught on my lips while he continued to choke me. On instinct, I reached for his arm, but he slapped me away as though I was a dog snatching snacks off a table. Isaac's fingers pressed into my skin and when I glanced up at him, his eyes were glowing so brightly, they looked like sunlight. Fur rippled from his skin and his ears stretched until they were pointed at the tips. Holy crap! This guy was literally mid-shift and holding his act together, and I couldn't even get my wolf to stop trying to kill my friends.

I really did have a lot to learn here.

My feet floated off the ground as Isaac raised his arm with me still in his hold. Deep inside, the wolf growled against my psyche and my lips curled into a smile. *Welcome, moron. Finally woke up, huh?*

The wolf vibrated against my skin, and I shut my eyes, waiting for it to make a move. It didn't take long for the beast to slither out of its dark hole, and while Isaac's hold on me was strong, my power was increasing. My arms shot out to the side and my fingers fanned out. The sound of them reforming filled my ears, and I snapped my jaw, biting on my tongue hard enough to draw blood.

"Don't let him tell you what to do," Isaac hissed. "Find the power he has and connect to it. Got it?"

I nodded. At least, I thought I did. I had no idea what my body was doing, but what he said started to make sense. I hoped.

As the alpha instructed, I pushed against my beast, picturing my fingers curling into fists. The wolf fought me every step of the way, but I wouldn't let it win. It howled, or maybe I did, I wasn't sure anymore.

Shut up and listen! I screamed at him in my head.

One by one, my fingers moved, and the pain made my skin burn. The sound of bones breaking rent the trees, and I could hear the other members of the pack grumble curses under their breath. I didn't pay them any mind. My thoughts were only on the damn beast inside me that thought it could tell me what to do.

The wolf howled in pain as I forced the last of my fingers tight and pushed my arms outward. At that moment, something shifted. It was as though I could sense the wolf, the same way I did when I fully changed, but all that power was trapped somehow. I was so much stronger, I could taste it. Wrapping my arms in, I slammed them over Isaac's hand, breaking the hold he had over me. My eyes snapped open, and I shot my leg up, hitting the alpha straight in the gut and sending him barreling backward. He skidded across the dirt, coming to a stop a few feet away from me.

His eyes met mine and there was something in them I hadn't seen before.

Respect.

Inside me, the wolf howled again, and I cursed it out. It answered to me, not the other way around. I needed the wolf to understand that. At my side, my fingers tried to uncurl, and my bones ached from the need to shift. Every part of me was torn between two worlds, and I didn't know which one would win. My knees hit the hard ground and I struggled not to crouch on all fours. At this point, I knew where that led, and I wasn't about to go wolf right now.

A powerful hand gripped my shoulder, and I looked up at Isaac's stern face over me. "It won't listen," I bit out through clenched teeth. "It wants me to shift."

"He," Isaac corrected me. "Not it. Treat him with respect and the rest will follow."

Was he joking? How do you treat something that vile with respect? I craved to punch Isaac's face in, but I stayed still, battling the urge to shift. My entire body shook, and my brain felt like it was melting in my skull. While I could still form distinct thoughts, I reached for the beast. *Come on, buddy. Let's do this. Show this asshole who's boss around here.*

My wolf seemed to like that, something I would definitely need to keep in mind, and he loosened his angry grip on my mind. *Interesting.*

Slowly, the feral need to shift and attack dissipated, and I heaved over my legs, holding my breath to keep from upchucking the coffee I had that morning. When I looked down, my half-formed paws were shifting back, and I could barely feel the pain of the bones breaking.

Thanks, man, I whispered to the wolf. The experience was much less traumatic this time. I had a feeling he had something to do with it.

Around me, the pack offered cheers of encouragement

and a few rushed to my side, patting me on the back like I just won a freaking race. Isaac said something before helping me up, though his words didn't reach me. All I could hear was the wolf panting inside me, and for the first time since the initial shift, I didn't hate the sound.

"Whoa..." Peyton's eyes were wide while she listened to me rehash the morning's events. "Can't believe you totally schooled your wolf like that. Bad. Ass."

I chuckled. "I don't think it's that simple, but yeah, it felt better this time."

"I'm glad Isaac helped," Raiden said, a dumb smile on his face. With how much he was beaming, you'd think it was him that got the wolf to calm the hell down. "What did the rest of the pack say?"

Lorelei and Mel trained their eyes on me, and I wanted to storm out of the room. For a short while there, I thought I could be friends with these people, but somehow, that wasn't looking to be an option anymore. They were leaders of the resistance and as badly as I needed their help in finding Billie, I could never pretend we were buddies helping each other out. Even Peyton was different now, glaring at me like she knew something I didn't.

It was ridiculous and annoying.

"Nothing much," I finally said. "I don't think I'm part of their dumb group, if that's what you're asking. But they helped, so I'm grateful."

"I could talk to Isaac," Mel offered.

I shrugged her off. "Don't. I can do it on my own. I have to get in with them, and soon."

"Attaboy!" Raiden cheered.

I swear, I will clock you, dude. "Don't get too excited," I said. "I don't want a pack, but I do need them."

The confused faces around me told me I should elaborate.

"Look, I know you two have Daria working with the shifters," I started, pushing the resentment I had my lack of involvement aside. "But no offense to her and her friends, it hasn't gotten us anything we can use. Whoever took Billie isn't going to raise their hand and admit to it. And they definitely won't talk to you two, if that's your next move. You're their leaders and no matter what their beef is with Billie, they fear you. Enough to keep their mouths shut. If we have any chance of figuring this out, the pack is the best way to do that."

"How?"

"It's really very simple. I get in on their good side, put on a perfect little wolf act, and use them to get information on the other shifters. If whoever took Billie thinks I am spending my time playing wolf, they might drop their defenses. It's our only shot here. Plus, the other shifters seem to be afraid of the wolves, so it's a good play."

"Isaac won't like that."

"I don't actually give a shit," I sniped. "And he doesn't have to know, so maybe don't say anything. I'll figure it out when it comes down to it."

Opposite me, Peyton kicked her leg up on a chair and stared me down like she was about to breathe fire. "That's gonna take too long. We need to find her now!"

"You don't think I know that?"

I liked Peyton, but her attitude was making me want to throw punches. Inside, the wolf agreed, and worry set in when I thought about losing control right now. Luckily, he was all bark and no bite, and though I could sense his anger, he did nothing about it. Good.

"Tyler and Abigail will be in Stamwick in a few hours," I said. "We'll know if the coven is behind this soon, but until then, I'll do what I can with the wolves."

"And if they are responsible?" Lorelei asked. The mind reaper had been silent since we met in the cramped dining room, so when she spoke, I listened.

The concern on her face was tangible, and though I wished to deny it, I felt it too. If Tyler and Abigail found out the High Coven was behind the kidnapping, we were in deep shit. No one in the house was strong enough to go against them. Hell, the last time we won was because Billie was there. But we didn't have a choice. At least I didn't. I had to get her back and I would die finding her. Coven or not, I was bringing my girl home and I would kill whoever took her from me.

Determination washed over me when I faced Lorelei. "If it was the coven, nothing changes. We kill them all if we have to. We're getting Billie home."

Chapter Fourteen

River

By the time the leaders left, leaving only Payton and me at the table, I was frustrated beyond belief. It had been days since Billie was taken and we were nowhere close to finding a lead. Why the hell did I think this would be easy? Nothing ever was in this damn town. If Billie was here, she'd have figured it out by now and I felt even more helpless when I thought of it. Finding needles in haystacks was a superpower of hers. It sure as shit wasn't mine though. Unlike my stubborn, brilliant girlfriend, I couldn't find a clue if my life depended on it, and I hated myself for being so incompetent.

Not that anyone else in the house was any better. It was looking like Billie was the only one of our bunch that had any sense, and without her here, we were screwed.

Across from me, Peyton sat with her legs crossed and a permascowl plastered on her face.

"What are you thinking?" I asked when she finally looked my way.

She forced out a loud sigh. "I'm seriously freaking out here."

That makes two of us.

"About the High Coven?"

"Yep. And all of it, really." She frowned, her eyes slinking into thin lines. "We're spinning in freaking circles here. It doesn't make sense that we haven't found anything so far. It's like whoever took her vanished. Like they're playing with us or something."

"People don't vanish, Peyton. We'll find them. Everyone leaves a trail."

Heavily lined eyes stared back at me. "You sound like her."

A searing pain shot through my heart, and I tore my gaze off Peyton to look at the wall. Frames upon frames of shadowers that were killed by the High Coven glared back at me, and it only worsened the dull ache that spread through my chest. *What would you do if you were here, babe? Where would you look?* My questions fell away, shattering me into oblivion.

"We'll find her," I said because it was all I could manage to think of.

"How, River? How will we find her? We've gotten nowhere so far! Literally nowhere!" The color drained from Peyton's face, and she dug her multi-colored nails into the table's wood. "I've never felt this useless in my entire life."

I tried to smile, failing miserably. "Yeah, me too. How's the leader thing going?"

She shrugged.

"That good, huh?"

"It's the freaking worst! Marcus had everything figured out and I'm scrambling just to keep up. I mean, you've seen the rest of them? Can we say intimidating? I don't even know what I'm trying to accomplish here. These people will never listen to anything I have to say. I'm a mess and they know it."

"Don't say that." I leaned in, ducking my head to find her eyes. When I saw the lines of mascara dripping down her face, panic swelled in me. Peyton had never cried before, at least not in front of me. Even when Savannah and Abigail gave her hell back when we were kid,s all she did was talk back. This wasn't something I knew how to handle, and I cursed myself for not getting a *Peyton Instruction Manual* from Billie. Resting my chin in my hands, I arched an eyebrow. "Are you telling me Peyton Ling is backing down from a challenge?"

"Shut up, River. It's not a game."

"Isn't it though?" I asked. "Remember that time Savannah made you trip in the assembly in front of everyone?"

Peyton sneered. "Dude! You really suck at making people feel better!"

"Stay with me here," I urged. "After you ate pavement, remember what you did?"

"Flipped her off and got detention for it?"

"Yep."

"Good talk."

Chuckling, I shook my head and found her eyes again. "What I mean is, you didn't back down. Sav is a lot to handle, and most people don't mess with her, but not you. You got yourself stuck in detention just so you can show her she can't hurt you. That's the Peyton I remember. Where's that girl now?"

"Not sure if you noticed, bro, but this isn't exactly the same as tripping in grade five."

"Actually, it kinda is. So what if Marcus set unrealistic expectations? The job is yours now, so what you do with it is your call. The soul suckers here need you and I know you can step up to do this, Billie knew it too."

At the mention of her best friend's name, Peyton's eyes got wet again, but she brushed the tears off with her sleeve. "I really miss her. Morgan does too. I guess we all do."

"You're lucky to have Morgan around. I'm glad you two found each other," I said.

Peyton smiled in the most genuine way I've seen in days. Her entire face pretty much lit up. "Me too. She's—" A deep blush spread over her cheeks. "She's really awesome. I know Billie was gunning for us to hook up, but I had no idea how on point she was. Little freaking matchmaker. I'll never hear the end of it when she's back."

The joy in her face dissipated into thin air and she dropped her eyes to the floor. "What if we don't find her?"

Not an option. "Look, Peyton, we both know our girl is not going down without a fight. We'll figure this out and to do that, we both need to get our shit together."

She was quiet for a while, staring into the corner of the room and biting her nails to the bone. After a few minutes of excruciating silence, Peyton squared her shoulders and blinked away whatever thoughts were haunting her.

"You really think getting in with the pack will help?"

I took a deep breath before answering. "No clue. But it can't hurt. I meant what I said. The pack could be useful in one way or another. Raiden was right about the wolves. They are one of the tightest shifter groups in the house and the others fear them. Having them on our side can't be a bad thing, especially if the High Coven are involved in Billie's kidnapping. We'll need all the help we can get."

"Yeah, no shit. Hope you're right, teen wolf."

"Okay, that's not a thing."

Peyton grinned. "Tell that to Savannah. Girlfriend is one step short of having t-shirts made for you."

An image of Savannah wearing a shirt with my dumb wolf face on it flashed before me and I gagged at the thought. "So, what do you say? Think you can stop the waterworks and help me figure all this crap out?"

"You got yourself a deal, wolf boy!" Peyton exclaimed. "No one messes with me or my friends."

Smiling, I nodded and let my body relax for a moment. Peyton was right. No one messed with us or our friends, and if they did, there would be hell to pay.

Savannah's hair was tied back so tight, it made her eyebrows rise higher on her forehead like she was permanently in a state of shock. To be honest, I wasn't sure why I was even noticing that. I should have been more focused on what she discovered when looking into the backgrounds of the resistance shifters.

She tapped a broken pencil against the wooden tabletop and every hit jerked my thoughts into a million different directions. The shifters were squeaky clean, all except one.

"When's Raiden getting here?" I asked, seconds before the door flew open and the lion shifter barged in.

His face was flushed, like he ran here, and I could tell by his confused expression that he had no idea why I called him. I wasn't even sure myself, but Savannah's discovery didn't sit well with me.

"What's wrong? Mel said you got something and wanted

to see me," Raiden said, his breath heavy. "Did you find a clue?"

"You can say that again," Savannah scoffed.

Raiden looked from her to me, his confusion deepening.

"This girl you have checking everyone's alibis," I said. "Daria. Why didn't you tell us her and Damen were a thing?"

The lion shifter breathed out a laugh, relaxing his shoulders and leaning back on the doorframe. "That's why you called me here? River, seriously, you have to work on your delivery. I thought this was important!"

"It is important," I hissed. "Your cousin, who wanted to kill us, was dating the chick you now have looking for Billie. What if they're in on it together?"

Raiden laughed again, and I fought the need to attack him. His eyes glistened, and he cracked his fingers so loud, the sound reverberated in my ears like thunder. "Damen messed that up like he does everything else. Daria is a good kid, way better than he deserved. When he started hanging out with the twins, she hit the road. Can't say I blame her, those two were trouble."

"The twins River killed?" Savannah asked.

"Yep. Listen, I get you want Damen to be the answer here, but he's not. I wish he was, trust me."

My back stiffened as I looked him up and down, trying to find the lies in his words. There were none. Raiden was so convinced of his cousin's innocence that it was making me question myself. Was I obsessing over Damen? Probably. I couldn't help myself though, and it made me uneasy. It also made me feel incredibly useless and stupid.

In all the movies I watched, the cops had some perfect theory worked out to find missing people and the clues just landed in their freaking laps. What they forget to tell you in those idiotic films was what happens when there are no leads or clues at all. How do you find someone that simply evaporated off the face of the earth?

Every small hope we got in the last while led us absolutely nowhere and we were no closer to finding Billie than we were days ago. Somehow, deep down, I believed it would have been easier. Maybe that was why I was so set on Damen being the one to do it. It tied everything up in a neat little bow.

That wasn't how life worked though. At least not my life.

There were no clues to lead me to the next destination and no breadcrumbs trailing straight to Billie. I was spinning wheels, we all were, and it made me mad as hell.

"I want to talk to this Daria girl," I said with determination. "Not that I don't trust you and Mel, but I want to hear what she has so far on my own. Can you arrange a meeting?"

To my relief, Raiden nodded. "I'll call her now. Be ready in an hour."

He didn't have to tell me twice. I was as ready as I ever was.

Chapter Fifteen

Billie

Daria had not returned for hours, and I worried she never would. My stomach growled, and I worked to think about the last time she brought me the stale bread that had become a staple in my meal plan. Twelve hours, maybe? I couldn't tell anymore.

"Hey, Naomi?" I asked. "You there?"

There was no answer this time. My head pounded and my mind raced as worry took over me. How long has it been since I spoke to her? Was she all right? What bothered me most was that the cavern's visions stayed away since they showed me the gruesome attack on Kai, and as much as I dreaded seeing them, not seeing them was worse. At least when the visions came, I could keep tabs on my friends and River. Dreadful as those tabs were.

My heart broke when I remembered River's broken body, and I shifted my weight, forcing the pendant to roll around so I could feel closer to him. It wasn't nearly enough to bring me peace, and soon, tears were blurring my sight. None of this was fair. River and I have only started whatever it was we had going on, and already, I was losing him. I didn't have a lot of experience with men, but I was pretty sure that getting yourself trapped in a cavern while witches pummeled your boyfriend to death wasn't standard dating procedure. Every time I thought I found some semblance of happiness, it was yanked away from me. Now, my bad luck followed the people I loved as well.

"YOU WILL NOT WIN!" I roared, my voice echoing down the cavern.

I had to get the hell out of this place, and for that to happen, Daria had to return. Ever since she left, I had gotten closer to reaching my shadows, but I couldn't attempt an escape in case she showed up in the middle of it. After Daria's next visit, I was going to fight through the spell and tap into my magic. I just needed her to hurry her sad ass up and get here already.

Something ran by in my peripheral vision, and I snapped my head in its direction. The tunnel I faced was as empty as always, and yet, when I moved my head, the darkness within it seemed to follow. I narrowed my eyes and faced it head-on, concentrating on making out some detail in the shadow.

It swayed slowly, spreading out over the tunnel's walls and then contracting together again. The darkness swelled and shrunk like a beating heart, and when it stopped moving, a gasp fell from my lips.

There, at the furthest point of the tunnel, the shape of a man appeared.

He was tall, not as tall as River, but fairly close. It was too dark, and I couldn't make out any of his features, but I could tell he had a broader build, with long legs that anchored to the rock beneath him. His hair had a curl to it, and it fell just past his ears, rustling in the light wind that blew through the tunnel. As he moved, the darkness followed him, keeping him encased in its cocoon and out of my sight.

Blinking rapidly, I shook my head.

This can't be real. I'm going freaking nuts.

"Hello, Billie," the man said, and my jaw hit the ground. "I didn't think I'd see you again."

"W-what?" I choked out.

The man leaned on the tunnel's wall, kicking a foot up behind him. "Your mother did an excellent job hiding you from me," he said, his voice like a song. "She was always so sneaky."

What in the actual hell is happening here? My mouth opened and shut, but no words came out. Mainly, because I had none. I must have misheard him because there was no way this guy knew Beatrix, and if what he was saying was true, why did she feel the need to hide me from this person. Unless...

"Dad?" I breathed out. *He's not your damn dad. What is wrong with you? This is just the cavern playing with your head again.* "No, this isn't real. You're not real."

The man tsked and cocked his head to the side. "I am very real, daughter. Sorry to meet under such awful circumstances."

"Screw you!" I bit out before I could stop myself. "If you're real, prove it. Get me out of here!"

"I cannot."

"Figures."

A low laugh drifted through the tunnel and the man took a step forward. The shadows floated behind him like a cape, and when he stopped, it rearranged itself to wrap around his body. "I see you got my gift."

His head tilted to my hand, and I followed his gaze to the moonstone ring. Memories of my last conversation with Beatrix at the prison crashed through me, twisting me up inside. She told me the ring was from my father, that it was the only good thing he ever did. But why not tell me who he was, and how did this guy know about it in the first place? I had a hard time believing this was my dad. Dads didn't show up when you were chained to a wall and then just stand around, refusing to help you. Well, maybe some dads did. Maybe mine did.

Fear gripped me when I remembered Beatrix's words. *You must never look for your father.*

Great going, Mom. Didn't have to look far, did I? He found me just fine on his own. If this was him in the first place, which I highly doubted it was. Even if I wasn't going completely nuts and this was my father, I couldn't let myself think about it. At least not while I was still stuck in this damn mess. *No distractions, eye on the prize.* I forced the tears that threatened to flow back down, narrowing my gaze on the shadow man.

"So, if you won't help me," I said, gathering the mess I was into a tight little package. "Why are you here?"

The murkiness around him spread, overtaking the entire width of the tunnel. When it reformed, he was standing at the edge, and though he was closer, I still could not make out his face.

"I wanted to see how you were, all things considering."

An uncontrollable rage filled my gut, and I kicked my legs up, straining them to bring myself to stand. This guy had some nerve. He showed up here after being gone my entire life, refused to help me, then asked how I was? I didn't think so. One absentee parent was enough, I didn't need to add a second to the mix. I had done just fine in my life without Beatrix around, and I would do fine without him as well. If this idiot couldn't free me, I had no use for him.

Shaking the chains that held me, I faced him. "Doing just great. Thanks for stopping by."

"The hostility is quite unnecessary, daughter."

"I beg to differ."

Though I couldn't see his face, I could sense a smile spread across his features. I hated that I pleased him somehow.

"You wanted to know why I came," he said. "I am here to offer some guidance that I believe will serve you well. You're powerful, Billie. More so than you know. There are parts you are yet to tap into, and if you have any hope of escaping this place, you must find them. Connect to the part of you that lies hidden inside, it is your answer."

"What part of me? What the hell are you even talking about?"

"The part that isn't witch," he answered bluntly, as though that explained anything.

I blinked. "The shadows?"

"Perhaps."

Oh, good, more riddles. Wonderful.

"Look," I said, acid in my tone. "Whoever you are, and whatever this is, it's not working. I can't use the shadows or any other magic here. There's some spell on this place that's keeping my powers blocked, so unless you know how to fix that part, I'm shit out of luck."

"It is no spell."

What does that mean now? "Then what is it? A charm, a potion, WHAT? Tell me!"

He laughed again, and I stifled the urge to kick a rock his

way. "The power here is yours, you must simply find it. Look inside, daughter, and it will all be clear."

Oh, yeah. Clear as fog.

"You are the key," he continued. "Your mother was mistaken to hide you from me, and now that I found you again, all will be right. Find the power, Billie. Find it and your true path will unfold."

Before I could ask more questions, the shadows dispersed, taking the man with them. The tunnel grew dim, and I slunk my shoulders, banging my head against the wall for support. My knees trembled, and everything in me told me I should fear this guy. If he was even real to begin with. There were so many questions running through me, I couldn't keep them all straight. My mind swam and my vision blurred as I fought to stay upright.

Deep in the tunnel, loud footsteps sounded, and a pang of hope rose in my heart. *He's back!*

When the figures emerged, every ounce of anticipation left me, and I pressed my back to the stone. Blinding terror spread through my bones as Daria stepped through the opening with four massive shapeshifters at her side. Their starved grins spread when they took me in, running their foul burning eyes over my figure.

Daria closed the distance between us and reached for the shackles. I tried to fight her, but she delivered two blows to my side, making me keel over myself. She undid the shackles and threw me to the ground. My knees scraped against the rough surface. Pulse racing, I scrambled to get up when another shifter slammed a boot on my back, forcing me down.

My arms spread out under me, and I pancaked on the cold stone, face hitting the rock last. In my sightline, a set of boots appeared, then another, until I was surrounded on all sides.

Shit! Shit! Shit!

Reaching out a hand, I struggled to grab a hold of someone's ankle to bring them down, but my arm was kicked away before I made contact.

Over me, Daria laughed, and her shrill voice carried over the cavern. Somewhere down the tunnel, Naomi listened in, I was sure of it. My eyes shut tightly and stilled, waiting for whatever came next with only one thought rushing through my mind.

Better me than her.

Chapter Sixteen

River

"Dude, that's rough," the brooding shifter I was talking to said. I think his name was Griffin. By now, I had met the entire pack, and the names melted together until I couldn't remember one from the other.

"You're telling me," I agreed. "We have no clue where she is and it's driving me crazy. As a fun bonus, my wolf hates my guts. So that's great."

Griffin, I hoped, slid back on the tree stump we sat on and looked over the horizon. His broad frame took up most of the seating space and I had to huddle in the corner like it was rush hour on public transport. At least that's what I imagined it to be. My mom forced a car down my throat as soon as I was old enough to drive and my experience with buses was limited. Beside me, Griffin retied the low bun at the nape of his neck, tucking a few golden strands behind his ears. His gaze was serious and gloomy, though, from my brief interaction with him, I could tell he wouldn't be a problem. Griffin was mostly a good guy, as far as I could tell.

The midday sun was high above us, blazing its rays through the dense trees. Even with the sunlight on my face, I was frozen solid. Fall in Shadowhurst had a chill to it that turned your skin blue, and it was one reason I hated the season. I thought most shifters ran hotter than lit fireplaces, but Griffin said that was a myth. Turns out only the air changed when we were around while our bodies stayed close to normal. *Fantastic.* As I sat next to him, watching the rest of the pack run off into the woods with their tails wagging behind them, my body tensed. Billie had been gone for almost three days and we were still at ground zero.

I craved to punch things.

"Have you tried to work on your control like Isaac said?" Griffin asked.

I shrugged. "Sort of. Honestly, man, my head's just not in this right now. I haven't slept in days and all I can think about is her."

Griffin shifted his weight, ripping bark off the stump.

"Sorry," I whispered. "I don't know why I'm laying this on you. Probably just exhaustion."

"It's cool. It's what packs are for."

Was I in their pack? The way things were going with Isaac, it didn't look good, but Griffin seemed to think I was in, so who was I to argue? I needed to be in. That was all that mattered.

The sun hid behind a line of trees, throwing deep shadows over us. "What's up with Isaac anyway? Is he always so—"

"Intense?" Griffin arched an eyebrow my way. "Pretty much. But he means well, so you get used to it. The pack is everything to him and he is our alpha. You should listen to his advice."

"I'm not sure I'm built to have an alpha."

Griffin's low laugh flowed through the forest. "Every wolf has an alpha. You're no exception. Unless…"

"Unless what?"

"Unless you're one yourself. But considering your ass can't even shift properly, I doubt that's true."

Shit. I really hoped that wasn't the case. The last thing I wanted was to be stuck leading these assholes. Griffin seemed to agree, looking me over then laughing again. *Great, now I'm a joke to these people. Amazing progress.*

"You wanna try it again?" he asked, gesturing to the small clearing before us.

The pack was long gone, likely hunting whatever poor animal they could find in their path. Isaac called these trips a pack bonding experience, though I begged to differ. Whether or not I could get a hold of my wolf, there was no way in hell would I ever kill another animal. The thought alone made me gag, and I ran my hands through my hair, forcing the bile down and rising to stand. "Just promise me you'll take me down if I try something stupid."

"Scout's honor," he said, holding up two crisscrossed fingers to his chest.

As I stood, I attempted to recall what Isaac told me to do, but my mind was not in the right space. Every time I had a moment of quiet, Billie's face flashed before me, and I was full of rage again. The wolf responded to that emotion no problem. It was one of our biggest issues, actually. If we were going to be sharing this body, my body, there had to be some ground rules. I couldn't shift each time I thought about her, or I'd be completely useless in our plan to get her back. What I needed was to figure out another way to trigger the shift.

Something that didn't involve me wanting to destroy every-thing in my path.

I struggled to think of the parts of my life that made me happy, anything that might get the wolf's attention. The more I thought about it, the more I realized that my life up until I met Billie pretty much sucked. I mean, sure, my friends were great, but other than them, I had nothing going on. Mom pushed me into witch-hunting so young that I didn't have a chance to figure out what it was that *I* wanted. Or who I wanted to be. It didn't help that my dad was on my case to pick a college and get over the hunting business, but he didn't get to have a sway on my choices. The guy left us without breaking a sweat, and it'd be a long while until I considered him a proper father figure. I squinted, recalling any activities I could remember where I felt like myself. Sports were a big part of my life growing up, though that only led me back to witch-hunting, so I dropped it.

Who the hell was I?

Someone that loves Billie. My brain seemed to be working against me today, and I squashed the feeling before the wolf took notice. I was too late.

I didn't even have time to register what happened when my entire body dropped to the ground like a sack of crap, and I convulsed as the shift took over. Inside, the wolf growled and scratched at the surface, and my blood boiled. My arms shot back, snapping into awkward angles as he took control of my body. His savage anger took me over, and though I couldn't be certain, I thought I felt him missing her as much as I did.

My eyebrows kissed. *So, we have something in common, huh? You love her too.*

The wolf whimpered, loosening his hold on my body. I

was still shifting, but this time, it wasn't the big event I had grown used to. It was slow and steady, poetic almost. Turning to crouch on all fours, I forced my gaze down and concentrated on the shift. Bones broke and skin stretched until every part of me was twisting inside out, yet I didn't feel any pain. *Got you now, sucker.* My lips spread into a sneer.

He did not love that.

As fast as it started, the shift paused and trapped me in the worst position possible. My legs were half-formed and I could feel a tail brush against them, but my upper body was still very much human. *Dude, what the hell? Finish the damn job!*

He did not.

Next to me, Griffin crouched on the tree stump, his eyebrows high enough to touch his hair. "This is new."

"HELP ME!" I screamed, annoyed with his nonchalant attitude. "How do I finish this?"

"No clue."

That's just perfect.

Panic rose in my gut, and I tried to run, but the back of my body refused to cooperate. The bastard inside me was literally holding my legs hostage. I needed to scream. In fact, I did. A lot. I cursed and huffed and puffed like a maniac, but nothing I did helped move the shift along. *Oh, no. Am I stuck like this forever?*

I didn't have time to dissect the thought. In seconds, an enormous hand swiped across my face, pushing me to my back. My cheek burnt from the slap and the anger I had before simmered to the surface. I attempted to fight back, but was held down. A minty scent filled the air, and I snapped my gaze to Raiden's large body crouching over me. He held one hand to my chest, pushing me into the ground while beating me with the other.

More cursing burst from me and I yelped as I fought to push him off. It definitely wasn't my finest moment. The wolf's body made it entirely impossible for me to have proper control, so I only flailed like an idiot making no contact at all. Raiden delivered another blow to my face, one that seemed to do the trick.

The wolf roared within me, forcing me to flip to my stomach so he could complete what he started. In a flash, my bones cracked, and my body reshaped to let the beast free. I buried my paws into the ground, facing Raiden and growling under my breath. My snout wetted, ready for attack.

Before me, a bright light submerged the usual blue of Raiden's eyes. He cracked his neck, facing me, and the wolf paused. Isaac may have been alpha of the wolf pack, but Raiden was something else entirely. He was the king of the freaking jungle, at least as far as the shifters were concerned.

My wolf whimpered, taking a step back and lowering his snout to the ground.

"Good," Raiden said, his voice low and heady. "Now shift back. Daria is here to talk to you."

The wolf didn't argue. One by one, my bones broke and mended until I was lying naked in the clearing with two giant dudes looking over me. If anyone else walked by right now, they'd probably call the cops on us. Luckily, we were in the middle of the forest with no civilization for miles. One of the perks of the location.

Raiden stretched an arm my way, and I took it, fumbling to stand up. The minty fresh of his cologne still lingered in the air, and I could sense my wolf retract as he sniffed it out. I wasn't sure why, but he feared Raiden.

Something I should have done as well, the guy was a freaking beast. Yet, for some reason, I didn't. Raiden was a friend, but it was more than that. A part of me couldn't grasp having to bow down to someone, and I clung to that part like glue. I may not know who I was or what I was meant to do in this life, but there was one thing I was certain of. I would not let anyone control me like my mom did again.

Taking a deep breath, I searched for my wolf. *Don't worry, buddy. We don't have to be afraid of this guy or anyone else again.*

I meant what I said to him. I was going to teach my wolf how to be one badass mother if it was the last thing I did.

When the fox shifter walked over to us, I recognized her immediately. She was the mouthy one Billie trained in one of the sessions she ran to get the resistance ready for any High Coven attacks that might befall them. I remembered Billie saying she was impressed with the girl, almost like she thought she would make for a good ally. The memory put some of my worries at ease. If Billie thought the fox was to be trusted, I had to believe that as well.

"Raiden said you wanted to talk?" Daria asked, a sly smile on her lips.

She moved with the swagger of someone who was not used to taking orders, and I liked it. This chick was hard, and if she was the one questioning shifters on Billie's disappearance, I had a pretty good feeling about it. Daria crossed her arms, making her cropped top rise up to reveal a part of the tree tattoo on her side.

"Nice ink," I said. *Nice ink? Don't be a creep. What's wrong with you?*

Luckily, Daria didn't seem phased by my odd comment and glossed over it. "Thanks. I got it after a bad breakup."

I probably should have kept my mouth shut, but I had to know.

"With Damen?" I asked, studying her reaction.

"Yeah. That guy was an idiot," she answered, devoid of all emotion. She pointed to the tattoo with a grin. "This is a reminder to choose better next time."

It looked like Raiden wasn't exaggerating. Whatever happened with Damen and Daria, she was not in league with him as I thought. *Great, another dead freaking end.* I scrunched my brow and turned back to the fox shifter. "Anyway, sorry to drag you out here. Just wanted to see where you're at with the shifters."

Daria's features got murky, and my stomach dropped to my feet. If she had something good, we would have heard about it already. I had no idea what I wanted to accomplish by talking to her. Maybe I just needed to feel like I was doing something other than sitting still. I was growing tired as hell of getting nowhere.

"Everyone's alibis check out," she said. "I already told Raiden and Mel that, though."

I tightened my jaw. "You seriously didn't get any vibes off anyone you talked to? Your friends either?"

"No, man," she bit out. "And talking to you is wasting my time. Like I told Raiden, I'll let you know if I find something out."

Her dismissive tone annoyed me to no small extent, but Daria wasn't wrong. All I was doing, all we were all doing, was wasting time. My fixation on the shifters was getting us nowhere, and the last hope I had to get Billie back was for Tyler and Abigail to find something in Stamwick. None of this made any sense. Billie didn't just disappear. Someone took her. Someone smart enough to know exactly how to cover their tracks. Someone way smarter than me.

My stomach turned and as I watched Daria walk away, I refused to meet Raiden's eyes while he glared at me from the distance. I didn't need to read his expression to know he was thinking the same thing I was.

The girl that risked everything to protect the shadowers in the resistance was gone and we were too dumb and weak to find her. Every minute that went by without a lead was one less minute we had to help her, and I couldn't stand it anymore.

We were so totally and utterly lost. Just like Billie. This was all my fault.

Chapter Seventeen

Billie

A hulking boot tip rammed into my stomach, sending me sliding across the cold ground. Rocks tore at my bloody skin, ripping layers off it and sending jolts of sharp pain over me. My tattered shirt clung close to my body and sweat soaked its thin material as the shifters continued their attacks. Somewhere amid it all, Daria shifted and was now snapping at my hair to pull me back. I slapped her away, only to be met with another smack across my face from one of her partners.

The taste of iron filled my mouth and I gagged on something hard. Choking, I clambered on all fours, beating at my chest to regurgitate whatever was lodged in my throat. After a few attempts, the object hit the rear of my teeth and I spit it out, panting to regain my breath.

It was a tooth. Another one.

By the time these bastards were done with me, I doubted I'd have any teeth left.

Mouth full of blood, I coughed and turned over to the side, shielding my head from an oncoming attack. The sound of bones cracking filled the cavern, and I didn't have to look up to know that Daria returned to her human form. Her bare feet strolled toward me, inching closer in my limited sightline.

"Easy on the head," she instructed. "We can't kill her."

Why? That was the only thing I could think of when another hard blow landed at my neck. My body tensed and a pain-filled shriek burst from my lips. *DAMN IT!* I really didn't want the assholes to see me cry, but after ten minutes of the beatings, I couldn't control myself. A thick mixture of spit and blood dripped down my neck and I choked back sobs while continuing to shield myself from their hits.

"I said don't overdo it!" Daria roared and the shifter that hit me took a step backward.

She crouched beside me, naked as the day she was born, and tilted my head to face her. There was a determination on her face, and I knew that she hated leaving me alive. If Daria and her friends had their way, I'd have been dead already. Still, something held them back. Or someone. I didn't know who the shifters were working for, but whoever it was, their instructions were saving my life here.

Daria held her hand up and the beatings stopped. "Ready to tell us where the book is?"

I shook my head and gritted my teeth.

"Wrong answer."

Her hand waved again, and fingers looped around my hair. An agonizing ache spread through my body as they pulled me across the ground. Large arms gripped my wrists, yanking them up to throw me against the wall. *Not the chains. Not now.*

Before I could fight back, the familiar cold wrapped around my wrists as the shifter secured the shackles. He laughed, tugging the chains to throw my arms over my head with such force, my shoulders almost dislocated. Sharp pains shot up my side and I looked down at my ripped shirt to see a blue bruise spread over my skin. Broken ribs, no doubt. I breathed through the pain, stealing glances around the cavern to figure out what would come next.

The shifters joined Daria's side but didn't make another move to hurt me.

"This won't stop until you tell us where that book is," she hissed.

I jerked my gaze over my attackers like a wild animal. "I DON'T KNOW!"

Daria was at my side in seconds. Her skin glistened with sweat, and I could smell the fox's scent rising from her. It filled my nostrils, overcoming my senses, and acid coated my mouth. The air was so hot from her shift that I couldn't take a full breath, and my head swam from the hits I took mere moments ago. My vision blurred and I was grateful not to see the details of Daria's unabashed nude body.

Crouching down, she reached for my hand, squeezing my fingers so intensely, I thought they would break. With a quick move, she yanked at the moonstone ring, ripping it off my finger.

"NO!" I yelled.

Daria chuckled, slapping me across the face with the ring still in her grasp. The crystal caught my skin, tearing through it, and I could feel warm blood ooze from the wound. Iron filled my nostrils. "I don't know why they chose you," she whispered, turning the ring over in her hands. "You're so weak."

The disgust in her voice sent shivers down my thighs and

I pressed my shoulders into the wall to put some air between us. It was only an inch or so, but it offered some relief.

"Give that back," I choked out, though the threat sounded futile considering my current position.

She didn't have to do anything, and I knew it. If Daria wanted to beat me to an inch of my life, there was no one here stopping her. My heart pounded in my chest, and I sucked in a breath as I watched her inspect the ring. It intrigued Daria, and I wondered why it drew her in. There was nothing special about the moonstone. In fact, it was one of the most useless crystals in the bunch. So why did she stare at it like it was her precious?

Struggling to breathe, I locked my eyes on hers. "It's just a stupid ring. Give it back."

Behind Daria, the shifters exchanged knowing looks and I snapped my attention to them, memorizing every detail of their faces. *When I get out of here, I'm coming for you. All of you.*

"The only stupid thing here is you," Daria said. Her face sank and shadows gathered behind her eyes. "If it wasn't for them, you'd be dead already. Be grateful you have this to protect you."

Another look of disgust and she was shoving the ring on my finger. The silver snatched on my skin, but as soon as the ring was in place, my shoulders relaxed. I sagged down, leaning my head back to watch Daria as she rose to stand. She looked at me with beady, squinting eyes, saying nothing as she walked away. Behind her, the henchmen she came with followed without another word.

When the cavern was empty again, I let the air I've been holding out and curled my knees into my chest. Blood, cuts, and bruises covered every part of my skin and it hurt to even think about it. I had no access to spells, so I would need to heal the normal way, which would take forever. I didn't think I had that long. There was no doubt in my mind that Daria and her pathetic crew would be back with more beatings in no time.

We can't kill her. Daria's words echoed through my mind as I searched for answers. Someone instructed them to come here and lay it on me thick. Someone that wanted the Book of Darkness. But who? And why?

I spit another bout of blood-coated saliva on the ground and fisted my hands. The ring was important somehow, or else Daria wouldn't have given it back to me. She wanted to see me suffer, and I knew it would bring her great joy to take one more thing away from me. It was connected to whoever orchestrated this entire thing, but I still had no clue who that was. Beatrix said the ring was a gift from my father, and the impostor claiming to be him confirmed that fact. Was he the one that held me here?

Nausea overtook me as I considered the option. Having Beatrix for a mom was bad enough, and now, there was a chance I had a dad willing to torture me to get some damn grimoire. *That's just freaking awesome.* I didn't think it was possible to hate my so-called family anymore, yet at that moment, I wished I never knew either of them. Not that I ever met my father, and I had a hard time believing that the shadow man was him.

It was a trick to get me to give up the book. It had to be.

Then how did he know about the ring? And how did Daria?

The shadow man said I needed to reach inside me to find the answers, but I was emptier than a silo. He warned me to find something in my magic that wasn't witch. What a dumbass! Witch magic was the only magic I knew, and everything else was impossible to fathom. Even my shadows must have been connected to the coven's teachings.

Unless they aren't...

The vagueness of the shadow man's hints rushed through me as I tried to put the puzzle pieces together. If my shadows weren't witch magic, what were they? There was only one other option, and I hated to even consider it. The shadows were unlike any power I've heard of before, and if they had no connection to the coven, they had to be related to the part of my bloodline I didn't want to accept.

They were fae powers. How I got them, I didn't know, but there was no other explanation.

Maybe the spirit fae blood that coursed through my veins triggered something in my magic and formed a mutation of sorts. I've never known of that happening, but weirder things have happened lately.

My head pounded as a realization hit me.

Was that what the shadow man was trying to tell me? To tap into the fae side of my magic? If it was, I was royally screwed. There was no way I could access any power at all down here, let alone something that dormant. The fae were the stuff of tales, urban legends amongst the witches, and here I was, trying to see if I could somehow manifest their power. It was a ridiculous idea.

Still, it was the only lead I had, and I needed to check it out if I had any hope of getting Naomi and me out of this place. I was about to try reaching for the magic again when another thought reared its ugly head.

Daria wasn't working alone, and whoever made the rules knew enough about the ring my father left me to deem it important. If my hunch was right and all of this was connected to fae powers, then the coven had it wrong all along.

The fae could still exist, and if they did, they wanted that grimoire. But why?

More importantly, what did my father have to do with any of it?

Chapter Eighteen

River

ornstalks rose high above me while I leaned in the grass, trying to keep my mind as empty as possible. Savannah suggested we get out of the resistance house for a few hours and meet at her family's farmhouse. And she was right. Getting away from that place was exactly what I needed. We had only been at her farm for an hour, and I was already starting to feel like myself again. My shoulders didn't creep up to meet my ears and the knots in my stomach lessened, if only by a fraction.

Across from me, Jayden laid flat on his back like he was making snow angels in the grass while Savannah kept her eyes out on the small path that led to her house. I knew who she was waiting for, but I still had no clue why we needed the company.

"Why is this guy coming again?" I asked.

This guy was Logan, the mind reaper Savannah had been spending time with. I wasn't sure what their deal was. I mean, every time he was around, all they did was argue so I knew they weren't hooking up. Something was off about that guy, and I couldn't put my finger on it. Having my best friend loop him in on all our plans made me uncomfortable, and as much as we needed the help, I wasn't sure he was the best man for the job. Logan rubbed me the wrong way and I didn't like it.

Savannah tore her gaze from the path to look at me. "He wants to help find Billie."

"And you trust him?"

Next to her, Jayden cocked an eyebrow in interest, then laid back down again. *Worst wingman ever.*

"Look," Savannah said, "Logan is an annoying tool, but I think he really wants to help. And he doesn't follow the leaders blindly like the other morons, which is good enough for me. The other day, I saw him tell Lorelei off. Lorelei! I mean, that chick is scary AF, and he had no problem letting her know where to put it. We could use someone like that around."

Jayden kicked her leg with his sneaker. "Someone's got it bad."

"Shut up!" Savannah sniped and kicked him back. "I just said he's annoying."

"Yeah, okay." Jayden snickered and turned on his side. His attention drifted to the path, and he wiggled his eyebrows. "There's lover boy now."

I followed his gaze to Logan's tall form strolling toward us. His silver hair flowed behind him as he walked, and I could see the grass bend under his heavy steps. For a mind reaper, this guy was jacked, and I wondered why he looked so different from the others. From my limited experience, mind reapers were fairly slim with long limbs and light demeanors. Like Lorelei, who resembled a freaking elf from some fantasy movie. Logan, on the other hand, was thick and full of muscle and he carried himself as someone who was used to throwing down in a fight. Maybe that's why I didn't like him. If it came down to it, I was pretty sure this guy could kick my ass without breaking a sweat.

"Hey, guys," Logan said as he approached, his British accent coating each word. He lowered to sit closer to me than Savannah, and I didn't fail to notice the irritated expression on her face. If Logan saw it too, he chose to ignore it. "'Sup, Sav?"

My best friend arched an eyebrow. "It's Savannah. We already went over this."

"Yeah, yeah. Whatever you bloody say, princess."

Savannah grimaced, but kept her mouth shut. That was a first.

"Anyway," Logan said, peeling his eyes off her. "I got some brilliant news. Well, Peyton does."

Interest peaked in me, quickly replaced with hope. I hadn't dared to let myself hope for days, but if Logan had something to share with the class, I was all for it.

"Did she get a lead?"

"Yep. A good one," he responded. "I mentioned Marcus' journal last I talked to her, and she said she'll go through it to see if we get lucky."

"And?"

"She got lucky, mate."

Jayden rose on his elbows and looked at the mind reaper. "Get to the point, pretty boy."

"He mentioned a place the shifters like to hang out when they're not in the house. Some trailer outside of town. Peyton thought it might be worth checking out, so she's meeting us there."

"And you had to come all the way here to tell us? Could've just called," Savannah bit out.

The reaper's lavender eyes drifted from her to the rest of the farm. "Wanted to see how the better half lives."

"You're a prick, you know that, right?"

"Been called worse."

Frustrated, I hopped to my feet and stood between them. My body was still in the field, but my mind was elsewhere. Peyton found a clue and it was the first one we had, so there was no time to waste on whatever idiotic thing these two had going on. I looked from Savannah to Logan, my face stern. "Save this for the playground. We have to go. Now."

Sweat beaded down my back as we marched through the vacant hilltops that spread over the west side of Shadowhurst. I had never ventured out this far from town and every step further in felt foreign, as though the hills had a life of their own.

There was nothing here but rocks and garbage left over from whoever was in this place last. As I looked around, I spotted beer cans scattered in the dead grass with remnants of food containers and empty bags of chips. Of course, this place was perfect for a party. It was far enough from town not to be trampled by locals, and the hills hid the area well.

My foot caught something hard, and I looked down to see the carcass of a small animal protrude from the ground. I had to hold my breath to stop from retching.

This was definitely a shifter hang out.

Before I could get disgusted with myself and my kind, a tiny figure appeared on the horizon. I looked up to see Peyton waving frantically our way. Next to me, Savannah stiffened, and we bolted for the hill, Jayden and Logan on our heels. The incline wasn't steep, and I was breathless and covered in sweat by the time we reached the top, likely because of sheer anticipation.

Peyton's face was pale, not unusual for her, but shadows were looming behind her heavy eye makeup.

"Anything?" I asked.

She shook her head, pointing to a small trailer close to us. "It looks empty. Morgan is checking it out still, but if I had to guess, this place hasn't been used in years."

SHIT! I scanned the trailer, noting the rust that crawled up the sides. There were no tires in its frame and the metal base sunk into the ground deep enough that the grass grew around it. Broken chairs spread out in a semi-circle across the small lawn next to the trailer, blending seamlessly into the barren landscape.

My back straightened and I pushed past Peyton to skid down the slope. Pulse racing, I checked every inch of grass on my way down, hoping to find something that belonged to Billie. The place was as empty as my heart. A frigid wind blew past me, cooling the sweat on my shirt and flinging it against my skin. Deep down, I could sense the wolf's disappointment as it mirrored my own.

This can't be all there is here.

I refused to believe it.

Reaching for the door, my heart rate skyrocketed and before I could turn the rusted handle, it swung open. I stumbled backward, shocked to see Morgan appear in the doorway. My eyes looked past her shoulder to the decrepit trailer interior and my hopes plummeted.

"It's totally empty," Morgan said, confirming my suspicions. "Sorry, River."

Tears threatened and the whimpers of the wolf in me did not help keep them at bay. I looked away from my friend, unable to see the sadness on her face. This place was a dead end. Any chance I had of finding Billie felt a million miles away and it shattered me into pieces. *Babe, I'm trying, but you have to help me out here,* I begged as though she could hear me. Never in my life had I begged for anything before, but if it meant getting her back, I would give up every ounce of strength to do so. I'd drop on my knees and pray to whatever deity was out there just to see her face again.

My hand reached for the trailer's side ,and I pressed into it to keep steady. Still in the doorway, Morgan took a step toward me but stopped. My shoulders shook and I hung my head low, keeping my face from her sight. The rest of our friends stayed still and let me have this pitiful moment to myself, and I've never loved them more for it.

Falling apart was not something I did well.

In my jacket pocket, my cellphone vibrated, and I rubbed my eyes before picking it up. "Tyler?"

"Hey, man," my friend said on the other line. His voice sounded frantic, and I let my dumbass heart leap to conclusions. Did they find Billie?

"Did you see her? Does the coven have her?" I fired off, already moving to leave.

Tyler was silent for a moment before speaking again, and when he did, I wished he hadn't.

"It's not them. We've been watching the townhouse for hours and nothing is off here. The high priestesses came and went like nothing's going on. They even have kids here. If Billie was here, we'd know it. She's not, man. I'm sorry."

Whatever was left of my heart exploded and I fell to my knees, pressing my side against the metal of the trailer's walls. I wanted to scream at him, shoot the messenger and all, but held myself back. Tyler tried to help, and it led us nowhere. Again.

I ran my fingers through my hair and brought the phone to my ear. "Thanks for trying. You guys should come back."

"River, dude, that's not why I called." Tyler's voice was strained, as though he just ran for miles. "We're trying to get back as fast as we could. Are you at the house?"

"No, we left to follow a lead Peyton had."

"You need to get back there now," he said. "We think something's up. The high priestesses left in the morning, and we haven't seen them return. They had head witches with them. I don't have a good feeling about this, Abigail either."

My jaw tensed. "You think they're moving on the resistance?"

"I don't know, but it's a good idea to be there just in case. Tell Peyton and the others to be ready."

Fumbling with the keys, I hung up and pushed myself up. The hairs on my neck rose as the wolf's awareness stood on edge, his worry seeping into my bones. We were a short drive from the house, so it wouldn't take us long to get back to warn the others, though something told me to move my ass faster.

They were coming for us. For all of us. My wolf could sense it and I didn't disagree.

This was going to be a disaster.

Chapter Nineteen

River

Magic filled the woods by the time we returned to the resistance. We crept around the sides, pressing against the trees for coverage so as not to be noticed by the witches. As we moved in on the house, a sense of unease washed over me. The trees were quiet and there was not a witch in sight.

Something was very wrong.

There was no doubting someone was here, I could smell their magic in the air, but if they were, they stayed hidden enough for us not to spot them. My head darted from side to side, the lines on my forehead deepening.

"This is weird," Morgan whispered behind me. "It's too quiet."

I nodded. "Agreed. There's magic here."

Near to us, leaves ruffled, and I jerked my gaze in their direction. From their deep green, a swirl of dust emerged. I shot my hand up to pause the others. As I turned, a cloud of purple swirled past me and I ducked to the side, remembering Billie's warning of the spell. One more second and it would have hit me straight on and paralyzed my body. My eyes scanned the forest, coming up empty. *What the hell?*

Quick as it appeared, the magic died away, leaving us alone in the woods again.

I could see the house through the trees and my mind raced thinking of the danger everyone inside faced. We rushed here so fast, I didn't get a chance to warn anyone. "Guys, we should—"

"Already on it," Peyton said, typing something on her phone.

One by one, we dared to move forward. My entire body screamed in warning, and I could feel my wolf rattle at my skin to be free. I wanted nothing more than to shift, but that wasn't the brightest of ideas. As strong as I felt in wolf form, we still had no clue what was happening or how much danger we were in. It was best to stay human as long as possible.

Behind me, a loud crack broke the silence, and I turned just in time to see Peyton's sneaker drop to the ground. Her body froze and when her eyes met mine, I knew shit was about to hit the fan.

Around her leg, a cloud of iridescent light burst in the air, encasing her shoe and locking her in place. Her face flushed as she tore at her foot, desperate to get free. Beside her, Morgan ducked down and began tearing at the ground like she was digging up a freaking grave.

"What is that?" I shouted, leaping to help them.

"A trap," Logan answered. His back pressed to Savannah's as the two moved to block Peyton from our invisible opponents. "Please, tell me the others are on the way."

Before anyone could answer, flashes of running figures filled the trees around us and I jumped to my feet, abandoning the futile task of freeing Peyton. Beside me, Jayden pulled two knives from his varsity jacket, his eyes narrowed on the figures.

To my surprise, a single head witch emerged.

She was tall, with gray hair gathered in a tight knot over her head, and her piercing black eyes stared directly at me. With a flick of the wrist, she summoned more of her magic and chucked it my way. I turned on my heels, just in time to dodge the hit, and reached for my own knives. Slicing them through the air, I hit the witch in each shoulder. Her body stumbled back, and she shrieked as pools of blood spread from the wounds.

Inside me, the wolf howled and begged to be set free. I pushed back on him. *Not yet, buddy. No kills.*

I knew better than to kill any witch attacking us. It would only end in more bloodshed on our side.

The wolf growled but listened. *Thanks, man.*

My attention turned back to my friends. "This can't be the only one here."

Man, I hated being right.

In seconds, a group of witches burst from the trees and rushed us. Spinning on my heels, I clocked one in the nose and sent her barreling backward. She rebound quickly, beckoning me forward. My legs moved on their own accord, and I was rushing for her when someone pulled me back.

"There's more of these traps all around the house," Morgan said. "Don't fall for it."

"Got it. We have this, help Peyton."

I didn't have to tell her twice. Morgan was digging up dirt again before I could even finish the sentence.

Close to me, Savannah and Logan stood back to back, slicing pieces off the witches that came at them as they neared. My chest pumped fast as Logan looped his elbows under Savannah's and spun her up and around. Her legs kicked out, delivering a brutal blow to the jaw of a witch and causing her to drop hold of her magic. While she was down, Logan pushed back on Savannah and kicked the second one in the gut. She skidded backward, bending over her knees and coughing blood on the ground. Whatever I might have said about Logan before, I was taking right the hell back now. The guy could fight, and he and Savannah made for a formidable team.

Good thing he's on our side, huh?

The wolf agreed.

Studying the formation the witches took, I glanced between their faces and feet. "Guys! Watch where they're standing and avoid coming near, it's where the traps are. They're trying to lure us in. I'll be back!"

"Where are you going, brah?" Jayden yelled out, kicking a witch that got too close to him in the gut. She catapulted away from him, landing on her back. When her body hit the ground, the same iridescent cloud exploded, trapping her in place.

Squinting past the trees, I squared my shoulders and frowned. "I want to find the high priestesses. They have to be here."

Carefully, I inspected the area, looking for another heat signature. Something caught my attention a few yards away and I snapped my head in its direction. Their glow was pale, but I knew it was the high priestesses. They were far enough away to stay safely hidden behind the house, but my eyes zeroed in on them, regardless. Sniffing the air, I latched onto their scent and snarled.

Something was off about their posture and when I

moved in closer, my mouth gaped taking them in. The four women crouched near the walls of the house, their palms planted firmly to the ground. The earth shook under them as they forced their magic into the dirt. Tearing my gaze away from the high priestesses, I looked to the windows of the resistance house and terror filled my mouth. Inside, shadowers slammed their bodies against the glass as they attempted to get free, but something held them back.

Magic.

Smoke rose from the ground and my heart leaped in my chest when I realized what the high priestesses were attempting.

They're going to burn the house down with everyone in it!

Sebyl told Billie that she started a war when she went against the coven, and she wasn't kidding. I wondered if the high priestesses knew that Billie was missing and if they did, was this their way of taking out the resistance while they were unprotected? It must have been. *They're dead!*

I had to move fast. The smoke had already filled half the small clearing that surrounded the house, and I could see sparks fly from the women's hands as they worked their magic.

With a final glance to my friends, I rushed for them. My bones creaked and groaned as I shifted and when I landed not far from the witches, I was all wolf.

The high priestesses took notice since my arrival wasn't exactly discreet. Their bodies moved closer together, clutching hands and whispering faintly between each other. I buried my paws into the dirt, rearranging myself to attack.

A flash of light spread over the priestesses, and they shot their palms in my direction, flinging their magic my way.

Lightening burst in the forest, surging toward me at an unbearable speed.

Before I could swerve out of its way, the lightning hit my side and sent me topping over. Pain unlike any I've felt before crushed through me and I growled and yelped as I righted myself to stand. My fur was charred black from the hit, but my resolve only strengthened. *They're going down!*

I bolted for the priestesses, cutting through the trees like arrows. Nearing them, I could smell the lightening the priestesses had thrumming in their hands. I refused to let it scare me. I would take any chance I had to save everyone inside that house.

The four women were all equally as petrifying but it was Sebyl that held my attention. Her black bob covered most of her eyes, though I could feel her gaze on me. She widened her stance as if to beckon me forward, and I obliged. Lunging through the air, I tore for her, letting the speed of the momentum carry me forward. I was almost at her throat when a blast of magic hit my side, catapulting me away from the high priestess.

Howling, I hit a nearby tree and my bones cracked as I dropped to the ground. The smell of singed fur hit my nostrils and I shuddered as the pain of the wound sank in. My eyes darted between Sebyl and the witch that approached, trying to decide who to attack first. The slight figure strolled toward me with so much confidence, I almost didn't realize how short she was. Something about her was familiar to me, and I tried to place her in my memories. Inky black hair bounced over her shoulders as she walked, and when she neared me, I remembered.

Victoria. Billie's friend from the coven.

My mind was torn between ripping her to pieces and

sparing her. The wolf howled, urging me to attack, but I stood still. Victoria loomed closer, and when she threw a ball of fire my way, I reacted on instinct. I dodged her magic and looped around her, using the distraction to catch her off guard. She turned, but I threw myself on her, pinning her to the ground. The young witch floundered beneath me, and I buried my weight into her back, pressing her face into the dirt. My lips parted and my jaw unhinged as I followed the scent of her blood all the way to the vein in her neck. The desire to kill rose within me and I snapped my teeth in anticipation.

You can't do this. A soft voice tugged at the back of my brain, and I froze. *I'll never forgive you if you kill her.*

Billie?

I was definitely losing it because there was no way in hell Billie was talking to me right now. Yet, it seemed so real. *What is this?* The wolf was as confused as me because he stood still for the first time since I shifted. Beneath me, Victoria tried to escape and against my better judgment, I loosened my hold on her. She kicked back, knocking me away and staring in bewilderment. Her eyes grew and she cocked her head to the side.

I mirrored the motion.

"What..." she asked, gasping. "Who are you?"

Not being able to answer, I only stared. My front paws dug into the ground, and I shifted my weight backward. The move was a lot more difficult in wolf form and I wished I could shift, so she could see I meant her no harm. Or did I? I wasn't sure.

Victoria started to stand, and I urged my wolf to let her. He fought me every step of the way, but soon, I was backing away to give her a wide berth. Victoria's narrowed eyes never left me as she took calculated steps to extend the distance between us. To my relief, she didn't reach for her magic and within moments, disappeared into the trees. I could still see the faint glimmer of her body retreating when a raging ache spread through my side.

My wolf cried in agony, trying to decipher what was happening to us. My ribs felt like someone broke them, and I wondered if it was from the hit I took earlier. One glance down, I realized the pain was on the opposite side from the singed fur. Whatever was affecting me, it wasn't from the magic I got blasted with.

The pain spread and understanding came with it. It was Billie's, just like last time.

Somewhere not far from me, I heard the howls of the pack and my eyes landed on a hoard of shadowers rushing from the house to attack the witches. Whatever I did must have torn the priestesses' attention from their spell because my friends were free. If there ever was such a thing as a silver lining, this sure as shit was it.

Heat rushed through my chest and howls burst from me as I imagined something awful happening to her and my screams attracted a few of the pack members. They left their post around the high priestesses and rushed in my direction. One by one, they invaded my space and I snarled at them to back up. I didn't need them near me when I wanted to rip the world apart. Billie was hurt, physically hurt, and I was powerless to help her.

Looking at the pack, all I saw was red. What was the point of having these beasts around if we couldn't help Billie? What was the point of me being around?

I howled again and locked eyes with the wolf nearest me.

His reddish fur rippled as he inched toward me. I bared my canines, signaling him to back off. He didn't.

That was a big mistake.

Unable to stop, I dove for him. My jaw snapped open and the growl that left me echoed through the woods. The red wolf stood his ground, and I was almost on him when a set of teeth tore through my skin. My body convulsed and I dropped. Above me, a massive gray wolf pinned down my paws as his jaw continued to tighten around my neck. I only got a glimpse of his burning eyes before the world went dark.

Chapter Twenty

Billie

"**W**ork, damn it!"

My frustrated shrieks drowned out any other noise in the cavern as I struggled to connect to my magic. My fingers gripped the chain so hard, I could feel the indents it left in my palms. Icy metal burnt against my heated skin, and I cried out in pain, yanking on the chains as hard as I could manage. My ribs pulsed with an agonizing ache, and I choked back sobs, struggling to connect to the shadows within me.

I had been at this for hours, and every attempt proved to be more excruciating than the next. Each time I came close to reaching them, the block placed on me tore through my body, destroying all will to continue. I wasn't even sure what I was trying to accomplish, but the shadow man said to find the power inside my magic, so I was willing to give it a shot. Unfortunately, my body wasn't quite as cooperative.

After repeated failed attempts, my brain was liquid and my legs spread out on the cold floor in a heap of uselessness.

Power, my ass.

I had no hidden magic to find, only the shadows the cavern blocked me from using. This was a lost cause.

Frustration tugged at the edges of my mind, and I groaned before trying again. When nothing happened, I sighed and slumped my head down.

Totally freaking useless.

Rearranging myself to sit on my side, I turned my head to the far end of the cavern. "Naomi?"

Silence answered me. I haven't heard from Naomi in a long while and as much I wanted to hope for the best, a part of me feared for her safety. Daria and her shifters were going to town on me, but at least they had instructions not to kill me. Somehow, I doubted Naomi got the same treatment. Dread spread through me as I considered the possibility that she might not be alive anymore, and I had to force myself to let the thought go. I would have heard something if she died. A commotion, a scream, even the sounds of the shifters dragging her body away; but nothing of sort reached my prison and I had to keep that at the forefront of my mind.

"I know you're okay," I whispered, or prayed perhaps. "I know you are."

She didn't answer. Of course, she didn't. That would have been too easy, and what were the chances of something actually going my way in this hell hole? Pretty damn slim, I'd say. Fighting the exhaustion that threatened to overwhelm me, I pressed my feet into the rock and slid up the wall. The wounds the shifters left behind had begun to heal, and while I was still in pain, at least I wasn't bleeding out on the floor anymore. The things I had become grateful for since waking up here were laughable, and I was seriously starting to doubt my sanity. *When people tell you to look on the bright side, I doubt this is what they mean.* Yet, here I was, completely and totally grateful that I wasn't shedding blood by the buckets. *Go figure.*

As I uncurled my back to lean against the wall, a new pain emerged, and I buckled back from its intensity. It felt like someone tore knives down my throat and I had to squeeze my shoulder in to test the theory. When my shirt came out clean, I was even more confused than before. *Did that bitch bite my neck?* I didn't remember her getting that close, but maybe I was wrong. It sure as hell felt like someone bit me, yet there was no wound to prove it.

"Idiot," I cursed myself through clenched teeth. "You have bigger things to worry about."

I cracked my neck, ignoring the throbbing feeling it left behind on the ghost bite. My legs shook under the weight of my torso, and I rolled my eyes at their incompetence. It was bad enough that I had no magic, now I also had legs that didn't work? That wouldn't cut it for me.

I kicked at the wall, wincing at the needles it sent up my shins. By some miracle, it worked and I found myself able to keep standing. Getting a better hold of the chains, I tried to picture all the movies I've seen where people were kept captive. They usually trained in secret, waiting until no one was around to get unnaturally strong and deliver a world of pain on everyone that wronged them. Goddess, how I would have loved to be able to do that. The catch was that not only could I not work out, what with my dumb arms chained above my head, but no amount of physical strength would get me out of here. What I needed was not something my body could provide. At least not with the magic block tightened over me like a noose.

With my legs solid, I strengthened my resolve and took a wider stance. "Okay, Naomi, here goes nothing."

Closing my eyes, I reached for the shadows again. This time, I could sense hints of them under my skin and a smile tugged at my lips. They were so close, I could taste it. My lids fluttered as I searched for their power, digging deep inside and poking around every crevice. On my finger, the moonstone ring cooled to the touch and a pang of hope blasted through me. I was almost there. Carefully, I pressed deeper, eager to feel the magic that craved to be free of the constraints of my body. The cavern fought me every step of the way, forcing the shadows back down as I tugged on them. My skin blazed and the agony of being torn apart ripped through my bones, but I stayed on it. I was going to get my damn magic back, even if it killed me.

I almost had a grasp on it when the air before me shifted and the golden glow I knew so well began to form.

"NO! Not now!" I choked out, refusing to give up.

The light intensified, and my resolve grew with it. As images swarmed before me, all I could think of was getting a grip on the shadows and yanking them out. My eyes burst open, and when the vision came into focus, I wished I had kept them shut. The porch I had spent so many nights on appeared in front of me, and I clenched my jaw, knowing what would come next. The cavern was showing me the Chandler residence. Or home, as I've come to know it. Lights were on in the living room, and I could see Silas tidying up the place as he often did when no one else was around. The man was seriously a saint.

Golden lights danced in my sightline as the vision spread out, revealing a front yard full of head witches. At their helm, the high priestesses stood with magic rippling between their fingers. I wasn't sure why they brought so many people,

Silas was one man and if they intended to hurt him, they didn't need a freaking army to do it. *Idiots.*

Vicious smiles covered every face in the yard and disgust filled my stomach. I hated these women. Hated them more than anything else in this world and if they thought they could take everything I loved from me, they had another thing coming.

My body shook as I pulled on the slivers of magic I felt before. Eyes trained on the coven, I gritted my teeth and ripped the shadows outward. The cavern vibrated around me, fighting my every move. One by one, the shadows crept, wrapping over my arms and legs in their beautiful darkness. My power was power, yet what I could feel, I loved fiercely.

Trembling, I concentrated on Sebyl's pointed nose and a scream bubbled to the surface. I yanked on the chains, shutting my eyes and pushing the shadows out. They blasted out of me, barreling into the golden light and straight for Sebyl's face.

In the instant before my magic hit her, I thought I saw her eyes snap to me, but that was impossible. She didn't know I could see her, could she?

The light dispersed and the shadows rushed through the cavern, covering the outer edges of the walls in their gooey thickness. My gaze landed on the rocks they clung to, and I imagined myself tearing them out, ripping them straight from the wall. As the image formed in my mind, the energy altered inside me. My hold on the shadows dropped and I clung to something else entirely. An elemental energy I haven't felt before, one that was so strong, it scared me shitless. There was no way to describe it. The closest I could think of was wielding crystal magic, and even that wasn't good enough. It was like I could control the rock itself like I was holding it in my hands even though it was several feet away from me.

I locked in on that thought, curling my fingers around the rock from where I stood. One quick breath in and I drew it toward me. Shock spread on my face as the small boulder groaned before shooting out of the cavern's wall and flying my way.

"SHIT!" I screamed and ducked my head out of the way.

The rock hit just over me, shattering on impact and raining pellets down my hair. Panting, I looked from the remnants of rock on the ground to the small hole in the wall it burst from. "Holy crap."

My eyes watered as excitement set in, and I jumped up and down, letting the tiny glimpse of joy overtake me. Sure, I wasn't nearly as strong as I was before all this, but it was a huge step forward. I got hold of some of my magic, and where there was some, there was more. Tears streamed down my cheeks, and I pounded my fists into the wall, not sure what to do with my body.

Billie...

I froze.

Billie...

Eyes red, I looked left and right, blinking through the tears. His voice slithered through me, and it sounded so close, I thought he was right there next to me. "River?"

The cavern was empty, as always.

"River? Is that you? Where are you?"

I listened, but he never answered. In my chest, my pulse sped up and a warmth spread over me, settling in a spot just above my heart. I looked down, slack-jawed as thin black lines crept over my skin. *What the...* My eyes bulged as I watched them twine through my chest, palpitating to match the quick beating of my heart. Small shapes emerged and I nearly passed out, but before I could, the lines brightened and disappeared.

Words caught in my throat and pressure built in my brain while I tried to make sense of what just happened. That was River, I knew it with every part of my body. Somehow, he was here with me. He found me. I didn't know how, but it was true. I could feel it.

River found me and now, he was gone again.

Icy air hit my face and I shivered at its touch. "Back to square one, Naomi," I whispered into the abyss. "Back to square freaking one."

Chapter Twenty-one

River

Opening my eyes was a close equivalent to ripping apart glued pages. My lashes clung together and when I finally got them open, an unbearable itch filled the corners of my eyes. I rubbed at them, bringing my blurred vision into focus.

The room I found myself in was dim with only a single lamp on the small side table next to the bed I lay in. Torn wallpaper lined the walls, and it didn't take long for me to realize I was in one of the spare rooms in the resistance house. Panic rose in my chest, and I shot up in the bed, swinging my legs over the edge and pushing myself to stand.

"Calm your shit." Isaac's gruff voice filled the room.

I turned to see the alpha reclining in the chair opposite me.

"What am I doing here? What happened to the coven?"

He cursed under his breath and pointed to my neck. "The pack and your friends drove them off. We dislodged the traps they set and most shadowers have been sent away until we're sure it's safe for them to come back. And you're here because I had to put you down."

Rubbing a hand over my skin, I winced, feeling the indents his fangs left behind.

"What the hell, man?"

"You attacked a pack member."

Disgust overcame me. "So you bit me?"

"I would have done worse if Raiden didn't step in. If you can't figure your shit out, you need to stay away from us." Isaac's voice was calm, but I could hear the warning in them. "We're trying to help you and you're being unreasonable."

Well, shit. It wasn't that I disagreed with him, I was most definitely being unreasonable. But who did this guy think he is? He wasn't there when I felt Billie's pain and I was willing to wager that if the tables were reversed, he'd do the same. Isaac didn't strike me as the type to talk things out. He was an angry prick, and I could smell it on him. Sure, attacking that wolf wasn't my finest moment, but I'd be damned if I had to apologize to this cocky bastard.

Biting my lip, I met his eyes. "You weren't there, so lay off."

Isaac's jaw tensed and I could see him fight the urge to hit me, mostly because his face looked a lot like mine as I battled the same feelings. It was clear Isaac and I would never get along. Maybe what Griffin said was true and I had a bit of alpha in my own wolf. Or maybe I was just stubborn as hell and refused to bow down to anyone. Whatever it was, this guy was getting a rise out of me, and I didn't need the added stress.

"If you can't follow our rules, you have no place with the pack," Isaac bit out.

"You mean *your* rules."

His gaze deepened and he crossed his arms over his chest, puffing it out for extra intimidation. It didn't work and deep inside, I could all but hear my wolf laughing. Looked like it didn't work on him either.

"I'm the alpha, kid," Isaac said. I wanted to beat the smile off his face. "What I say goes. Get with the program or keep moving. No one will miss you here."

Oh, this is on now.

I took one long stride to lean over him. My hand reached around, curling over the back of the chair he sat in so I could come face to face with the alpha. As my hot breath spread over him, I could see Isaac's shoulders tense. *Good, I have your attention.*

"I don't have an alpha. That crap might go over with the rest of the morons, but it won't work on me. You want to flex your power, I don't care. I came to you for help with Billie and that was a mistake. You're nothing but dumb animals playing by rules that don't matter."

The alpha's hand slapped my arm away and he straightened his back, putting his annoying face right in mine. "Watch your tone, kid. Raiden isn't here to cover for you."

"Who says I need him to?"

I curled my lip in a snarl and immediately felt like an idiot. The move might have worked when I was in wolf form with fangs to threaten with, but right now, I was basically standing over the guy and smiling. *Great job. Just stellar.*

Refusing to back down, I pressed my lips into a thin line but stayed in place.

Isaac did the same.

"Good luck finding your witch without us," he hissed. "By the time you figure it out, she'll be dead already."

His words reached my wolf and for once, I was glad the

angry bastard was paying attention. Before Isaac could utter another word, my hands gripped his shoulders and I pulled him from the chair, slamming his back into the wall. Dust rose and I could see it twirl in the light. My legs shook as I picked Isaac up and smashed his body against the drywall. His eyes reddened, glowing as his wolf recognized the threat.

Isaac's arms jerked outward, and he brought them down against mine, trying to break my hold. It did nothing. My grip stayed steady, and I pummeled him into the wall again, then pressed an elbow to his throat. He gagged, but his gaze stayed fierce and angry. The alpha in him wanted to tear me apart. The feeling was mutual.

A guttural growl escaped him, and I pushed my elbow in deeper, cutting off his air supply.

"You don't talk about her," I said between clenched teeth. "Understand?"

When I felt him try to nod, I snaked my arm behind his head and threw him to the side. He spun away from me, rubbing his throat where a red mark was spreading over his skin. The rage in him was palpable and I could taste it in the surrounding air, finally understanding what Billie meant about the heat shifters gave off. I could feel it baking off him. The room felt like a sauna, and I kept my attention on Isaac, waiting for him to shift.

To my surprise, he didn't.

The alpha cracked his neck and cleared his throat. "Don't come back to the pack. Don't even look at them. You're done here."

"I'm just getting started. Why don't—"

My words caught in my throat as a sharp pain stabbed my chest. I bent over my legs, clutching my heart to stop the ache, but it was pointless. The pain spread and I tore the t-shirt I wore over my head, eyes widening as I watched black lines swirl over my skin. They pulsed, spreading up my neck and down my abdomen. It felt like someone was cutting me with a knife. I choked on saliva filling my mouth. My hands rubbed at the skin, but every time I touched one of the lines, a blinding spasm filled my brain.

Knees hitting the wood, I jerked my head back and let out a howl.

"What the..." Isaac whispered over me, his eyes as wide as mine.

I panted. "MAKE. IT. STOP."

"I-I can't," he breathed out. "I don't know what that is."

Horrified, I faced him. "Aren't you the big bad alpha?" I choked out. "What the hell is happening to me?"

Isaac gripped my shoulder and pushed me back to get a better view of the lines. When he touched my skin, my wolf growled and I had to talk him off the ledge. *He's trying to help, we can hate him later.* My words did little to calm the beast, but he stayed still regardless.

"It looks like a mate bond," Isaac said. "But not like one I've ever seen. And it doesn't usually happen this way."

"How does it usually happen?"

The pain was unbearable, and my knees shook as I tried to stay upright.

Isaac grinned, he actually freaking grinned. *What an asshole.* "Well, normally, whoever you're mated to is with you when it happens so unless it's me, this is something else." He lowered the top of his shirt and pointed to a swirl of red lines over his chest. "Besides, they never spread that much, and I'm already taken."

One of these days, I'm going to break this guy's jaw.

Shutting my eyes, I breathed through the agony, swiping

his hand off my shoulder. My body curled inward, and I huffed over my thighs, trembling as the lines continued to race up and down my torso. It lasted for another minute, the longest one in my entire life, and then, as quickly as it started, the pain disappeared. Sweat beaded down my brow and I looked down at my chest.

The lines were gone.

A massive hand touched my back. "You all right?"

I was still reeling from the phantom pains left behind but managed to push Isaac away from me. With as much confidence as I could muster, I rose to my feet until I was face to face with him. A light green hue illuminated his face as the shifter in me made an appearance and he took a step back. It was a smart move.

"I don't need your help. I'm not in your pack, remember?" I sniped, turning on my heels to storm out of the room.

Anger fueled my every step as I left Isaac behind and walked down the narrow corridor. The alpha was becoming a problem, one I would need to resolve. There was only one way I could think to do that, and I shuddered at the thought of going through with it. But what choice did I have?

One way or another, I was getting the pack on my side. I needed them to get to the other shifters and Raiden was right about one thing, wolves needed other wolves.

Inside me, my wolf snarled in agreement.

Isaac had to go, and the only way to do that was to take his place. I had to challenge his role as an alpha. I had to fight him for control of the pack.

Chapter Twenty-two

Billie

Hope fluttered feathery wings against my heart as I clutched onto the memory of River's voice. I heard him, I knew I did. Not understanding how it happened or what the black lines that appeared on my chest meant was driving me crazy, and I replayed the event over and over until it blended into a slick mess of thoughts. The closest thing I could think of was Mel and Raiden's mate bond, but this couldn't be it. River and I could not be mated. I wasn't a shifter, and Mel said the bond must occur between two identical bloodlines. Still, it was much too coincidental for me to discard the theory, especially when I wanted it to be true so badly.

That's not it, I tried to convince myself. But could it be?

"Ugh," I groaned and faced the emptiness before me. "If this is some trick you're playing, it won't work!"

The cavern answered in its usual manner, with melodic drips and a reminder I was still nowhere close to escaping. "Thanks for nothing!"

Looking down to my chest, it disappointed me to see it

clear of markings and my heart grew heavy in my chest. Hearing River's voice offered a burst of energy I hadn't expected, yet now that it was gone, I was back to feeling sorry for myself like a complete loser. When did I become this pathetic? It was infuriating and I shook the weakness off, concentrating on the rock wall in front of me.

My head pounded as I attempted to reach for the stone with my mind, imagining it bursting outward like it did before. When nothing happened, again, I slumped my shoulders and let out an annoyed huff.

"What a waste of time."

"I wouldn't be so sure," a euphonic voice said from the gloomy tunnel.

I strained to see through the dark, my eyes focusing on the outline of a man in the distance. "Oh, look who's back! Dear old Dad," I hissed, sarcasm dripping off my lips like molasses. "Came to give me some more bum advice?"

Shadow man chuckled and the surrounding night dispersed for a brief moment. I had given up on trying to make out his face. Whoever this man was, he didn't want me knowing his true identity. Which was fine by me; I had no intention of making friends with the dad imposter.

"You're very close, daughter," he said, taking a few steps inward. "Yet you're still fighting it."

"Fighting what?" I bit out. "I found my power like you said and nothing happened. I moved a freaking rock, big deal."

"A very big deal indeed..."

Grinding my teeth, I let out a low growl. "You're honestly insufferable. Anyone ever tell you that?"

"Some," he mused. "I have my moments."

"Look, not that I don't appreciate the company, but

unless you have something to help get me out of here, I'm kind of busy."

His head whipped around the cavern. "Yes, clearly."

What an actual ass.

Fighting the scowl that refused to leave me, I trained narrowed eyes his way. "Seriously, what do you want?"

He was silent, taking the chance to try and scare me, no doubt. I wouldn't fall for it. My gaze remained on his figure as he shifted his weight from foot to foot, swaying. The shadows around him moved in a choreographed dance, and vertigo overtook my senses as I watched them. If I wasn't so pissed, I'd have been impressed with this guy's ability to look so effortless in a place that was nothing but death and suffering. That wasn't the case though. Mostly because I was mad as hell.

Frustrated, I yanked on the chains to get his attention. "Well?"

"What I want," he finally said, "is for you to realize your full potential."

"Yeah, yeah. I heard it all before. You know, you sound just like Sebyl when she thinks I'm not trying my best. Doesn't work on me."

"Do not compare me to that weak sorceress."

So he knows of the High Coven. Weird.

My interest had officially peaked, and I perked my ears at his words. "You've met Sebyl?"

"A story for another time, daughter. A time that will come soon, I am certain."

Yep, I'm over it. "If you won't tell me why you're here, you might as well move along. I know I look like I have all the time in the world, but I'm pretty busy here. You know, trying not to die and all."

The man's shoulders tensed, and he leaned on the wall as though to keep steady. His fingers twitched and a line of shadows burst from his hand and shot toward me. Their icy grip tightened over my ankles, yanking to pull me down. Butt scraping on the cold stone, I slid forward, grasping for the chains to keep me in place. The shadows pulled, and I kicked back at them to gain control, but he was too strong, or I was too weak, and they had me splayed on the floor in seconds.

I shrieked.

He laughed.

"It is unpleasant to have such a disrespectful child," he said while I squirmed against his magic. "Beatrix should have raised you better."

"She'd have to be around to raise me."

I kicked again, and this time, the shadows gave way. Their hold on my ankles dissipated and they flew back to the man, vanishing as quickly as they appeared. Horrified, I clawed to sit up again, my eyes studying him intently. His magic was like mine, albeit much stronger, yet similar nonetheless. This was absolutely crazy. Not only did this weirdo have the same unusual magic I possessed, but he was a man. *There are no male witches in the world.* My heart raced in my chest; was there a chance he wasn't lying?

Was this really my father?

The idea disturbed me to no small degree, and I cringed at the thought of having to call the stranger 'dad'. It was a foolish thing to think about. Just because someone showed up and told you they made you didn't mean you were one big happy family. I didn't know much about having proper parents, but I was pretty certain one had to stick around to have that claim. At this point, the Chandlers were more parental as far as I was concerned. At least they didn't leave me chained to a wall and tortured me with half-truths and pointless chit chat.

Before I could challenge him again, the man spun off the wall, vanishing in a pool of night. He reappeared a moment later in the tunnel to my farthest left, giving me whiplash from trying to follow him.

"Do you want to be free of this place?"

I nearly doubled down laughing. "You're joking, right? No, please, keep me here forever. Best vacay I've ever had. Seriously, this is better than a cruise around the world."

"Then give them what they want!"

His roar reverberated through the tunnel and the sudden outburst made me shrink back. So far, the shadow man had been cool and collected, and hearing him yell was unnerving. I wasn't sure why, but I expected better of him. *He's not your dad, moron. You can't expect something from a stranger.*

Okay, I was definitely losing it. This time for sure.

Hairs stood on end as I worked past his tantrum to discern the meaning of his words. "The Book of Darkness?"

He nodded.

"Why do you care about it? Why do they? Whoever *they* are."

"That is not your concern," he said. "Yet."

"Then what—" I started to ask, but he cut me off.

"Think of the elements, daughter. They will lead your way."

In the blink of an eye, he was gone, leaving only an empty tunnel behind. My eyes scanned the surroundings, hoping he would appear again as before, but after minutes of waiting, I gave up. Much like the first time he came to me, the shadow man evaporated into thin air before I could get any real answers from him.

"Great! Excellent advice!" I shrieked. "Really getting the hang of this dad thing I see!"

My words fell into nothingness, and I breathed out an annoyed sigh before resting my back against the wall. The stench of dirt and blood reached my nostrils and I fought back a gag reflex. I needed a shower and I needed it days ago.

Refusing to give up, I turned over his last words as one would a Rubik's cube. My brain latched onto them, inspecting every angle as though it would change their true meaning. What elements was he talking about? The only ones I knew of were what us witches pulled power from, but that couldn't be it. All I had to use as a conduit were the pendants on my neck, and even with them, the block on my magic wouldn't let me tap into any power at all. The only success I've had so far was with my shadows, and even then, it was minimal. Just enough to pull the rock out.

Wait, is that what he meant?

No, it couldn't be. I forced myself to recall what happened and a gasp burst from my lips. When I reached for the rock, I felt it. It was almost as if I was holding it in my hands, and it wasn't the shadow magic I held inside me that connected to the rock's element. It was something else. Something new and something very, very unsettling. Unlike the magic taught to me by Beatrix and the coven, this wasn't power I was manifesting. It felt like a core part of my being. Almost as if the element itself was etched into my blood.

My mind raced as I pieced the puzzle together.

"Not witch magic," I whispered.

A question bubbled to the surface and my eyes widened

in response. Was I able to control the rock because of my fae bloodline? "No. Freaking. Way."

My weak muscles tensed, and I crossed my legs to sit comfortably as I considered the option. If I had some crazy dormant fae powers, it wouldn't make sense for them to connect to the element of earth. I was a spirit fae, something I still had a hard time accepting, and spirit fae could only wield that particular element. So how did I move the rock? And why did it feel like it was an intrinsic fragment of my magic? Witches didn't move rocks willy-nilly. We needed magical items to help us wield magic, this was how it had always been. Even the original witches used powerful items imbued with fae magic. So how did I do it?

I looked around, trying to spot something I may have missed. A crystal, a bushel of herbs, anything. I came up empty.

Too many pieces were missing for me to understand any of this, and I was running out of time to figure it out. I had to keep my head in the game. It didn't matter why I could move the rock, what mattered was that I did it.

I looked through the cavern, a determined smile breaking to the surface.

Sure, I was chained and with minimal power, but what I had was not without use. However it happened, I could move stone, and it was the best discovery I've made in days. The entire place was one big rock, and I had the magic to command it.

My gaze drifted up, past the chains, and to the metal pin bounding them to the wall. The pin was buried deep inside, but I noticed a few protruding edges, and my resolve strengthened. I only needed to move one rock. Just one.

Loud, heavy footfalls carried through a tunnel, and

Daria and her crew stepped out to greet me. Their vile eyes took me in, and I noticed one of the men crack his knuckles. They've come for another beating, and it should have scared me shitless.

It didn't.

This time, I would not let them get their hits in so easily. I finally had something to fight for.

Chapter Twenty-three

River

"You're sure that's what you saw?" Raiden asked, his brows scrunched into one thick line. "Maybe it was a side effect of the shift somehow, one we haven't encountered before."

His broad frame spread over the padded wall of the training room, creating a Raiden-shaped indent in the soft fabric. Across his chest, Mel's hand drew idle circles over the markings of their mate bond, her eyes never leaving mine. After I told them about the black lines that appeared on my chest, they hadn't stopped questioning me and it was starting to seriously annoy me. I wasn't making it up. I knew what I saw.

"It wasn't the shift," I said sternly. "This was different. Isaac saw it too and it felt... I don't know... It felt like Billie was there. I know it sounds crazy."

"Maybe," Mel said. "Maybe not."

Hope butted up against my heart and I let myself get carried away in it. The shifter leader wasn't exactly telling me that Billie and I were mated, but she also wasn't denying it and that was good enough for me. At least for the time being. Across the room, Savannah inspected a set of knuckle dusters she picked up from the weapons room like she was admiring a piece of jewelry. Her large eyes briefly met mine and she glanced away, avoiding the connection. With everything that went down between Billie and her, I had the feeling my best friend did not care for the conversation and was grateful she stayed quiet for once.

Savannah mumbled something I couldn't make out and retired her attention to the weapons in her hands, not bothering to look at me again.

Next to her, Logan was busy talking to Peyton and Lorelei, giving me the chance to question Mel further.

"You think it might be the bond?" I asked, ignoring the disapproval on Raiden's face.

The lioness pursed her lips and ran a hand through her purple locks. "Could be. I won't be able to tell for sure until I see the effects you described, but I don't want to rule it out."

"She's not a shifter." Raiden shook his head to dismiss the notion. "For all we know, it was someone else from the pack."

Tension built in my neck and shoulders, and I had to force my jaw to relax. The thought that my wolf was attempting to mate to someone other than Billie was not something I was willing to entertain, and while I understood Raiden's reasoning, I was disturbingly close to biting his head off.

Fists clenched, I started for the lion.

"Weirder shit has happened in this stank place."

Savannah's annoyed tone gave me pause and I peeled my enraged glare off Raiden, twirling to face her. "Thanks," I mouthed, slinking against the padded wall.

Finally acknowledging my existence, she winked and looked back to the silver adorning her knuckles. Her hazel eyes twinkled as she turned over her fists, testing the weapons. Was it just me, or had my best friend become even scarier since we'd been spending time at the resistance house? Savannah was a force to be reckoned with on a good day, one reason we got along so well, but in the last little while, she was nothing but anger and attitude. I wondered if Billie's disappearance affected her to a degree. The two weren't friends, at least not yet, but Savannah had been on edge ever since we realized Billie was kidnapped.

Maybe she was more worried about my girl than I realized.

Savannah balled a fist and drove the knuckle duster into the concrete beneath her. The weapon didn't leave a dent and she scowled, ripping it off her hand and tossing it across the room. A loud pang rose in the air when the metal hit something in the weapons room and everyone's shocked faces turned to my friend.

"What?" She shrugged and waved her hand dismissively. "You got any proper weapons here or just this crap?"

Yep, she's definitely a freaking terror.

Opposite us, Raiden stiffened and refused to entertain her theatrics, choosing instead to revert his attention to Mel and I. "Let's find Billie first, then we'll deal with whatever's going on with you."

Finally, we agreed on something.

"I need to talk to Damen," I announced. "He might know something that he isn't telling you."

"He does not," Raiden argued. "You need to let this crap go."

I couldn't. For some ridiculous reason, I just couldn't.

"Look, man. You're his cousin, and his leader, what are the chances he'll talk to you at all? Maybe I could threaten him to talk. Now that I have some control of my wolf, I can be useful. He won't expect me to have shifted and it might give us a leg up. Catch him off guard, or whatever. We need something, anything at this point. The High Coven didn't take her, so we have to play the only hand we have here."

Raiden's brow twitched and he looked past me. "I'm telling you he won't talk. Damen is hot-headed and wolf or not, he won't budge. Believe me, I tried."

"What about the other shifters? The ones that aren't in the house anymore. Let's round everyone up again. After the coven attack on the house, it might sway them to give Billie back to save their own asses."

"None of them have anything to do with this. Daria already checked."

"Well, I'd like to hear it from them."

Raiden sighed and shook his head. "Listen, kid. I know you're trying to do the right thing here, but this isn't the way to do it. The ones that aren't in the house anymore are missing for a reason. They have families, children that are not safe staying here. We went to a lot of trouble keeping them hidden in case the High Coven decides to return and I can't let you show up guns blazing and scare them all to death. It isn't going to happen."

Why was Raiden trying so hard to dissuade me from seeing his cousin or the other shifters? Discomfort tugged at my mind, and I tried not to jump to conclusions. Whatever reason the lion had for defending these people must have been good. Raiden wouldn't jeopardize us finding Billie to protect someone that threatened to kill her in the first place.

Still, something didn't sit well with me, and I needed to figure out what it was.

"I still want to talk to him," I said, pressing further.

"It's a waste of time."

Dude! Seriously, what's up with you? My hands fisted and my back tensed as I faced the lion. Inside me, my wolf fought the urge to hit Raiden every step of the way, and it annoyed me to the core. The beast caged in my body may fear the enormous man before us, but I wasn't the least bit worried. No one told me what to do, definitely not when it came to guaranteeing Billie's safety. If Isaac couldn't get his filthy paws on me, I would be damned if I let Raiden succeed in the same.

A vein popped across my brow, and I stepped in, only to be met with Mel's curvy figure leaping between us. Her palms pressed to my chest, nudging me away from Raiden. The lioness was smaller than me, but I knew if it came down to it, she'd kick my ass if I so much as dared to make a move on him.

"We're on the same side here," she whispered, continuing to push me away. "Think it through."

I wanted to tell her that I *was* thinking it through and that her mate was acting like a grade-A douche, but kept my mouth zipped. My lips crashed into a thin line, and I could feel the eyes of all our friends piercing my back. The room had grown so quiet that I could hear their heartbeats speed up. Deep down, my wolf whined, begging me to back down.

It only made me that much more upset.

Tightening my fists, I cracked my neck and looked past Mel to Raiden. "We're not done here."

"Hey!" Savannah yelled out, freezing me in place.

"When you two are finished with your dick measuring contest, Logan has something."

I twirled on my heels, forcing the anger I felt for Raiden away. It remained, despite my best efforts, and I had to bury my feet into the concrete to keep from swinging back around. My shoulders rose to meet my ears and I kept my hands fisted in case the guy came at me while I was turned away.

He didn't, and relief rolled through me, giving me enough leeway to keep my attention on Savannah.

"What did you say?"

"He found something in Marcus' journal," she said, motioning to the book in Logan's hands.

I had been so obsessed with picking a fight with Raiden that I hadn't noticed it until that moment. Guilt spread through me, and I let the tension in my neck dissipate. I really had to get my head in the game here. "Marcus knew something?" I asked.

"There're some notes in there about—"

"Thanks, princess," Logan interrupted her. "But I can explain just fine on my own."

Red spread up Savannah's neck, and I could see her battle the urge not to hit the mind reaper. Her features darkened and she gritted her teeth so loud, I could hear it from where I stood. Is this how ridiculous I looked when I spiraled out of control? I certainly hoped not.

"Can someone explain already?" Mel asked. "I seriously don't care who at this point."

You and me both.

Logan flashed his teeth and opened the leather-bound journal, flipping through pages until he found what he was looking for. He strolled toward me, a shoulder knocking

Savannah's to get past her. My best friend crossed her arms and shook her head in annoyance before leaning back on the wall. When my gaze met hers, she nodded lightly. Whatever Logan found had to be good for her to put her shit aside and not retaliate.

The mind reaper shoved the journal my way and pointed to a passage. "This part here."

Marcus' handwriting was impeccable and I had no trouble reading his notes. Curiosity piqued as I took in the words, scanning through them several times to make sure I read them correctly. When I had the passage all but memorized, I looked up at Logan. "He thought the shifters were working with someone else? Someone not in the resistance?"

"Looks like it, mate," Logan answered. "It doesn't say who, but he wrote several times that some shifters had been acting odd. The first mention was about four weeks ago."

He flipped the pages back to the date and tapped his long finger to a short entry.

"That lines up with the threats we received," Peyton said. "Lorelei, do you remember him saying anything about whoever might be working with them? Maybe something about a little girl?"

The leader shook her head. "Not at all. Though Marcus often kept things to himself until he was certain he had enough proof to bring it to the rest of us."

Great. Just great. Lorelei was the closest to Marcus from all the leaders, and if she didn't have any information, there was little chance we'd get it elsewhere. All we had was the journal which wasn't much to go by.

"Is this all you could find?"

"For now," Logan said. "I'll keep looking. Maybe I missed something. Actually, I could use your help on this,

Lorelei. You knew him better than most and you might see something I didn't."

"Of course," she said.

At her side, Peyton stiffened. "We have another problem."

Of course, we did. Didn't we always?

"The Chandlers are back from their trip on Sunday and fall semester starts the next day." Her eyes landed on me, and knots formed in my stomach. "If Billie's not back by then, they'll figure out something is wrong."

"So, no pressure then?" Savannah asked.

The nerves I locked down before were back in full force and my fists tightened as I thought about what was at stake. We had four days to find Billie and bring her home before the entire town started looking for her.

There was no question about it. This would not end well.

Chapter Twenty-four

Billie

Strong hands pulled the chains that held me, dragging me across the floor. Above me, a male shifter grinned like an idiot as he yanked at the shackles with all his might. My back scraped over the stone, and I cringed as pieces of skin ripped over its jagged edges. Inch by inch, the shifter heaved my body to the center of the cavern, kicking my side when he had me in place.

The remaining shifters surrounded me, and the anticipation to beat me down rolled off them in waves. Two men parted, letting Daria walk through to tower over me. The fox spread her lips in a sinister smile and closed her eyes. Her thin arms outstretched, and her fingers snapped in unnatural directions as she began her shift.

My back froze, though only for a second. This time, I was ready for her.

Before Daria could complete her shift, I wrapped my fingers over the chains and jumped to a crouch. Raising my arms over my head, I whipped the metal out and around, slamming it over her ankles to knock her down. Daria's back hit the floor with a thud and air escaped her lungs. Hot breath rose over her lips in a puffy white cloud, and she yelped, staggering to stand.

I raised my foot, bringing it down over her neck, and Daria shrieked when the heel of my boot collided with her windpipe. Coughing and spitting up on the floor, she turned herself over.

Thick, sausage-like fingers wrapped around my neck and pulled me back. My boots skidded as the shifter who kicked me earlier dragged me from Daria. The chains scraped over the rocky ground, and I fought to grasp hold of them. Air was scarce, and when the shifter tightened his grip on my neck, my skin grew cold. Eyes bulging, I kicked back my leg, burying my boot into his groin. He doubled over, dropping his clasp on me and stumbling backward, his hands cupping his jewels.

Seizing the chains, I swung them around and landed a brutal blow to his jaw. Blood burst from his mouth, and I heard something whip out and hit the wall behind him.

A tooth for a tooth, jackass.

My lips twitched as I turned back to Daria and the other shifters. "Not so easy when I fight back, is it?"

She snarled and leaped for me, her henchmen on her heels. Their bulky frames took up most of the cavern and when they moved in unison toward me, I took a step back. My shoulders collided with the wall, and I twirled the chains around my fingers to tighten my bearing on them. As Daria neared me, I jerked my arms out and pushed the chains into her neck. Twisting on my heels, I whipped around her and wrapped a chain over her head. Pulling back, I brought

Daria close to me. Her legs kicked out from under her, and she tore at the metal noose I held securely.

I took another step, dragging her with me.

Gaze landing on the shifters that approached, I pulled again, cutting off Daria's air supply.

"One more step and she's dead," I hissed.

They froze in their tracks. *Good choice.*

Keeping my back to the wall, I walked the perimeter of the cavern with Daria's limp form in my grasp. She kicked and fought me with every step, but I continued to move. Each step got me closer to the tunnel that led to Naomi, and I kept my eyes locked on the shifters as I crept toward it.

"Naomi! I'm coming!" I yelled out.

In my arms, Daria's eyes jerked from the shifters to the tunnel, shock clouding her features. Before I could catch her, she drove an elbow into my broken ribs, and I dropped my hold on the chains. Daria pushed us back, slamming my body against the stone with so much force, I had to let go. My bones cracked and I shrieked, clutching my fingers to the wall for support. Knees trembling, I yelped as an agonizing pain extended through my lower back.

"Get that bitch!" Daria shrieked.

In seconds, all five shifters were on me. Even the one who's balls I likely broke stumbled my way with a furious glare trained on my shaking legs. Their teeth bared and the sound of bones breaking filled the cavern. One by one, they dropped to all fours and completed their shifts. Horrified, I scanned the beasts before me, calculating my chances.

Two of them were foxes, much like Daria, but larger in build. There was a coyote and a black panther, but my gaze tore from them to land on the gargantuan bear standing on its hind legs behind his friends. The bear let out a growl and I noticed a missing fang in his disgusting mouth. At least I got a good shot in already.

The foxes lunged for me, and I swerved out of their path just in time. Moving with the weight of the chains dangling off my wrists was difficult, and I nearly faceplanted while twisting out of the way. My shoulder hit the wall. I gritted my teeth from the dull ache that stretched up my side. Shaking it off, I turned my body again to face the remaining shifters.

With a grunt, I whipped the chains over my head and snapped them outward. They hit the floor, bouncing off and swiping the panther in its shins. In a flash, I yanked the chains back and repeated the motion, this time aiming for the coyote. The metal hit its front paws with enough force to send it scrambling backward, and a wide grin stretched over my face.

"Moron," I bit out and readied for the next blow.

I was about to hit the panther again when something sharp pierced my shoulder blade. A blood-curdling scream tore from my throat, and I hit the ground, fighting against whoever dragged me back. My skin felt like it was on fire, and when I looked up, I saw a fox's canines buried deep in the flesh of my shoulder. It bit down harder, and I roared in response.

The second fox rushed to my other side, its jaw open wide. When his teeth penetrated my arm, I almost blacked out. Blood pooled from its vile mouth as it tore at my skin, pinning me to the ground. My head rolled back, and I tried to keep my vision from blurring.

Eyes opening and shutting, I compelled myself to look

up just in time to see the bear's nasty face in mine. It growled, jaw tearing apart while it lunged for my neck.

My body jerked back. I pulled my knees into me. As the bear's teeth neared me, I gathered all the strength I had left and kicked it square in the chest. On any other day, the blow would have been pointless, and I'd have been a goner. Yet today, the bear catapulted away from me like I'd just hit him with a speeding car on the freeway. Its eyes spun around the room, landing on the shadows spreading from me to its chest.

At my sides, the foxes yelped but kept their hold on me.

The bear rose clumsily and started my way with the panther close on his heels. A few more seconds and they'd rip into my skin, and this time, I wasn't sure I had the strength to stop them. My head shot up, gaze landing on a boulder protruding from the cavern's ceiling. *Here goes nothing,* I thought, bringing my attention to the rock.

Body trembling, I reached for the stone's element, begging for it to hear me.

At first, nothing happened, and I was about to give up and face my fate when a trail of dust fell from the ceiling and landed on the bear's ragged fur. The beast didn't register it, but I knew better. Mind clearing, I pushed myself to keep my eyes on the boulder despite the wild animals charging my way. With everything I had left, I pictured the rock in my hands and my fingers spread wide at my sides. The boulder vibrated, sending more dust to set over the bear, covering his entire head in debris. His pounding steps slowed, and he looked up in confusion.

The idiot was still staring when I tore the boulder from the ceiling and sent it straight down on his head. Dust and dirt spread out before me in a thick cloud as the ceiling gave way. The enormous boulder I pulled free barreled down, landing on the bear's massive skull. A loud thud echoed down to me, and I heard a snap, cringing as I pictured the shifter's neck snapping from the weight.

When the dust cleared, his thick body lay idle in front of me. Blood and brain matter surrounded its colossal form, and the smell penetrated my nostrils, making me gag.

"NOOOOO!" Daria screamed and tore through the cavern to the bear. As she neared it, its body twitched and thrashed, shifting back to human form.

If I thought seeing a bear with its head bashed in was bad, seeing the limp body of the man was so much worse. His arms splayed out in unnatural angles, and I tried not to look past his chest for fear I might retch from the sight.

Daria's outraged eyes snapped to me, and she rose to stand, fuming. Tears poured down her face, making me almost feel sorry for the girl. Sure, she was a huge bitch, but I just killed her friend in the worst way possible. Whether or not he deserved it, I felt bad it had to go down this way.

"Billie!"

Naomi's panic-filled voice reached me, and I snapped my neck toward the dim tunnel it came from. "Naomi!"

Before I could say anything else, sharp teeth pierced the soft flesh of my neck and warm blood ran down my chest. My vision swam and my head pounded as flashes of orange fur danced before me. I tried to focus on the face of the animal that attacked me, but my eyes darted around the cavern with a mind of their own.

Coldness spread through my bones, and I felt myself weaken by the second. My arms fell to my sides, too heavy to move. Lashes fluttering, I took in a raspy breath and gazed into the distance. Somewhere in the tunnel, shadows formed, bringing forth the blurry shape of a man.

I breathed in again, fighting against the heaviness of my lids. The shadows spread wide, slowly disappearing from my vision with the rest of the cavern. As blackness overtook me, I locked my eyes on the shadow man, and terror engulfed me whole. Though I couldn't be sure, I swore I could see him smiling.

Chapter Twenty-five

River

The fresh scent of colder weather crawled up my nostrils; winter was on its way. Leaves crunched under my sneakers as I made my way through the forest's foliage. Every step reverberated back into me, and nerves shot up my body, getting me closer to where the wolf pack gathered for their daily hunts. I could hear their howls in the distance, and my heart raced thinking of what I was about to do.

Having realized how little time we had put me in an impossible position.

I swung a tree branch out of the path and stepped out into the clearing. They were all here; some shifted, and some still in human form. As soon as my heavy body staggered past the trees, all eyes snapped in my direction. From where I stood, I saw Griffin raise a questioning eyebrow my way and I shot him a sheepish smile before inching closer to the pack.

My pack, I had to remind myself. *I just have to take Isaac down, then they'll be mine.*

When the alpha crossed the clearing toward me, every fear I had laying idly inside rushed to the surface. Was I seriously about to challenge the wolf alpha in front of the entire pack? Who the hell did I think I was? Doubts clouded my thoughts and I worked to keep them tucked away. This had to be done. If the pack would not let me in, I was going to leave them no choice.

Isaac threw a death glare my way.

I returned the favor.

In three long strides, he was in front of me.

"I told you not to come here," he said. "This is not your pack. No one wants you here."

Scanning the clearing, I could see he was right. The shifters in wolf form bared their teeth and the rest of the pack refused to look at me. Even Griffin stood off to the side with a confused look on his face. *They're not going to make it easy on me, are they?*

My wolf shrugged. *Thanks for the vote of confidence, bud.*

Squaring my shoulders, I faced Isaac. "Why don't we let them decide that for themselves?"

Heat unfurled inside me, and I could sense the blood boil in my veins as I called my wolf forward. My jaw unclenched, and I ran my tongue over the pointed edges of the canines that pushed through the gums. The shift took over my body, dropping me to all fours before Isaac's dumbfounded face. I kicked my legs back, gritting my teeth while my bones reformed. My shirt ripped at the seams, falling to the ground in tethered pieces, and fur shot out from my arms in patches of gray. When the shift was complete, I let out a howl and rose on my hind legs, pushing my front paws into Isaac's chest.

He stumbled backward, anger replacing the hesitation on his face.

So self-assured.

In moments, his wolf was before me and snarling like a wild animal. Isaac's jaw snapped in a pathetic attempt to make me back down, but I didn't let it bother me or my wolf. Around us, murmurs rose from the pack as they watched us with shock-stricken eyes. The few in beast form inched closer, but no one dared to interrupt. They all knew what this meant.

A challenge. One I intended to win.

Isaac's wolf was larger than mine and he knew it, his growls deepening as he flashed his fangs in my direction. I could feel my own beast pause for a moment, as though he was questioning our ability to take the alpha down. With a snarl, I urged him forward, burying my paws into the ground. Warm saliva dripped from my mouth, and I trained my sharp eyes on Isaac, beckoning him in.

The alpha let out a long howl and charged for me. His hind legs pushed off the earth and he flew forward with so much speed, I couldn't swerve out of the way even if I wanted to. Our muscled bodies collided, chests smashing together and teeth snapping as we fought. His jaw unhinged and he sunk his teeth into my side, tearing at my flesh.

Whimpering, I twisted my body and latched onto his neck.

Gasps resounded through the clearing, the brutality of the event spreading like wildfire. I jerked my head back and forth, shaking Isaac's wolf as though I could tear his hide off. He snarled but didn't back down. As his teeth sank deeper into my side, I winced at the pain. My wolf cried out, and I dropped hold of Isaac's neck to stumble backward. Blood matted my fur, and I felt a piece of skin missing from where he ripped into it.

Agonizing pains ran down my side, and I swayed back and forth, vertigo overtaking me.

In a flash, Isaac pounced on me, pushing me down and burrowing a bite into my shoulder. My body twitched as he munched down harder, and my legs kicked out from under me. A yelp escaped me, and when Isaac's fiery breath filled my nostrils, my anger returned.

I twirled beneath him, rearranging my body so I could force his grip off. Frustrated, I ripped from Isaac's clasp and threw myself on top of him. My front paws beat into him while I unlatched my jaw to spread over his fur. When my teeth penetrated his skin, and I could taste his blood on my tongue, I pressed further.

Isaac twitched, a cry filling the void between us. He fought to throw me off, but years of wrestling in Shadowhurst Academy taught me one thing. Once you had them down, you didn't give an inch.

Burying my snout in his filthy fur, I gnawed harder until his blood ran like a river. It fell down his neck, staining the gray of his wolf a sordid red. Iron filled my mouth, and it surprised me to know the taste didn't make me gag. Instead, I was overcome with a hunger I haven't felt before. Snarling, I dug my teeth into his flesh, shoving my snout into the warm liquid that poured from him.

Inside, my wolf smiled.

Looking to Isaac, I saw his eyes glaze over as life left him. If I didn't back down now, I'd kill the bastard. A part of me wanted to do just that, but something intervened. I needed the pack to accept me as their alpha, and I wasn't sure that would happen if I let Isaac die. No matter how much I craved for it to happen.

Steadily, I unhinged myself and stepped away.

Warm blood dripped from my lips, and I breathed heavily, turning to face the pack. Behind me, Isaac's body stilled as he slumped, defeated.

A light brown wolf dared to inch closer, and I growled under my breath. He stopped cold in his tracks, whimpering and lowering his head. *Good.*

When I was certain I had their attention, I reached for my wolf, urging for the shift. One by one, my bones reformed and in moments, I was standing tall with blood covering me and my privates out for the world to see. Under any other circumstance, I would have been mortified, but not this time. This time, I couldn't care less about who saw what.

I wiped Isaac's blood off my chin and uncurled my back. "Your alpha has been beaten."

Silence filled the clearing.

"I won't force you to follow me," I continued. "Whatever deal you had with Isaac, I don't want the same. Whatever just happened, I'm one of you and I hope that's enough. If you're looking for an alpha that's more reasonable than that fool over there, we can work something out. I need your help and I don't want to take it by force. Some shadowers have left the house and I know I'm new here, but most of you have been around long enough to know them. Are friends with them even. What I'm asking of you is a lot, I realize that, but I don't have a choice anymore. One of those shifters took the girl I love, and I will do anything I can to get her back. Help me find the missing shifters and find out which one of them took Billie. Once she's back, I promise to stand by you and be the leader you deserve to have. Whatever that means."

The pack stood still.

"You have until tomorrow to decide. I hope you'll help me."

With that, I turned on my heel and walked away from them. Blood trailed behind me, and as I marched by Isaac, I fought the urge to look at him. Taking him down as alpha was a good first step, but what I told the pack was the absolute truth. I had no intention to take his place. All I needed was them on my side to send a message to the shifters who took Billie. With the pack, I would show them I meant business. Enough to spread fear through the house. If there was one thing I knew, it was that fear was a powerful weapon. It created tension, and I hoped that tension would be enough for whoever took her to make a mistake. When they did, I'd be waiting.

I'll find you, love.

My knees buckled and heat flared in my chest, making the hairs on my arms stand on end. Eyes bulging, I watched the thin black lines spread over my skin, pulsing so intensely, I thought I might pass out. They burnt into me as I clutched my hand to my heart, feeling it race under my palm. My vision blurred, and when it refocused, all I saw was black.

Stumbling, I swung my arms around me to spin in a circle in an attempt to see through the darkness. My eyes narrowed, and something caught my attention near to me. A few feet away, I noticed the figure of a man lying on the ground. His body was battered, and where his face should be, a giant boulder lay covered in blood. Bile rose in my throat, and I battled the urge to vomit. Beneath my eyelids, tears pooled as I tried to make sense of what I was seeing.

It was so quiet. So quiet and cold.

My bones rattled when a gust of chilled air wrapped

around me. Blinking, I let the tears fall down my cheeks. I felt like a complete sack of shit, shaking and crying, but no matter how hard I tried, the tears kept coming. A faint sound pulsated somewhere past me, and my ears perked up.

Drip. Drip. Drip.

WHAT IS THAT?

Jolting my head around, I attempted to find the source, but nothing came into view. All I saw was the man's corpse. My arms whirled around me, and I tried to move, but something held me down. Pain traveled up and down my body while my legs stayed glued to the ground. In the distance, the drips I heard before continued, and their melody drove me insane.

I dropped down, shutting my eyes and convulsing uncontrollably. Leaves whipped around me, and when I snapped my eyes open, I was back in the forest again. The body I saw was gone and I could hear bird calls rise from the surrounding trees.

My head pounded and my chest felt like someone held a burning candle to it for hours on end. Looking down, I noticed the black lines disappeared again, replaced only with reddened flesh and the dull ache of residual pains.

Rubbing my eyes, I wiped the tears off and tipped my head back, letting my howl permeate the dense forest around me.

Chapter Twenty-six

Billie

When I came to, Daria and her shifters were gone, and I was chained to the damn wall again. They had cleared the man I killed out, yet I could still see the pool of blood left behind from where the boulder hit him, and my stomach turned at the sight. Tearing my eyes from the deep red stain on the ground, I cringed at the spasm the movement sent up my neck.

Whichever one bit me left a deep gash on my throat and I could feel it pulsate as it healed. *Wait, what?* Jerking my gaze to the rest of my body, I noticed the wounds that adorned my pale skin were almost gone. Even the sickeningly blue lesion on my broken ribs was lighter and I could see it mending before my eyes.

What the...

Confused, I blinked and watched as the bruise shrank in size until it resembled more of a mosquito bite than something that impaled me for days. Don't get me wrong, I wasn't one to look a gift horse in the mouth, but this was actually insane. Wounds didn't heal overnight, not without a healing potion, so whatever was going on with me couldn't be anything good. Could it?

Eyes darting around the cavern, my brain ran at a million miles a minute.

Somehow, and I had zero clue how, I was tapping into the fae magic that swelled within me. The fae were notorious for their healing ability, what with the whole living forever thing, so it would stand to reason my ailments weren't disappearing naturally. Magic was involved, and since it wasn't mine, it had to be theirs.

I felt it all around me now. *This is new.*

Clawing at the wall, I inched upward until I could comfortably press my palms to the stone wall. As my skin connected with the rock, energy shot through me, and I all but collapsed on the spot. My blood bubbled in my veins, pulsing as it clung to the earth element in the wall.

Terrified, I yanked my hands away.

The energy settled, but I could still feel it hum in my body like the ghost of Christmas Past coming to visit. Bringing my palms to the wall again, I stilled my breathing and let my jaw drop open when I felt the rock's element rush through me. This magic was so different and so powerful that it made my knees buckle and my brain want to explode. There was no block on it, not like when I tried to reach the witch magic inside me, and instead of tiring me out, it gave me strength I didn't know I had.

Inside me, the shadows swarmed, and before I knew it, I was covered head to toe in their oblivion. *Seriously, what in the hell?*

Panic clouded my mind, and I battled the need to rip my hands from the wall again. As much as the power I felt scared me, it was also invigorating. It was as if a part of me had become unlocked when I tore that boulder from the ceiling, and now, my body was an open vessel for the energy that pushed into it. The shadows thickened, blocking my view of the cavern and forcing my jaw to relax. Around me, the cavern shook. Lightly at first and then with a force so mighty, I thought it might collapse on itself. Dust and dirt fell from the ceilings and walls, shooting up my nostrils until I was choking to spit it out. My mouth dried, and I stomped my feet into the ground as I imagined the cavern stilling.

It rumbled and fear gripped me.

Closing my eyes, I pressed my palms deeper into the stone, bringing the image to a more vivid state. Little by little, I visualized having control of the earth and rock around me, breathing my energy into the vision as one would breathe air. In response, the cavern calmed its rumbling.

Holy. Freaking. SHIT.

Not breaking a sweat, I unhinged myself from the wall and let my palms cool off in the icy air. My skin burnt and I swore I could feel boils forming on the surface, but when I looked down, I was completely unharmed. Whatever this recent development in my magic was, I loved it!

"Naomi?" I yelled out and waited.

A few seconds later, my friend's voice carried back to me, tugging my lips into a relieved smile. "Yes? Are you all right? I think there was an earthquake or something."

"Yeah, that was me," I said. "I don't know what's going on or how I'm doing any of this, but I think I can get us out of here now."

A light rustle reached my ears as Naomi moved around in her prison. "It's too dangerous. The others, they'll be back soon. We can't take them all on, they're too strong."

She fought back sobs and it all but killed me.

"Trust me, I can do it. I'm not sure how to explain this and I have no clue how much you know about what's happening to us, but this isn't your run-of-the-mill kidnapping. The people that took us are shapeshifters, and I'm a witch."

There was complete silence from her end, and I bit the inside of my cheek while waiting for a response. I had hoped I didn't just drop a bomb in her lap, but if Naomi and I were getting out of here, she needed to know what we were up against. *Dear Goddess, please, don't let her be freaked out.*

"I kind of figured they weren't human," Naomi said.

Thankyouthankyouthankyou! "On a scale of one to ten, how freaked out are you right now?"

"About a hundred and seven," she choked out. "But whatever gets us out of this place. You sure you can do it?"

"I think so. Or I hope so. I don't know."

"You have to try," she begged. "I can't do what you can, so you're our only chance of getting free. Isn't there a spell you can use? I mean, I know little about witches and magic, but that sounds like something you do, right?"

I tried not to laugh, I really did. "Yeah, that about sums it up. I can tell you more when we're out of here. I don't think I can use my witch magic, though."

"What? Why not?" The fear in her voice was heartbreaking.

"There's some kind of block in this place to keep me from using that part of my magic. There's something else... Hope you're ready for another shocking revelation."

"Hit me with it."

Biting my lower lip, I took a deep breath and faced the tunnel. "I think this cavern has some sort of connection to the fae."

"Fae?"

I could all but see her eyes bulge out of her head.

"Yep. They're like my ancestors, or whatever," I tried to explain, doing a shoddy job of it. Obviously. I had a hard enough time coming to terms with my theory that having to explain it to another person, a human nonetheless, was overwhelming. "Anyway, I think because I have some fae blood in me, I can somehow tap into their magic. Haven't accomplished much yet, but I'm getting the hang of it."

Naomi moved around again, and the sound of her chains rang through the tunnel. "What have you tried so far?"

Wow, this chick is handling this oddly well. Even though I barely knew her, I was proud of Naomi. She was a freaking champ in my books, no question about it.

"I'm trying to form a connection to the earth element in this place. I could pull out a few rocks before." An image of the boulder crushing the bear's skull flashed before me, and I shook it off. "So I thought I'd wedge the rock that's holding my chains in place out."

"And?"

I frowned. "It's not working. The damn thing is really jammed in there, and the rock won't budge."

"Hmm..."

My eyebrows rose. "Naomi? What are you thinking?"

"Not sure yet," she answered. "I don't get how any of this works, but can you hear that water dripping somewhere close to here?"

"Oh, thank the Goddess you hear that too!" I shrieked. "I thought I was going nuts. What about it?"

A deep sigh reverberated through the cavern as Naomi collected her thoughts. "I was just thinking if you can move rocks around or whatever, maybe you can do it with water?

Caverns have liquid running through them for the most part. I think it's trapped in the rock or something. If you created enough of a force, do you think it would help push the stone out?"

"Naomi! You're brilliant!" I screamed. "When we get out of here, I'm going to hug the crap out of you!"

Her light laughter made me tear up, and I had to work to keep my mind on the important things. Naomi may have known little about magic, but this girl was as smart as they came. In a way, she reminded me of Peyton, which likely explained why I was a sobbing mess at the moment.

Filling my lungs with as much air as I could muster, I let out a long breath and placed my palms on the wall. When I searched for the water's element in the cavern, my pulse raced through my body, pounding into my skin like a drum. One way or another, I was ripping these damn chains off the wall and getting us free. I didn't care what magic I had to use to do it. Fae, witch, damn unicorn magic for all it mattered.

Naomi and I were going home. We were going home *now*.

Chapter Twenty-seven

River

"How did she even get my number?" Peyton screeched, waving her cellphone in my face and stomping back and forth in my front yard. "This is some stalker shit right here is what it is."

Trying to follow her movements was dizzying, and I had to look away after her third round. By the time Peyton was done with her drama, the lilies my mom planted would be stomped to the nothing. I stretched out a hand and waved her over. "Can I read what she said again?"

With a huff, Peyton chucked the phone in my lap, tapping her foot on the ground. Right over a freshly propagated plant. *Just perfect.*

I convinced myself not to worry about it. Dad didn't care about the garden and Mom was, well, gone forever. *It's just a freaking plant; get a grip!* I wasn't sure why it was affecting me so much, but if Peyton didn't calm her shit down, we were going to have issues. To my relief, she eased the stomping and slid to sit on the stairs beside me. Her foot still danced, but at least it was on gravel now, which was fine by me.

Scanning the text, I read over every word as though I didn't already have it committed to memory.

Hey. You don't know me, and this is probably hella weird. My name is Vic, and Billie was a good friend of mine. We need to meet up. I can help you.

Peyton was right to worry. A text from a junior coven witch was alarming. That it was from the girl I almost killed when the High Coven attacked the resistance made it even more questionable. Why was Victoria messaging Peyton and promising to help? I shivered, thinking of what her help might look like. Billie told me that the witch almost killed her when she caught her taking the Book of Darkness, and Billie had to erase her memories just to get away. Did the spell backfire? Is that why Victoria was messaging Peyton now?

"It has to be a trick," I said, handing back her phone. "The coven could have put her up to this to get closer to us."

"Okay, yeah, fine. But like why? What's the end goal here?"

I shrugged. "I don't know, but I don't trust this girl."

"No kidding, wolf boy."

My back stiffened at the annoying nickname, but I let it go. We had bigger fish to fry at the moment, like figuring out why Victoria was crawling out of the woodwork to help us out. Junior witches didn't betray the High Coven. The only one we knew of was Billie, and I remembered how difficult it was for her to accept that her coven was up to no good. No way in Hell Victoria was suddenly on the same page. She was up to something, and I didn't like it.

Reaching for the phone, I ignored Peyton's side-eye and unlocked the screen. "Should we respond?"

"And say what? 'Hey, girl, long time! Wanna grab a latte and chill?' Are you insane? I am not talking to this chick!"

"No one is asking you to bring her home for dinner," I said, irritated. "I just want to see what she says so we can figure out what the High Coven is up to. We know nothing about her except that Billie considered her a friend back when she was a part of the coven. It can't hurt to text her back."

With an angry growl, Peyton snatched the phone from my hand and tapped on the screen. Her fingers scrolled across it, and her eyes danced as light illuminated her pale face. Jaw ticking, she tapped a few more times before turning to face me.

"Victoria Hatzi. Eighteen years old, attended Humberview High School, graduated with honors. Has no plans for the future and is likely taking a leap year before settling for a college. Single, by choice, and loves baby turtles. She has one sibling, an older sister that she doesn't talk to, and was raised by her mom and grandmother until she moved out two months ago."

Peeling my jaw off the floor, I faced Peyton. "How the hell do you know all that?"

"Social media. What are you, a hundred?"

"You know, for someone upset about getting stalked, you sure do enough of it yourself."

Peyton's lips smashed together. "Don't test me, furball."

I knocked a swift elbow to her side and motioned for the phone. Hesitantly, Peyton handed it over and continued to sigh obnoxiously. Her dramatics didn't go unnoticed, but I refused to let her get to me. Victoria's message was most likely a trap, and we both knew it. Still, it wasn't something I was willing to leave alone. Not when there was a chance the witch wasn't lying and wanted to help us. It wasn't like we were doing a stellar job of finding Billie on our own.

"What if she's telling the truth?"

"No chance."

I nudged her leg. "Come on, you're telling me there isn't a shot in hell another witch might be over the High Coven's lies?"

"Dude!" Peyton yelled, bursting my eardrums. I slid away from her, though it did little to drown out her shrill voice. "Billie said junior witches are basically brainwashed bimbos. Judging by what I found on this chick, she isn't much better. This is a trap and I'm not falling for it."

"Okay, fine. Just do me a favor and think it over. I'll talk to the others and see what they have to say. We need a break here, and we need it bad. Maybe this is it."

Peyton looked past me to the destroyed flowers under the porch. From where I sat, I could see uncertainty weigh down her shoulders and it mirrored my own feelings to perfection. We have sunk so low that I was hoping a rogue witch would come to our rescue. It was pathetic enough to make my skin crawl.

Disgusted with myself, I looked past the driveway, then glanced at my watch. Dad would be home any moment now, and I dreaded having to explain why I will be gone all night again. The last few days had me torn between fleeing to the resistance house to chase down dead ends and lying to my father. I had grown tired of both. I wished I could be honest with him, but that wasn't in the cards. My father thought witch-hunting was a dumb belief passed down by our ignorant ancestors. I doubted that finding out that magic and shadowers exist, and that his son was a damn shifter, would help his grievance. As far as Dad was concerned, my friends and I were wasting our time playing with weapons and I had to keep the charade up, no matter what happened. At least for another year until high school ended and I could move out.

Thinking of the future twisted my stomach into knots, and I leaned on a post to keep from sliding down the porch. My limbs were liquid, and the onset of a pressure headache pulsed my temples.

"Still nothing from the pack?" Peyton asked, breaking me out of the self-pity I was drowning in.

I shook my head. "Not yet. I gave them 'til tomorrow, so we'll see. It's not looking good though."

"What are you gonna do if they refuse to help?"

The question sat heavy in the air. I was pretty sure we both knew what I would do if it came down to that. I'd tear the town apart and kill every shifter that got in my way.

Peyton's phone vibrated in her lap and we both jumped at the sound. Our eyes locked, darting to the screen. *Shit. Not Victoria.*

As she fumbled with the keys to answer, I could see that despite her arguments, Peyton was as disappointed as me. That familiar frown was back on her face and wrinkles sat deep under her eyes. Her voice was steady, despite the unease I could smell off her, and it surprised me to hear the strength of it when she finally answered. "Go for Peyton."

What a drama queen.

"Uh-huh. Uh-huh. Uh-huh," she recited. One more 'uh-huh' and I was going to tear the phone from her hand and stomp my foot on it. "Okay, yes. We're on our way."

"Who was that?" I asked.

"Savannah," Peyton answered, a broad smile on her face. "They found something in the journal."

Chapter Twenty-eight

River

Peyton dropped me off at the edge of the woods before rushing away in a mad dash. "Where are you going?" I yelled after her as the Jeep smoked out of the parking lot.

"Had an idea! Be back soon!"

That was ominous. Peyton was notorious for having out of the box ideas, and whatever this one was, it had her peeling out at lightning speed. *Please, don't let her crash. please, don't let her crash.* I recited the words, knowing Billie would kill me if I let anything happen to her best friend.

Making my way through the trees to the house was quicker than normal, mostly because I was pretty much running the entire time. By the time I reached the front porch, Savannah and Logan were waiting, their voices carrying over the foggy forest. They were arguing, as always. One of these days, I had to figure out what was up with those two before they killed each other. Today, however, was not that day.

Because today, my annoying friends did something right for a change.

"Hey, guys," I said and crouched next to Savannah. "Peyton said you found something?"

Their heads shot to me in unison, and I stumbled back. Between Savannah's fierce stare and Logan's eerily lavender eyes, the two had a *Children of the Corn* vibe going that I didn't care for. I straightened and settled cross-legged between them, hoping to cut the tension by some small amount. "So, what did you find?"

Savannah leaned over me to pluck the journal from Logan's hands. It did not go over well.

"I thought we agreed I can speak for myself?" the mind reaper sniped, clutching the journal with his long fingers.

"Maybe when you learn more than two syllables."

Angling my body, I twisted to block Savannah's sneer from Logan and shook my head. "Can I just see the damn journal?"

She rolled her eyes.

Logan growled.

Off to a great start, here. "Guys, come on! Cut it out! This is important. If you have something to help us, I need to see it. You can deal with your bullshit later."

That seemed to settle them down and after a few huffs, Savannah let the journal go and motioned for Logan to start talking. The reaper flipped a silver lock of hair over his shoulder before opening the book in his lap. As he whirled to face me, a glimmer of hope pushed up my throat and I swallowed it down.

"You know Billie's shadow thing?" he asked. I nodded. "Lorelei said Marcus was looking into it for her, but she didn't put the pieces together until we started going through his notes. She gave the journal to Billie the night of the party because Marcus figured out that her magic is somehow related to the fae."

"But we already knew she had a fae background in her family," I said. "I'm not sure how this helps us find her."

"That's not all. What Marcus believed was that she wasn't just related to fae. He thought her magic was fae magic."

My neck tensed. "That doesn't make sense. Billie is a witch and all the magic we've seen her use has been the one taught by the coven."

"Not the shadows," Savannah whispered.

"Exactly," Logan said, winking her way. Judging by her disgusted face, my friend did not appreciate the gesture at all. "Anyway, Marcus mentioned in his notes that the shadows are a form of fae spirit magic, which would make sense because that's where her ancestry lies. He even found sources to prove that the original witches had similar shadow magic they picked up from their fae counterparts. There was other rubbish I couldn't understand, but that was the gist of it."

"...okay," I said. *So not okay.* "How does that help find her though?"

Savannah and Logan exchanged knowing looks, then turned to me.

"You know how we found out that there were students in Shadowhurst that all had distinct fae bloodlines?" Savannah asked.

How could I forget? My mom killed those students and got herself locked up in a magical prison for it. It wasn't something that was going to leave my memory for a long time, if ever.

"In one entry, Marcus wrote that the shifters he'd been suspecting of treason let something slip about a shadow creature. That's what he was trying to tell Billie before he died. That she wasn't the only one with spirit fae magic."

My jaw dropped and sweat beaded down my back. These two officially blew my mind. I wondered if Billie had a chance to read the notes Marcus left before they took her, knowing it didn't make the slightest difference in the end. Fae magic or not, someone still got to her.

Sucking in a breath, I turned to Logan. "Do you think whoever took her was just like her? Someone with the same fae background?"

His lips crashed together, and he lowered his head. "I think so."

Just then, the sound of leaves breaking underfoot rose from the trees and we turned to see two figures emerge from the woods. Smiling, I waved to Peyton as she made her way to the porch, but my mouth dried when I noticed the other person following her.

The woman ambled, riddled by age, and the messy bun on her head was covered in loose twigs she'd collected in the forest on the way here. Her brow creased, and she studied my friends and me with so much intensity, I shrank back.

"Yo, bitches!" Peyton screeched. "I brought back up!"

Ms. Broussard scowled at her cursing and focused a sharp gaze on me. "Hello, everyone."

Was it just me or had Peyton completely lost it? Why would she bring a human into the resistance house knowing full well how the shadowers inside would react? This was a bold move, even for her, and I shuddered to think what the other leaders might think of her actions. The resistance lived in strict secrecy. It was what kept them safe. Peyton bringing

Ms. Broussard here violated so many rules, I couldn't count them on all my fingers.

She's dead.

"Um, Ms. Broussard," I said awkwardly. "Hello. Peyton, can I talk to you for a sec?"

The spunky weirdo brushed me off with a sleight of hand and ushered the shop owner toward us.

"Later, furball. This is important."

I frowned. "So. Is. This."

"Dude!" Peyton shot her hand up like she was going to backhand me across the face. "Savannah said we might be dealing with someone of fae descent, and if anyone knows anything about the gross history of this town, it's Ms. Broussard. She's willing to help, so let's let her get her mojo on."

I definitely couldn't argue with that. If Peyton was willing to risk her neck with the leaders to bring the shop owner here, she must have had a good reason. And she wasn't wrong, Ms. Broussard was a walking encyclopedia in Shadowhurst history, so we needed her eyes on this. I still didn't feel comfortable having a human at the house, especially considering how the shadowers reacted to the hunters being here, but this was a necessary evil.

Reluctantly, I slid to the side, having only now realized that I was guarding the damn journal with my body. When Logan handed it over, his eyes zeroed in on Ms. Broussard and I could swear I saw a hint of recognition in them. Recognition and possibly fear.

The shop owner glanced his way, clenching her jaw before she snatched the journal from his hands.

"Uh, you two know each other or something?" Savannah asked, catching on to the same odd exchange I did.

"Nope," Logan said.

"Not at all," Ms. Broussard agreed. I didn't fail to notice how quickly they dismissed the idea and filed away my suspicions to be dissected at a later date.

Ms. Broussard skimmed over the pages, nodding slowly as she read.

"You think you can help us find out who the shifters meant when they talked about the shadow creature?"

Her lips curled at the edges, and she slammed the book shut. "I believe so. Though, it will take some time. I will need to cross-reference everything in this journal with the books in my shop. Is it all right if I take it with me?"

"No problem," I said. "But Ms. Broussard?"

"Yes?"

"We're running out of time."

The look on her face told me she didn't doubt it and she bid good bye before following Peyton back through the trees again. As her back retreated, I slunk into the wood beneath me and listened to Savannah and Logan resume the argument they started earlier. Catching only pieces of their conversation, I lost interest quickly and drifted off into deep thought.

With Ms. Broussard's help, we finally had a lead worth exploring.

My pulse quickened as I pictured Billie's face in my mind, imagining what it would feel like to hold her again. I couldn't wait to bring her back to me, to run my hands through her hair, and to taste the freshness of her skin. Damn, I missed that girl so much, I even couldn't wait to fight with her.

I was still lost in fantasy when a firm hand gripped my shoulder and pulled me back.

Inside me, the wolf growled, and instinct took over.

Swinging my arm around, I aimed for whoever grabbed me and threw a loaded fist in their direction. My knuckles connected with skin and a roar pierced my eardrums. As I focused my eyes, the wolf whined, and I had the urge to scold the bastard for making me paranoid enough to attack. Looking into the eyes of the person I clocked, my shoulders sagged.

Well, this is most definitely not going to play out well.

Chapter Twenty-nine

River

"What the hell, kid?" Raiden howled, rubbing the spreading red spot on his jaw. "You looking for a fight here?"

My hands shot up, waving an invisible white flag. "Sorry, man. I didn't mean it, you just startled me. Why are you sneaking up on people, anyway? You know my wolf has a mind of his own right now."

"You're lucky it was me and not Mel, she would have kicked your ass for that." Raiden flashed his teeth, making me feel a little less guilty for hitting him. "And your wolf would be just fine if you followed my advice and got yourself in with the pack instead of challenging Isaac. When were you planning on telling me about that, by the way?"

The lion's tone was stern, and I didn't appreciate being scolded like a child. This guy wasn't in control of my actions. Hell, even my own father couldn't tell me what to do. That he thought I had to clear things with him was annoying, and despite my wolf shivering like a coward, I had the mind to hit him again.

Rolling my shoulders, I faced Raiden. "Didn't realize I had to give you a play-by-play of my every move."

"Watch it, kid," Raiden said, his words cold as stone. "I may not be your alpha, but I am still a leader in this house. I get you're upset, so I'm willing to let it slide, for now. You try something like that again though, and we're going to have a problem."

Near us, Logan was immobile, but I noticed Savannah reach for the knives tucked into the hidden holsters of her jeans. I shook my hand in warning, and she stopped in her tracks, crossing her arms over her chest. She wasn't pleased with me telling her what to do, no question about it, yet her ability to listen was astounding. We didn't need Raiden to have enough of our crap and send both of us packing. At least not until we found Billie. After that, all bets were off.

Fighting against myself, I forced a smile and turned back to Raiden. "Noted," I said. "And sorry for the punch. You caught me off guard and it was wrong."

"No worries. So, you wanna tell me why you took down Isaac?"

Not really.

"I guess," I breathed out. "I figured we need the pack's help and they sure as shit wouldn't do anything with Isaac pulling their strings. They needed motivation."

"And your idea of motivation is to challenge their alpha after you've had, what? A couple of days practice at being a wolf?"

Well, when he put it that way... "Yeah, sorta."

"Listen, River. I won't be telling you what to do and what not to do with others like you, but I can guarantee that nothing good will come out of this. Shifters are not like the rest of the shadowers—"

"No shit," Logan said.

Raiden's massive shoulders rose, but he moved past the comment. "As I said, shifters are different. Isaac may not be someone you can get behind, but the pack chose him. That means a lot to those of us who have tight bonds with our animal counterparts. Not all shifters run in packs, though most lean on their own kind, and when they do, it's a heavy bond. One that doesn't get wiped out with a fight."

"If you're trying to tell me I have no chance in hell of making them choose me as their alpha, you can spare the lecture. I don't even want the role. All I want is..."

"What?" Raiden arched a bushy eyebrow my way. "To use them as a weapon against the other shifters until someone talks? It won't work."

"How do you know that?" I shouted.

The leader sighed and patted me on the back before I could back away. "Because I've been where you are. Pack or not, if it was someone from the house that took Billie, they won't talk. No matter how much fear you can instill in them."

Those were some big words from someone that had done very little to help so far. Raiden hadn't raised a finger to threaten any of the shifters, hiding them from me instead, and I was over his bullshit. All he did was ask them some lovely freaking questions. What good was that? People didn't respond to niceties. What they responded to were threats, and I was full of those lately.

My muscles tensed and I shook his hand off my back. "I want to talk to your cousin. I need to know who else he ran with, playing nice hasn't worked so far, so it's time to beat the answers out of those asshole friends of his. I'm not asking again."

"No."

"What is the matter with you?" I roared. "Are you seriously choosing that bastard, the one that threatened Billie's life, over her? You're pathetic!"

With glowing eyes, he took a step in and shoved his round face in mine. His warm breath washed over me, and I had to tilt my neck to look up at his almost seven-foot frame.

"Damen is not responsible for what happened to Billie. This conversation is over."

He was so wrong, I could barely stand it. I didn't care what Raiden had to say in defense of his cousin. I knew Damen had something to do with Billie's disappearance, and even if he didn't, he knew who did. But why was Raiden defending him? Something was amiss, and it made my brain hurt when I thought about it. The only reason I could imagine for Raiden to prevent me from questioning Damen was that he had something to hide. *What? What are you hiding?*

Skin paling, I looked at the lion shifter.

Are you the one that took her? Is that why you won't let me near Damen? Because he might give you up?

My vision swam. This piece of garbage was acting high and mighty and pretending to be my friend while the entire time he was the reason she was gone? No! It couldn't be! Still, I couldn't stop the outrage that grew as I looked into his eyes. Raiden didn't let his shifter side out unless it was important, and the only reason he was this pissed off right now was because I hit a nerve.

You son of a...

I lunged for him, my fist connecting with the same spot I hit before. At my attack, Raiden doubled back, putting some distance between us, and sending me toppling over. My body skidded forward, hitting the dusty wall of the house with a shoulder. I curled in on myself, breathing into the pain. Deep down, I could sense my wolf's confused emotions as he tried to calm me down. Somehow, our roles reversed, and it was me that needed the calming.

Nostrils flaring, I shouted for him to come forward, and it only took a moment for him to obey. My body dropped, hitting the porch with an echoing thud. Bones cracked and fur grew as I reformed. When I whirled around, River was gone, and I was a wolf again.

And the wolf was angry as hell.

I leaped in the air, barreling toward Raiden with so much speed, the landscape blurred in my peripheral vision. My ears pulled back and I snarled, barring my pointed canines as I moved for his neck. Raiden's eyes burned brighter, but he refused to shift. He stepped out of my way just as I reached him, making me crash into the pole holding up the porch's slanted roof.

Wood splintered and I jerked backward, twisting to face him again.

This time, Raiden began his shift and the need to kill multiplied within me. His lion was huge and full of muscle, and I could feel the wolf hesitate.

Wolf up, moron, I growled at him.

Raiden roared, shaking his mane and slamming his thick paws into the wood. The floor creaked under his weight and my legs shook as his heavy body landed. Growling, I threw myself at him. Our bodies collided and we spun around each other, my teeth in his mane and his chest pushing me back. Someone screamed my name, and I whirled my head to see Logan running in our direction. Behind him, Savannah jumped to catch his arm, but she was too late.

The mind reaper wrapped his fingers over my tail and yanked me back, causing a blood-curdling yelp to rip through me. He was still latching on when I spun to pin him to the floor. Beneath me, Logan thrashed violently to get free, but my hold was too strong. I unhinged my jaw and aimed for his jugular only moments before someone knocked me away.

My wolf howled, and I scrambled to right myself, then pounced at whoever stopped me from killing Logan.

I had realized my mistake too late.

Under my weight, Savannah looked like a broken doll. Her arm was twisted at an odd angle and a bluish hue I haven't seen before replaced the bronze of her skin. *What did I do? What's wrong with her?* My body shook as I looked over my friend's body, realizing all too soon that my paw was pressing into her throat, stopping her from breathing.

About to dismount, my fur rippled as an agonizing pain seared into my brain. My eyes widened and I tried to howl, but nothing came out. I dropped to Savannah's side, losing my hold on her throat and relief rushed through me when I heard her choke on air. Head still pounding, I shot my gaze wildly around when I spotted him.

Towering over us, Logan's broad frame stood tall and relentless. His eyes were shades lighter, making them look like two orbs of light against his skin. Logan smirked, and I gagged on the pain that followed. *What is this guy doing?*

I wanted to shift back, but he locked every part of me in place. All I saw was Logan and his grin. The bastard was enjoying this.

His power soaked through me until I could all but taste it on my tongue. It tasted of lilacs and I shook my head to gather my thoughts. I must have been going crazy because, for a second, Logan's power felt so foreign and unreal, I wasn't sure he was a shadower at all. Beside me, Savannah groaned, and I peeled my gaze from the reaper to face her. Her eyes begged me to stop fighting and I obeyed.

As I shifted back, Logan's low chuckle echoed over the porch, followed closely by a lion's roar. It was enough to make me pass the hell out, which was exactly what I ended up doing. My eyes rolled back into my skull and my head thudded on the floor while I fought the need to sleep. I was too weak, and sleep was much too tempting.

The last thing I saw before shutting my eyes was Logan's hand pressing into my forehead. The last thing I smelled was lilacs.

Chapter Thirty

Billie

Shadows encased my body and they swarmed in and out of my skin as I shook, the strain of reaching for the water in the cavern's walls overpowering me. Breathing through clenched teeth, I struggled to hold my weight, grinding my feet into the ground to keep standing. My cheeks puffed out and the red in them spread over my entire neck.

Almost there, almost there, almost there...

Little by little, I weakened.

Around me, the cavern groaned and trembled, covering me in its dust from head to toe. The debris settled in my hair and eyes, and I had to breathe through my mouth to keep it from crawling up my nostrils. I had been at this for hours. Long, unbelievably infuriating hours. While Naomi's plan was solid, I was beginning to doubt my ability to tap into the water element around me, and though I couldn't feel the cavern's block against me, using this much of my energy was debilitating. My legs were numb, and my wrists bled so profusely from the pressure of the shackles that I couldn't move my fingers anymore.

I slunk down, letting the shadows creep back into my skin.

"Almost had it that time!" I yelled out to my friend.

"Good! Keep trying!"

Her words were all I needed to continue. Closing my eyes, I pulled myself up and reached for the magic within me. In a flash, it snapped to attention and covered me in its darkness once more. Each time the shadows passed through me, my smile widened, as though their presence was feeding me the energy I so desperately needed at the moment.

Silencing my heavy breathing, I steadied and closed my eyes, waiting for my cue.

In the distance, a low drip sounded, and my focus drew to it. I pictured the water droplet in my mind, slowing it down as it fell from the rock. Wet bubbles glistened in the faint light, and I trailed my inner gaze upward, envisioning the source of the water. My breathing slowed, matching the honey-soaked movement of my imagination. Carefully, I reached for the water's sediment inside the walls.

Its energy was so weak, I could barely feel it, but it was there, and I was coming for it.

Unlike the stone surrounding me, grasping hold of the water element was proving to be an impossible task. Either I was an idiot to think I could control it, or it refused to cooperate. Whatever the reasoning for my failure was, it wasn't doing me any good. Somewhere out there was our salvation, and I was too incompetent to find it.

"DAMN IT!" I roared, slumping back down. "I can't get it."

"You can do it," Naomi responded. "I know you can."

"And if I can't?"

She chuckled. "Not quite an option, is it?"

It really freaking wasn't. I had to figure this out no matter what it took. Mind racing and pulse humming, I tried to remember what I knew of fae magic to help me tap into the elements in the cavern. As it turned out, I knew very little. Actually, I knew so little, it was downright embarrassing. For someone as obsessed with digging up secrets as I, my ability to remember anything to do with the fae was more useless than ice in a sauna. I had no doubt the High Coven was to blame for the lack of knowledge I possessed, but worrying about why I was in this position was not helping matter one bit. Having learned nothing of the fae in all my years of studying magic was no one's fault but mine.

Something zoomed in my peripheral vision, and I jerked my gaze to it. Emptiness unfurled before me, though for a second, I swore I saw a shadow move. *Probably just remnants of my magic*, I thought, shaking off the paranoia.

Shadow man had not returned since the last time I saw him while the shifters beat me down and I wasn't mad about it. I didn't need his riddles and vagueness. What I needed was to get my shit together and to keep trying.

Squaring my shoulders, I glanced at the ceiling. "If I was fae, what would I do?"

Laughter burst from me, and I instantly felt like an idiot.

"What would I do? Seriously?" I asked the empty cavern. "Well, for one, I wouldn't let some dirty shifters chain me in this damn place. If I was fae, I probably would be frolicking around, free as a freaking bird while everyone else played with the half-assed magic I allowed them to have. I would..."

Ohshitohshitohshit! My eyes widened and my jaw

slacked as the epiphany struck me down. Fae taught the original witches. That was what Sebyl said. So, if they did, it stood to reason that whatever elemental magic they had could be passed down through learning and practice, not bred the way the coven explained magic to be. The original witches were just humans, and it was the fae that gave them the magic modern witches now possessed. I always thought that it was because they provided the witches with powerful items to help them connect to the magic of the elements, but what if I was wrong?

What if we were all wrong?

If that was the case, it changed everything. Perhaps it wasn't the crystals and herbs and spells that gave the first witches their magic. Maybe the fae taught them how to tap into the elements their bodies held hidden inside and use it to their advantage. These days, witches relied heavily on item magic for that connection, but what if that wasn't necessary at all? What if the objects we used only amplified what was already there in the first place?

I didn't need to look for the water element in the cavern. I needed to look for it in myself.

Flushing, I jumped to stand. "Naomi, I think I got it. I'm gonna try something new."

Deep down, the shadows pounded at my skin, and I pushed them away. The power surged through me, begging me to set it loose. I didn't budge. Gradually, I tapped into my shadow magic, logging the way it felt and setting it aside. My shoulders tensed as I searched within myself for energy that felt out of place. One that was different from the shadows. Heart racing, I tore myself apart, pulling open every inch of my body to look deeper than I've ever reached before. Something tugged at me, and I latched onto it, twisting my greedy fingers around it. Around me, the cavern shook with so much force, I could feel it at my back.

Nope, wrong one.

I grimaced, letting the energy go. The cavern stopped moving and I smiled. With the shadows out of the way and not tainting the magic inside me, I could control the earth element with ease. *So, this is how I moved that boulder...*

Still grinning ear to ear, I continued to dig deeper in search of the water element I was hoping to find. Without the shadows, I felt empty, but I knew I couldn't stop. It had to be in there somewhere. If the original witches were able to do this, then I could too.

The shadows scraped against me again, and I fought to keep them at bay. When they subdued, I shut my lids tightly and pushed on. The water element was so distant, I almost missed it, but one glimpse and I was reaching for its magic like a hungry shark. Its energy was foreign, similar to the earth element, yet still distinct. It was wet and sticky, and it wriggled in my blood as I tried to hold on to it. My fingers curled as I connected to the water and a relieved breath broke free. As the water's magic coursed through my blood, I ignited. The magic charged me like a battery, flowing through me and reconstructing my entire being. Body stiff, I let the new magic consume me until I was liquid myself. My skin glistened with sweat, and I could feel droplets stream down my forehead.

I dared to open my eyes.

The sweat fell into them, and I blinked it away, annoyed with the interruption. It wasn't until I looked up that I realized the water coating my body wasn't sweat at all. My eyes wetted as I cried with joy, gaze never leaving the small stream pouring from the rock above my head.

Chapter Thirty-one

River

Could not begin to describe how over I was of waking up after someone knocked me out. It was becoming a regular event in my life and each time felt worse than the last. It looked that I was a danger to not just myself, but everyone around me, and the thought scared me stiff.

This time was no different.

My bones creaked as I rolled over to the side to find my body splayed out on the front porch like a sack of garbage. Unlike the last time I got my ass handed to me, no one bothered to drag me to a bed. Not that I deserved such treatment. Not after what I did to Savannah. Waking up on a porch with the cool winds of Shadowhurst whipping around me was better than what I should have received.

Rising on my elbows, my attention landed on the person keeping watch over me, and I froze.

"Rise and shine, chap," Logan said, his face blank. "No hard feelings, I hope."

Groaning, I sat up straighter. "Is Savannah okay?"

"She's fine. Dislocated shoulder. Raiden took care of it."

I did not want to know what that meant.

This was the second time I almost killed my best friend, and to say it upset me was putting it mildly. Savannah always seemed to be in the wrong place at the wrong time with my shifts, and it was a massive problem. Deep down, I knew she was only trying to help, but if she couldn't understand how dangerous I was, I had to keep my distance from her. I couldn't allow myself to hurt her again.

Against the wall, Logan raised an eyebrow. "You should stay away from her."

What the... "Are you reading my thoughts right now?" I demanded, fuming.

"Sorry," he whispered. "It's just a residual connection from using my powers on you. It'll pass. I hope."

"You hope? What the hell, Logan?" I shouted. "You could have killed me!"

"You could have killed her."

My mouth was a desert as I took in his sentiment. Logan had an excellent point, but I still despised him for making it. Actually, what I despised most was myself. I almost hurt Savannah, again, and the guilt was drowning out any other thought I had running through my mind. All except one. "What was that anyway?" I asked, urging myself to calm down. "Your powers, they felt different."

"Had a lot of run-ins with mind reapers, have you?" He smirked.

"I mean, no, but Billie explained it to me and that did not feel like anything she said. It was messed up, man. Like you were literally squeezing my head inside out."

The reaper's face grew murky, and his eyes darkened as he took me in. Running a hand through his long hair, he fanned out the ends, eyeing them as though he was due for a trim. His nose pointed up and the tension in his jaw intensified, making it appear even more chiseled than before. From where I sat, I could see veins pop on his neck and worry set in. Raising my head, I found his eyes and cleared my throat. "You okay?"

"Yeah, fine," he responded nonchalantly. "Whatever you may have heard, every mind reaper's powers are different. Mine, including. I really didn't mean to hurt you that bad, but I thought you were going to kill her. Had to be done."

Did it though?

"I get it, I think," I said. "What's the deal with you two, anyway?"

Logan's eyes darkened. "No deal. She's the most frustrating person I ever met, but that doesn't mean I want her dead. And I'm pretty sure you don't either."

I shook my head. That we agreed on, at least.

"Oh, not to kick you while you're down, but Griffin stopped by while you were getting your beauty sleep."

The sudden urge to wipe the smile off his face was excruciatingly difficult to battle and I had to bite the inside of my cheek to keep from lunging for him. Logan wasn't exactly number one in my books right now, but he wasn't wrong to knock me out. I would have done worse if the tables were reversed and it was him about to kill Savannah. Whatever betrayal I may have felt had to take a backseat to what was at stake, and I was certain that what Logan said next would require mental strength I didn't think I could gather. Leaning over my legs, I peered up at him. "And?"

"It's not happening, dude. The pack wants nothing to do with you."

"Guess Raiden was right." I grimaced. "Still can't believe they'd rather follow that moron Isaac than me. We're screwed, man. Idiots or not, those wolves are strong. I could sense it when I was around them. We could have used their help to flush out the others since Raiden is clearly not doing anything about it."

I looked around the porch, finally noticing how quiet it was. "Where is he anyway?"

"No clue," Logan answered. "He rushed off right after you went night-night. Man's a serious nutter these days."

The hairs on the back of my neck rose and knots formed in my stomach. That damn lion was keeping things from us, and I was going to find out what it was before it cost Billie her life. If the asshole was protecting his cousin, or worse, had something to do with her kidnapping, I would get to the bottom of it. *Some leader!* I scoffed and brushed a hair off my face. *He talks a big game, but when it's time to follow through, the guy is as shifty as they come.* My stomach twisted and I gritted my teeth in frustration. Raiden was definitely hiding something.

Across the porch, Logan crouched down, bringing himself eye to eye with me. His lavender gaze found mine and I tried not to shake when I remembered the last interaction we had.

His shoulders rolled and he took in a hollow breath before speaking.

"You're wrong about the pack, you know."

Here we go again. "Why does everyone keep telling me that?" I asked.

"Because it's true. And like it or not, you're lucky to have them. Some of us shadowers have nothing close to a pack and trust me when I tell you, it can be a lonely world out there. Shifters got the better end of the stick with their weird little pack bonding thing. The rest of us are in this alone, and unless we have blood ties, we're basically screwed."

"Blood ties?"

"Family. Parents and whatever."

Studying him, my heart beat a little faster when I thought about what Logan said. Did he mean he didn't have parents? Is that why he was here at the resistance? I had so many questions for the guy I couldn't pick which one to ask first, so I settled on the easiest. "What about Lorelei? She's a reaper too. So that's someone."

"Lorelei is Lorelei," he responded, explaining nothing at all. "She's not exactly easy to get close to and I'm not even sure I'd want to if I could. That woman is dark, I can feel it. Besides, Marcus was the only one she ever let in, and with him gone, she's pretty much impossible to talk to. I don't know how he put up with her."

I chuckled, imagining what that odd relationship must have been like. Sure, I was no picnic myself, but Billie and I made it work by always being honest with each other and not holding back. I couldn't picture Lorelei having the same rapport with Marcus, though what did I know? Until Billie, I wasn't *Mr. Bright Side* either. In all honesty, I wasn't sure I was much better at that even with her around, but I was trying and that had to count for something.

Thinking of her shattered my heart and it wasn't long until I could feel tears prickling behind my eyelids. Blinking them away, I turned my attention back to Logan, worried he might see me fall apart like a complete weakling.

"So, what else did Griffin say?" I asked, hoping to change the subject.

"Not much. I don't think you should worry about Isaac, though."

"Oh?"

Logan smiled, and this time, I didn't completely hate him for it. "Guess your beat-down did something good and he's no longer their alpha."

"Who is?"

"No one."

Wait, WHAT? A wolf pack without an alpha was unheard of, even I knew that. My thoughts blurred together as I imagined what the future held in store for the wolves, and I couldn't come up with one solid scenario. It didn't make sense for wolves to run alone. Someone would step up to lead them, and I didn't care who. Now that they were no longer useful to me, I was finished with them.

Who needed those jerks anyhow? I was strong enough on my own, and if they wouldn't help me find the missing shifters and scare the living daylights out of them, I'd do it myself. Besides, once Ms. Broussard figured out who we're looking for, it would give me a better idea of which of the furry assholes were involved. Maybe I didn't need to rip everyone's faces off; just the select few. I could do that. *Right?* Right.

Now all I needed was for someone to tell me where the shifters that Raiden was so unabashedly protecting were hiding, and I'd be set. Luckily, I knew exactly where to get that information. That asswipe cousin of his. A plan formed in my mind and my lips twitched as resolve sank in. Raiden refused to give up where he was holding his cousin, but that didn't mean I couldn't find another way. All I had to do was make the lion believe his pathetic family member was in danger and wait for him to make a move. Then I could follow Raiden's tracks straight to that bastard and make sure he told me everything I needed to know.

This was going to work. Definitely. Maybe.

Rising to stand, I was already halfway across the porch and to the front door when Peyton's shrieks stopped me dead.

I turned, taking in her slight form bursting through the trees and running toward us. She waved her cellphone in her hand like she was practicing a dance routine and her heaving breaths carried through the foliage in loud bursts.

"Peyton?" I asked, horrified. "What happened? Are you all right?"

"NO!" she screamed. "No one is all right!"

She skipped two steps to land on the porch in front of me, and I squeezed her shoulders, urging her to collect herself before speaking. When she was finally somewhat calm, I let her go. "Okay, easy now. Tell us what happened."

"I... I..." Peyton tried to speak, but words seemed to be trapped in her throat. "I got another text from that Victoria girl."

My jaw slacked. "What did she say?"

"They're coming again!" she shrieked. "They're coming NOW!"

Chapter Thirty-two

Billie

The water's stream intensified, and I continued forcing it through the wall until it soaked me from head to toe. Overhead, a rock came loose, giving me enough leeway to wiggle the chains and move the pin. As it scraped against the rock, I pushed more water through the crevice. My arms ached from the strain, but each time the pin shimmied further, perseverance kicked in.

I can do this!

Little by little, I got the pin half out, and though it was still firmly lodged in place, the hope for escape flourished in me. Half out meant halfway there, and it was good enough to keep me going.

I dropped my hold on the water element for a moment, taking a quick break before returning to the task at hand. After this much exertion and magic use, I'd have thought my power would be drained, yet that wasn't the case at all. Instead, I was rejuvenated. Almost as though I was stronger when I used magic. The idea brought discomfort with it, and I twirled the moonstone ring over my finger in repeated circles to calm my nerves. Each loop around sent shivers down my back. Even my ring felt more powerful now that I could wield the elemental energy around me. Was the ring the reason I'm able to do this? Maybe a moonstone crystal wasn't as useless as I always believed. Damn, I wish I knew that earlier on. I could have used it to my advantage on many occasions. In the end, it didn't really matter if the ring helped me tap into the power I was now using. Whatever did it, a part of me had unlocked and it would change everything. This new magic I had was unlike anything I've seen before, and it made me wary of its presence in my body.

There was no point worrying as long as it got me the hell out of this place, but I still couldn't stop the unease that settled in my gut when I thought about it. Magic had a balance, and if I wasn't draining my own energy using elemental powers, it was coming from someplace else. I only wished I knew where from.

"How's it going?" Naomi asked from her side of the prison, jarring me back to reality. "Did you get it free yet?"

I glanced up at the protruding pin. "Not yet, but halfway there."

"Good, good, good. Keep trying, a little more and you can yank it out!"

Having Naomi to cheer me through this was a blessing I didn't think I deserved. Every time I felt lost and hopeless, she helped me discover options I hadn't considered, leaving me beyond grateful for having found her down here. Not that I was glad she was suffering alongside me, but I doubted I would have gotten this far without her regular words of encouragement. I couldn't wait to escape and introduce her to all my friends. And River.

Thinking of him sent me spiraling again, and I had to

force the images from my mind to keep from crying. The bright green of his eyes was so clear, I swore he was right in front of me.

"Hold on," I whispered, focusing on his face. "Is he here?"

It took only a second for me to understand what was going on. The visions the cavern had shown me before had not reappeared for so long, I almost forgot about them entirely. Now, staring at River's eyes, there was no mistaking what was happening. All around him, a golden light swelled, spreading to reveal River's sagging body laying idly on a metal floor. His hand clutched his side, and horror flashed through me when I noticed the dark stain that spread from his stomach. As River's skin grew ashy before me, I understood what I was being shown.

"NO! River, stay with me!" I screamed into the vision, knowing full well he couldn't hear me.

His eyes rolled back, and his head clunked against the floor, making the hair on my arms stand straight. Tears stung at my eyes as I watched River take his last breath, fighting against the deadly wound in his abdomen. He was barely moving, and I wondered if this was the last time I would see him, my heart breaking at the thought.

Slowly, River lifted his head, and when his gaze met mine, I fell apart.

My shoulders shook while I sobbed, begging the Goddess to let him live. I screamed his name into the frigid air so many times, my voice had grown coarse and my throat felt like sandpaper. River's eyes never left mine. His lips quivered and he took another heavy breath in before letting the slightest smile break.

How could he smile right now? Did he not understand what's happening? Could he—

Eyes wide open, I glared at River's deathly face, and the tears that blurred my vision dried. Before me lay the boy I loved more than anything in the world, but it wasn't him at all. My attention fluttered between his full lips and his left cheek, focusing only on one thing. The dimple that drove me crazy on so many occasions. The dimple that wasn't there now.

"What the hell is this?" I screamed.

I didn't need to ask the question. The answer stared at me straight on. Whoever this dying person was, it wasn't my River.

My head slumped and I laughed into my chest. "It's all a lie. None of this is real."

Before me, fake River coughed up blood, and despite my realization, I winced at the sight. His lips twisted, forming words I couldn't hear, though I had a pretty good idea that he was begging. Watching someone die, even if it wasn't my River, was excruciating and I had to look away to keep it together. Around, the glow of the vision glittered, unfurling to cover every inch of empty space in the cavern. It wanted me to look, and it wanted me to break.

I wouldn't give it the satisfaction.

"You can quit the charade!" I yelled into the vision, yanking at the chains for emphasis. "I know it's not him! This isn't River, it's a lie. Just like everything else you showed me was! My friends are FINE!"

It seemed my outburst did the trick because before I knew it, fake River was gone, and I was all alone again. I never thought I'd see the day when I'd be happy not to look at his gorgeous face, but today was full of new developments.

The tears I cried for the stranger dried, and a renewed sense of accomplishment filled me to the brim. River wasn't in danger, neither was anyone else I loved. This day was finally starting to turn around.

Pulling myself up, I twirled to face the wall.

My neck lengthened and my eyes landed on the pin I was working on as I settled into my magic and reached for the water again. This time, when it flowed through the crevice, I let my shadows loose. They broke free of my body and swarmed the chains, obstructing them entirely. While the shadows twirled, I forced my mind to grab hold of the jagged rock that held the pin in place. The force of the water rushing outward and the pull I had on the rock caused the pin to creak loudly with each tug.

I wrapped the chains over my fists and brought the soles of my boots to the wall as I readied for the last heave. In one swoop motion, I wrenched the shadows into me, using their momentum to tug at the chains while I continued to pull on the rock. The pin scraped against the stone, and when it jerked outward, I flew back across the cavern.

Landing with a heavy thud on the cold floor, I choked on saliva and scrambled to lift the weight of the chains off me.

Every muscle in my body hurt, but I didn't let it settle. Laughing, I brought myself to stand, dragging the heavy chains behind me and looking up at the empty slot that used to hold them in place. My eyes darted around the space to make sure I was still alone. When I was satisfied, I made my way to the tunnel that led to Naomi.

"I'm coming for you!" I shrieked. "Get ready to go!"

Chapter
Thirty-three

River

We surrounded the house, more bodies emerging through the front door to join us as Lorelei and Logan ushered shadowers out into the small space beyond the porch. The hunters flanked my sides, and it shocked me to see Savannah among them. I guess Logan wasn't kidding when he said Raiden took care of her dislocated shoulder because my friend had her bow trained on the trees like no one's business. She met my gaze, shooting a quick wink my way before returning her attention to the forest. On either side of her, Tyler and Abigail held massive knives in each of their hands while Jayden cocked a rifle behind them. Close to the hunters, Peyton and Morgan stood side by side, their eyes narrowed in the same direction we all faced.

Victoria's message was clear, and we weren't about to take any chances. If the High Coven was coming for us, we would be ready.

Scanning the others, I found Raiden and Mel a few feet to my right. Their arms were locked, and I could see their eyes glowing as they got ready to shift. Past them, I spotted the pack, relieved to see Isaac missing. My body swayed as I shifted my weight from foot to foot, nerves overtaking me.

There weren't many left in the house, and looking around the shadowers that stepped up to join my friends and me, it was easy to see we would need to fight hard to make up for the dwindling numbers of our defense. I counted a total of eight shifters, not including the pack, six mind reapers, and one soul sucker. The numbers were not in our favor, and I shuddered to think what would happen if the High Coven brought more witches with them this time.

The element of surprise was all we had going for us, and I hoped it would be enough.

Receiving the warning from Victoria gave us a leg up. The coven wouldn't expect anyone here to know they were coming, so I was praying the high priestesses would let their cockiness get the best of them. I was also praying this wasn't some scheme they concocted by using Victoria as a pawn to get to us. Whatever it was, we were about to find out.

We heard their steps only moments before the trees parted and thirty witches rounded the clearing. Their faces dropped when they met us, shock registering across their features as they realized the surprise of their visit was shot to hell. The edges of my lips curled while I glanced over each witch until I found them.

Not over fifteen feet from me, the four high priestesses stood side by side with their feet dug deep into the ground. Sneers adorned each one of their features, masking the disappointment I knew they felt at the moment. Eagerly, I searched for Victoria but couldn't spot her in the crowd. Army was a better word for what surrounded us, but I chose not to think of it.

My insides boiled as I brought my attention to Sebyl.

"Leave before this gets out of hand."

She tsked. "Well, if it isn't Billie's greatest weakness. I truly don't see what she sees in you."

"Leave. Now."

Sebyl and the blue-haired priestess, Theodora, I think, exchanged glances before breaking out in hysterical laughter. Beside them, the other women chuckled, and I noticed the scary looking one reach for the sword strapped to her side. *So that's how you want to play this? Cool.*

It took only a moment for me to shift, and before they could finish laughing, I was already halfway through the clearing in my wolf form. On my heels, Savannah and the hunters ran, arrows zooming past me as my friend took out witch after witch. Screams rose through the trees. The witches retaliated, chucking handfuls of magic our way.

To my right, the pack shifted and was keeping pace with Raiden and Mel leading the way, the other shifters close behind them. I had no time to track everyone and concentrated on avoiding the lightning and fire that blasted all around me. A loud bang sounded near to me, and I whipped my head around to see smoke rise from the barrel of Jayden's shotgun. His face lit up, and when I followed his gaze, I saw a middle-aged witch fall to the ground. Blood poured from her leg, and she dragged herself backward, hiding her plump frame behind the foliage of the trees.

I growled at Jayden, hoping he registered my appreciation for him not shooting to kill.

My friend nodded and reloaded the gun before aiming at his next target. Hit after hit, he nipped the flesh of the witches that came for him and each one crawled away to nurse their injuries. With Jayden clearing the path for me, I was almost to the high priestesses when something wrapped around my tail and jerked me back.

Yelping, I twisted my frame to look back and alarm overcame me.

Brown, decrepit roots tightened over my fur and pulled me back toward a tree larger than a blue whale. My paws clawed at the ground and my body thrashed to be free, but the roots twisted over my tail so tightly, I would need to rip it off my body to get loose. Not an option, though I did consider it for a moment. A very brief moment. The thought alone sent my wolf into a fit and I had to talk him off the ledge in my head and assure that no tails were going to be ripped off any time soon.

Still sliding backward, I turned my head right and left to find the witch that was holding me hostage. When I found her, I wished I hadn't.

While the other three high priestesses carefully watched over the witches like the cowards they were, the one commanding the roots that bound me vibrated with a speed so fast, her body looked blurry. Her eyes were closed, and her arms stretched forward as she moved the roots to do her bidding. One look at her and I knew exactly who this was. The long lace dress she wore trailed behind her in silky layers and a crystal-encrusted head covering adorned her small head. Her face looked peaceful, despite the strain I knew she was experiencing to wield magic, and when she tightened her lips into a thin smile, all I could remember was Billie's description of the coven seer.

Luna. The prophecy-telling nut job.

Wonderful.

Fighting off head witches was one thing, but I didn't know how to break free of the hold the high priestess had on me. According to Billie, these were the most powerful witches in all the world and judging by how little effort it took Luna to drag me, I knew she was right to think it.

My back legs gave way and I toppled down to my belly as the next pull yanked me back. Teeth bared, I struggled against the tree roots, but the more I fought, the tighter their grip became, and the further they drew me away from the high priestesses. Behind me, the massive tree exposed more of its core and branches flew high in the air before shooting down all around me.

Terror flashed before my eyes as I watched the tree encase me in its twisted form. A prison cell forming to hold me in place.

I yelped, burrowing my paws into the dirt, but my attempts were pointless.

Through the wooden bars, I could see my friends holding their own against the witches. More witches retreated, taking their disgusting magic with them, and relief blasted through me.

We might stand a chance here.

The thought barely registered when the ground shook and thunder rose all around us. My eyes squinted to see clearer, and I froze when I noticed the high priestesses lock hands and raise their arms upward. Wind blasted around them, throwing locks of hair over their sinister faces while they collected their magic.

Sebyl shot a sly smile my way before all four dropped to a crouch and slammed their adjoined palms into the ground.

Lightning filled the forest and sparks flew as the priestesses set their magic loose. The ground quaked and gaps formed where the women's palms met it, spreading in deep gashes toward my friends. Everyone tumbled, trying to keep their footing strong while the soil cracked around them.

Something flashed in my peripheral vision, and I shot my gaze in its direction to see a bolt of lightening fly straight for Savannah's chest. She ducked to the side at the same time as Logan threw his body over hers, toppling her over before the lightening could make contact. In the distance, screams sounded as fire spread over the clearing to block everyone in.

My eyes jerked to the high priestesses, and I focused on their content expressions. Acid filled my throat. *We're not going to make it.*

Suddenly, the tree roots around me trembled and slithered away, leaving enough of a gap for me to slide out. I didn't hesitate, leaping out into the clearing with so much force I had to skid along the cracking soil just to stop. When I was far from the tree, I turned back, cocking my head in recognition.

A few feet from where I was held stood Victoria, her cheeks puffed out and red crawled over her neck as she spread her fingers wide to rise the roots into the air. When her eyes met mine, she smiled.

"Get everyone in the house!" Victoria commanded, still holding the roots in place. "I'll secure it!"

Not waiting for further instruction, I bolted.

I was running so fast that I could hear the pulse pounding in my chest. Mid-stride, I forced my wolf to shift and in seconds, my body was my own again. Taking long leaps, I reached Raiden and Mel in no time, careful not to startle them while they were in their lion form.

"In the house," I urged with as much strength as I could muster. Telling a lion what to do was as counterintuitive as it sounds, and if we weren't knee-deep in shit, I might have laughed about it. "Get everyone inside, NOW!"

Their bright eyes settled on me, and they were herding the pack before I had the chance to speak again. Briskly, I made my way to the hunters, shouting commands as I ran. Under us, the ground still shook and the fires the witches were commanding continued to spread. We jumped around them, careful not to trip over the gaping cracks as we rushed for the house. When everyone was inside, I looked for Victoria.

It didn't take long to spot her.

Running backward, her ponytail swung side to side while she trailed the tree roots toward her. They twisted in mid-air, slithering like snakes and inching closer to the house. When she reached the porch, Victoria threw her arms wide and brought more of the tree into the center. My jaw dropped as I watched her encase the entire house in the same prison I was trapped in only moments ago. The surrounding space grew darker until I saw nothing but wooden tentacles before me. At my feet, Victoria crouched, tearing bottles filled with multi-colored liquids from her small backpack. She moved so fast, I barely noticed when she drew a circle of salt beneath the front door. Her thin fingers dipped into one of the bottles and she drew several runes at five points of the circle then smashed her palm in the center. Victoria's eyes closed and her body trembled as she whispered something into the air. Beneath her, the runes lit up a bright yellow and Victoria raised her palm to crash into the tree. The yellow glow spread from her fingers and all across the wood, making the entire wall light up like a Christmas tree.

I looked over it, baffled.

"That was..." I whispered, not finishing the sentence.

Victoria swung around to face me. "Kickass. I know. I put a protective barrier around the house, it should hold them off for a while." She flipped her ponytail and extended a hand. "Victoria. Glad you got my message, or this would have gone a whole other way."

"I-I..." I mumbled. "Thank you. And yeah, we did. I'm glad you warned us."

Steadily, she ran her eyes over me, and I cupped my hands over my genitals before she reached them. This was definitely the most embarrassing way to meet someone for the first time. No competition.

"So, you're Billie's guy," she said like I didn't already know that. "Good for her."

I grimaced. "And you're her friend from the coven. What made you switch sides?"

"Many things," Victoria answered. "We have a lot to discuss, but not right now. Right now, we need to make sure the coven leaves and then I'm going to help you find Billie."

"How? We have no clue where to even start."

Victoria's face brightened and she patted my exposed shoulder. "That's not true, big guy," she teased. "I'm assuming you have the grimoire here?"

"Grimoire?"

"The Book of Darkness." Victoria shook her head. "Ugh, seriously, boys are the worst."

Confusion rolled through me, and I shrugged before locking my eyes on hers. "Why do you need the Book of Darkness?"

"Because I can use it to find Billie, but you might want to put some pants on first."

Chapter Thirty-four

Billie

The weight of the chains dragged me down and my legs shook as I walked through the tunnel toward where I had first seen Naomi. Each step shot exhaustion through my bones and I had to lean against the cold, wet walls that for balance. In the darkness, the cavern resembled a creepy setting from a horror movie and agitation engulfed me with every shaky breath.

Somewhere in the distance, the sound of dripping water echoed down to me and I clawed at the stone to help move me along. *Get to Naomi, use your magic to free her, find the water, and get the hell out.* I repeated the plan over and over until motivation flowed through me in waves.

Ahead, I noticed a familiar bend in the tunnel and my heart leaped in my chest. This was the turn we took when Daria—or bitch face as I now called her—led me to use the bathroom. Naomi's cell must have been closer than I thought.

Picking up speed, I rearranged the chains across my shoulders and bounded down the tunnel.

As I reached the turning point, my pace slowed. Pancaking into the wall, I peeked around the bend to make sure the coast was clear before continuing further. A light wind brushed past me and I froze in my tracks.

Silence.

"Almost there, girl," I whispered into the murky path before me and stomped forward.

When I could see the space I used for bathroom breaks I slowed down further and ran my gaze over the walls. My eyes widened, and I exhaled the breath I was holding when the entrance to Naomi's cell came into view.

It was as dark and gloomy as I remembered; a hole in the wall. Literally.

One more glance around and I was running for the spot that held my friend captive, the chains falling from shoulders while my body bounced up and down. When they slid down my back, I shook them off, letting the hefty metal drag behind me as I ran. Their screeching sounds echoed down the tunnel, but I didn't dare to stop.

I was too close.

Tears flooded my vision and white clouds rose from lips as fast breaths escaped. My hand reached around the entrance to her cell, and I pulled myself into the opening, crashing through like a bat out of hell.

When I fell in, my heart stopped.

Naomi's cell was empty.

"Naomi?" I choked out. "Where are you?"

No one answered me, and panic gripped my bones. My eyes darted around the space, looking for something to guide me to her location. The wall rose high to the ceiling, and when my gaze met the empty chains dangling from it, a gasp tore from my throat.

"Where is she? Where did they take her?"

The spot I saw Naomi in before was deserted, and from the looks of it, it appeared she was never here to begin with. The ground was undisturbed and unlike my own cell, there was no sign that someone had been by to leave food and water. *Had she been starved this entire time?* No, that didn't make any sense. Naomi couldn't have survived this long without being fed and she definitely couldn't have been strong enough to keep talking to me.

Something wasn't right.

Chains in tow, I toed closer to the wall, running my hand over the metal shackles. I picked them up, studying the locks to compare them to my own.

My skin paled and my jaw slacked.

The shackles were rusted over with age and they flopped open in my trembling hands; I couldn't force them closed, no matter how hard I pushed. They have not been used for a very long time.

Uncurling my fingers, I let the chains slip from my grip and they hit the stone wall with a bang. My chest constricted with shivering breaths and tears poured freely down my face and neck. Brushing them off, I sniffled and dropped my gaze to the floor. "You were never here. You didn't exist. It was all a lie."

My mind raced as I tried to recall every conversation I had with Naomi. She was always there when I needed her to be, saying exactly the right thing. That wasn't normal. People who were trapped and tortured didn't just show up to help you out, and they definitely didn't act like they could read your mind. All this time, I thought she was some poor human girl stuck in this hellhole with me when she wasn't anything close to it. No wonder she was so calm when I told her about my magic; Naomi didn't freak out because she couldn't. She wasn't even real.

"Shitshitshit!" I cursed, punching the wall with my fist. "How could I be so dumb?"

I'd been alone for so long, I made up a freaking imaginary friend. *WHAT AN IDIOT*.

Exhaustion and defeat threatened to overtake me, and I worked not to let negativity cloud my judgment. Pressing back from the wall, I stumbled, my eyes catching something lying on the floor where I imagined Naomi crouch before. I bent down, picking up the small rock, and brought it up to my face. It was a perfect circle, like someone had carved it by hand, and in its center, sat a hole the size of a penny.

I brought the stone to my eye, peering through the small opening as one would a window. My gaze focused on the cavern and I huffed out an annoyed sigh before lowering the stone and tucking it into my pocket. I should have thrown the damn thing out, but it felt important somehow; like it was a part of imaginary Naomi I couldn't leave behind. It called to me and standing here in the middle of yet another disappointment, I couldn't bring myself to leave it behind.

"Whatever you are, Naomi," I whispered, "you're coming with me."

Patting the stone through my jeans, I focused my attention back to the tunnel outside and the distant sound of water that trailed through it. Real or not, Naomi got me this far and I'd be damned if I didn't follow through with our plan now.

With renewed determination, I heaved the chains over my shoulders and walked out of the cell, tossing a last look at the abandoned chains before moving on.

Reach the water, find the stream, get the hell out of here. My knees shook and my bones ached, but I kept going. Nothing was going to stop me from leaving this awful place, not when I was this close. Not when I was almost free.

Chapter Thirty-five

River

Watching Victoria study the grimoire reminded me so much of Billie that I had to walk away. Leaving her with Peyton and Savannah, I walked down the rickety old steps of the resistance house and made my way to the front door. Outside, the blasts the coven pounded against the barrier Victoria spelled had died down and my shoulders slumped as I took in the silence surrounding the house. I still couldn't believe we made it through that.

Granted, if Victoria hadn't shown up when she did, we'd likely all be dead by now.

I pressed my face to the massive roots, finding a hole to peer through, and inspected the forest that loomed in the distance. The soil remained cracked and charred marks covered the spots where the lightning hit and the fires spread. The area resembled the center of Armageddon and I frowned when I thought about the damage the coven did in such a short time. These witches were powerful, and we were definitely screwed if they came for us again.

Pushing the apprehension away, I turned tail, disappearing into the house. The hallway that was once bustling with shadowers was empty and grim, filled with a hollowness that spread over the walls and straight into my heart. As I rounded the stairs, I glanced back, shaking my head at the disappointment of having to hide out like a coward. Somewhere in the depths of the house, those that fought beside me stowed away in darkened rooms and I was sure their anger was no less than mine.

The resistance had not been built for hiding.

My attention caught a crooked frame dangling from a nail in the wall and I stopped before it, trailing a finger across the ornate etchings in the wood. Inspecting the ancient photo of an ocean shore, I tipped the edge, righting the frame back into position. After a while, I took a long breath, faced the room I wished to escape and walked in.

"They're gone?" the witch asked, eyes never leaving the book in her lap.

I looked past her to Peyton and Savannah, who sat on the floor beside Victoria. "Looks like it. It's a dead zone out there."

"Good," Victoria said. "No guarantee they won't come back, but I think I bought us enough time for now."

"Enough time for what exactly?"

Victoria was silent, nodding as she ran her fingers over the passages in the grimoire. Her eyes danced over the words, and she flipped page after page so fast, I wasn't even sure she was reading them. She had made it through almost half the book by the time I returned, and either this girl was a speed-reader, or she knew what she was looking for.

Nearing Victoria, I placed my hand on the grimoire to get her attention. "What are you looking for?"

The witch looked at me with beady eyes, as though it surprised her to see me there.

"Something that mentions the fae," she said. "I didn't really know what to look for at first, but then Peyton said you guys thought someone with fae blood might be after her, so now I have a starting point."

"And you think this book would have that?"

Victoria's face twisted in an expression that told me she thought I was a complete idiot. "Hello? It's a grimoire written by one of the original witches. If anyone knew anything about the fae, it was this chick."

Okay, yeah, I was an idiot.

"Any luck so far?" Peyton asked.

Her body twisted to inch closer to Victoria and I noticed that her features no longer had a darkness to them as they did before. If Peyton doubted Victoria's motives, that doubt had vanished now, and it eased some of my worries. Similar to Billie, Peyton didn't trust people easily, so if she was willing to take a chance on the witch, it was a good sign that we weren't about to get the rug pulled out from under us. Victoria came here to help, and I was grateful for it.

"There are some spells that refer to darker magic, but I'm not seeing anything that mentions any person in particular," she said. "Most of this book is instructional, which isn't surprising. This is a grimoire, after all."

"So, to sum up, you got nothing," Savannah sniped.

"Not nothing," the witch retorted. "Just not something that could help find Billie. The spells in here are intense, though. Like nothing I've ever seen. No wonder the high priestesses kept this thing under such safeguards. This stuff is out of this world."

"Literally," Peyton joked.

Lowering to sit, I looked from her to Victoria. "You know, you never told us why you're here. Why you went against the coven, I mean. Last I remember, you were trying to kill Billie for stealing the book, so what changed?"

Sadness settled over Victoria's eyes, and she put the book aside before looking back at me.

"First of all, I wasn't trying to kill her," she said. "Billie was my friend. My only friend in the coven. We didn't have sleepovers and go on shopping sprees or whatever, but when it came down to it, I knew I could count on her. After the coven sent her away, I wanted to reach out so many times, but I couldn't."

"Why not?"

"Because I was scared. Everything Billie told you about the coven is true. The high priestesses have us believing a lot of bullshit and we let them control our actions because it's all we know. For me, it was even worse. My family comes from a long line of witches, all of whom have a high standing in the coven. When my sister left, saying she wants nothing to do with it, my mom cut her off. Like completely. Believing they would do the same to me if I disobeyed wasn't something I could handle. I was a jerk, obviously."

Close to me, Savannah rearranged her legs and leaned over Victoria. "Yet you're here now. And not to freak you out or anything, but that little trick you played to protect us from them won't go unnoticed. Girl, if you wanted to keep your mom on your side, that totally wasn't the way to do it."

"Yeah, no kidding," Victoria said. "It's not important anymore. Billie thought she wiped my memory after I attacked her, but it didn't work. I have tricks up my sleeve even she didn't know about. So when I woke up, I remembered everything she said. I was initially pissed, but then I started looking into her accusations. The more I searched, the more I realized she was right. The coven is up to something, and I want to help her figure out what that is. It's the least I could do after abandoning her when they shipped her off like that. But by the time I came to my senses, she was gone."

My jaw ticked. "How did you know she'd been kidnapped?"

"Boy, please! There isn't anything the High Coven doesn't know. If a witch is harmed in any way, we all feel it. It's some weird connection we have, happens right after our first initiation into the coven. It's actually good news, if you think about it."

My eyebrows arched in surprise, though I didn't need to raise my concern. Victoria was already one step ahead of me.

"She's still alive," she said. "If she wasn't, I'd feel it. All us witches would."

The ache in my soul subsided and I let myself get absorbed in her words. Not having Billie around was tearing me apart, but Victoria's reassurance that she was alive gave me a small fragment of strength that I desperately needed at that moment. If the witch thought Billie was all right, it meant I hadn't failed her as badly as I thought I did. At least not yet.

My fingers played with a loose strand on my shirt, and I kept my gaze downward for a long time before facing Victoria again. "You should go see Ms. Broussard," I suggested. "Bring the book with you. She's looking through all the families of this town to find another fae bloodline like Billie's and—"

"Billie is a fae descendant?!?" Victoria shrieked.

Right. We haven't told her that part yet.

I nodded.

"For Goddess's sake! You start with that!" she yelled, making Peyton laugh. "If Billie has fae blood running through her, it changes everything!"

My eyes bulged so far out of their sockets, I nearly lost them to gravity. "How does that change anything?"

"Honestly, River," Victoria said. "Cute but stupid is not a good look for you."

"I like her," Savannah said under her breath, and I fought the urge to knock her sideways.

Before I could say anything else, Victoria was on her feet with the Book of Darkness tucked under her arm. "The fae taught the witch that wrote this grimoire," she said, explaining nothing at all. "If Billie has fae background in her family, I need to know every person's name in her lineage. This whole time I was looking for mentions of fae when I should have been looking for mentions of Billie's family. The original witches were a small group, making them a tightly knit coven. Whoever wrote this book knew the witch that Billie's bloodline came from. I need to figure out who it was."

All three of us struggled to keep our mouths closed.

"You think Billie is related to the original witches?"

"Obviously!" she yelled out. "She'd have to be to have fae blood in her veins. Those elemental creeps got hella busy with the witches, couldn't keep their grubby hands to themselves. Not that I blame them, witches are awesome!"

At that moment, I couldn't agree with her more. "Okay, this is good. Peyton can take you to the Crystal Cauldron and you guys can look for clues in the grimoire together. If we can find mentions of Billie's family in there, we can connect them to another witch that may have—" I paused.

"—gotten busy with a spirit fae. It might give us a location for someone in town."

"That's the plan," Victoria agreed.

"Oh," I added. "Not sure if this helps somehow. I can feel Billie. Don't ask because I have no answers, but the last time it happened, I think I saw wherever she was being held. I couldn't make it out clearly, it was really freaking dark, but I could hear water in the background. So, look for anyone that fits the profile that lives near a water source. It's not much, I know."

"No, this is good," Victoria said. "Come on, P-town. Let's get this show on the road."

"Yeah, we're not in the nickname stage of our friendship yet."

"Suit yourself," Victoria said, grabbing Peyton's hand and dragging her out of the room.

When they were gone, I reclined by Savannah and sucked in a breath. "This is good, right?"

"Really good." She nodded. "More than we've had so far. So, what do we do until we hear from them?"

I looked at her through hooded eyes. "I have something I want to try. You won't like it."

Getting Savannah to convince Raiden his cousin was in danger was easier than I thought. All she had to do was put on a stellar act, which was a specialty of Savannah's, then tell him I was out of my mind and figured out where he was hiding Damen. It was close enough to the truth that it was believable. I was very much out of my mind these days.

To our luck, Raiden fell for her performance, which was

exactly why I now skulked through the dark suburban streets of Shadowhurst on Raiden's tail.

The lion shifter left the house in a hurry, making his way through the forest with so much speed, I had trouble keeping up. In the end, I stayed behind him far enough that he didn't hear my steps as I lurked in the shadows, but close enough that I could pick up his scent in the night. This whole smelling thing was becoming more useful than I imagined, and other than the disgusting aroma of garbage that wafted through from time to time, I was beginning to like having this much control over my surroundings.

Raiden rounded a corner, facing a path that led to the hiking trails Billie and I used to frequent on our dates. The air had grown cooler as night settled over us, and the faint lights of the street lamps that illuminated portions of the path made me feel like an even bigger stalker than I was. Seriously, if someone spotted me creeping around, I'd look like a straight-up serial killer. Luckily, the trails were empty this late in the night, leaving only Raiden and myself walking along them.

And soon, Damen as well.

I couldn't wait to find the bastard that threatened Billie's life, yet something did not feel right. The deeper into the trails that Raiden walked, the more I got the feeling that Damen wasn't as safely locked up as Raiden made us believe. If anything, it was looking that the lion shifter never caged the asshole at all.

Whatever happened there, it didn't matter anymore. I was about to get my hands on Damen, and not even his giant cousin could stop me from beating the answers out of him. Despite all the work Victoria, Peyton, and Ms. Broussard were putting in, I still believed the shifters were responsible for Billie's disappearance.

Call it a hunch, but somehow, I knew I wasn't wrong.

Raiden made another sharp turn and I sped up to catch up with him. My feet padded lightly, and little noise escaped as I slithered between the trees. Controlling the rising speed of my pulse, I stepped out into the path and stopped dead in my tracks.

Before me, darkness spread. Darkness and nothingness.

"Shit!" I cursed, jolting my gaze around to see which way he might have gone.

High above, the moon shone brightly, illuminating the trees and casting deep shadows over the small path that unfurled before me. There were no street lamps here, and I had to rely on my failing eyesight to see ahead. The further I stared, the more disappointed I became.

Raiden had just vanished into thin air.

I was about to turn back and try a different path when a loud growl sounded to my right. My head jerked and my body tensed as I spun on my heels to face the direction it came from. I only had a second to blink when an enormous chest collided into me, sending me flying back to land on my ass. Standing over me, Raiden's muscled figure unfurled and the death glare he shot my way told me everything I needed to know.

This was not going to end well for one of us.

Chapter Thirty-six

Billie

"We're close, Naomi."

You would think that talking to an imaginary person would have puzzled me, yet I wasn't floored by it at all. Somehow, I had grown used to having Naomi's company, whether or not she was real. Now, trailing into the depths of the cavern, I needed her more than ever.

The water's dripping tones grew closer, and I picked up my feet, drudging along the rough terrain of the tunnel with as much speed as I could muster. On my shoulders, the chains slipped and fell to the ground.

"For the love of..." I snapped, rearranging them once more.

My boots slid across the mud and sent me falling to all fours before I could rebound. Stumbling about, I skated over the filth beneath me in a sad attempt to stand up. When I finally made it, a gray sticky residue covered my entire lower body and my hands looked like I had spent the last few hours digging up a grave.

Pressing a mud-coated palm to the wall, I stared ahead. "It's getting wetter, Naomi. We're almost there."

The tunnel I followed went so deep into the cavern, I had to stop several times to make sure I was going the right way. There was no other direction to take as I knew this was how Daria came and went each time, so I knew it was the correct choice. Still, every step I took made me question myself, and I needed to urge my racing mind to slow down on more than one occasion.

What if I had it wrong and this wasn't the right way at all?

Not too far off, water danced along the rocks and I squared my shoulders. *Follow the water, don't freak out.*

The cavern's walls glistened with wetness, adding oomph to my internal dialogue, and pushing me forward. When my boots slid again, I held my balance with a smile on my face. On my neck, the chains creaked as I marched onward, and each time I inched further in, their weight lessened.

Time ticked in my ears with every agonizing step onward. Little by little, the drips morphed to a new sound, forcing me to move faster. I could hear water flowing and it was so close that the cool freshness of its scent invaded every part of my senses. Around me, the air grew frigid, and a light wind rushed past me. Its icy fingers tore at my skin while I walked, deepening my hope for salvation. I held onto it like a lifeline, following the gusts of air as one would follow a compass.

The tunnel made a sharp turn and as I rounded the corner, my heart jumped in my throat.

To my right, a small stream of water ran along the jagged edges of the rocky wall and when my gaze slid down, I gasped in relief. Falling to my knees, I ran my hands through the torrent, following its direction outward.

"This is it, Naomi," I whispered, stumbling to stand. "This is the way out."

My boots stomped the cold water. Further, in the distance, the wind howled and a sliver of light emerged. My eyes widened, anticipation building. I was all but galloping to follow the current.

The walls spread wider as I walked and the tunnel expanded, making my lungs swell in my chest. I gulped fresh air and let a laugh escape me. My body ached, but there was no stopping now, not when I was this close.

Still giggling like a psychopath, I made a beeline for the light up ahead.

I was almost at its edges when a dark shadow emerged, and four bodies entered the tunnel.

"Going somewhere?"

My gaze drifted over the monsters that blocked my path and I tightened my grip on the chains, looking Daria up and down. Her gargantuan friends flanked her sides, and each one had the same evil smirk plastered on his face. Gritting my teeth, I faced them head-on.

"Get the hell out of my way!"

Daria threw her head back to laugh and I lunged for her.

Muscles tensing, I rushed through the tunnel and called for my magic. Shadows burst from my skin, and I flung my arms outward, battling against the chains and blasting my power into Daria. She twirled on her heels without breaking a sweat. At her side, the other shifters didn't wait to make their move, and before I could swerve out of the way, they barreled into me.

My back hit the rough ground and air expelled from my

body. Thrashing beneath the men, my jaw tensed as I pulled the surrounding rock into me. The cavern quaked and walls caved inward, covering us in rocky debris.

"Hold her down," Daria commanded, walking over to tower over me.

I hissed when she reached down, unsure of what to do. With each struggling breath, I grasped at every element I could feel in the cavern, but before I could let myself loose, Daria's bony fingers wrapped around my own. My skin burned as she tore the moonstone ring off my finger and brought it up to her face.

"Let's see how you do without your little toy," she sneered, dropping the ring to the floor.

When she stomped on the crystal, a part of me died.

"NOOOOOOO!" I wailed, twisting beneath the men who held me down.

Tears threatened to blind me, though I refused to let them fall. My body weakened and my arms lay limp at my sides. The loss of the ring overcame me. It was just a piece of jewelry, and some rational part of me knew that, but it was also so much more. Memories of Beatrix handing me the ring flashed before my eyes and I stifled a sob, curling my hands into fists.

One shifter rose over me and brought a heavy boot down, crushing my arm. Blinding pain shot up my body and I winced as the other shifter wrapped his fingers in my hair. He dragged me back, scraping my weak body over the muddy ground while I kicked my feet violently. Someone grabbed my boots, and I could feel myself rise in the air. Something hard hit the back of my head, distorting my vision and making black dots dance before me. My eyes rolled back, and no matter how much I fought to stay lucid, my brain was swimming in my skull.

In a flash, I was flipped in mid-air and tossed over a shoulder.

Swaying side to side, I listened to the echoing steps of the shifters while they carried me back, my failing sight trying to stay focused on the light we left behind. It got smaller and smaller until I could barely see it in the distance. Despite my struggles, my arms sagged, and my head slumped down. The scent of musk and sweat filled my nostrils and I zeroed in on the ground below, counting the steps it took to rip me away from freedom.

Chapter Thirty-seven

River

The night was bitter and in its darkness, Raiden's blue eyes burned like stars. The lion shifter cracked his neck, looking me up and down with so much hatred, I barely recognized the man. His clean-shaven head reflected the moonlight, glistening as he cocked his head to the side.

"What are you doing here, River?" he asked.

"I had the same question for you. Thought you locked up your cousin, but that was a bullshit lie, wasn't it?"

My fury had no bounds, and Raiden's betrayal tore at my emotions like a knife in the back. "If you or Damen hurt her, I'll kill you."

A few feet away from me, Raiden's mouth gaped open, and he took a step in.

I backed up.

"You think I took Billie?" he asked, shock coating his face. "You can't be serious."

"I'm dead serious," I snapped. "Why else are you here skulking around at night? I knew if Savannah made you believe Damen was in danger, you'd come running. Didn't think you'd run here, though. You did nothing to protect her after that bastard tried to kill us, did you?"

With a shaking head, Raiden turned around and looked over the path leading away from us. The glow of his eyes receded, leaving only deep blue dots the color of oceans. As he trailed his gaze past the path and toward a corpse of trees to our right, his chest moved up and down with heavy breaths.

Not bothering to look at me, Raiden stepped off the path and meandered into the dense foliage. His hand motioned me to follow. "Come with me."

I did as I was told, even though each step filled me with dread. For all I knew, Raiden was marching me to my death, and I called on my wolf to be ready. If I was about to walk into a trap, I wasn't going down easy.

We walked in silence, Raiden a few steps ahead of me and always facing forward. His shoulders slumped lower and lower as we moved deeper into the trees. I studied his back, trying to prepare myself for whatever came next.

When Raiden finally slowed to a stop, I caught up to him and peered over his wide back. We stood between five large trees and their thick branches intertwined over our heads. Beneath them, the ground looked fresher, as though it had been recently disturbed. Three flat rocks stacked one atop the other in the center, reminding me of a totem pole.

"What the hell is this?"

Raiden closed his eyes. "You wanted to see Damen. Well, here he is."

"I don't get it."

Peeling my eyes from Raiden, I looked to the rocks and

my stomach turned. No, this couldn't be what I thought it was. Damen was his cousin, he couldn't—

The thoughts tangled in my head, but one look at Raiden, and I knew it was true. I came here looking for Damen, and I got what I wanted. Damen was here, buried under those rocks.

"He's..." I choked. "Dead?"

Raiden nodded.

"Why? Why would you kill your own family?"

It was an odd thing to ask considering I very much wanted to kill the bastard myself, yet I couldn't imagine Raiden going through with it. Sure, his cousin was a prick, but he was still his blood. Raiden was loyal to a fault, and I knew whatever forced his hand in this could not have been pretty. "Raiden, what happened?"

"You were right. That's what happened."

I blinked fast to clear my spotty vision, so I could focus on his face. When I did, the knots in my stomach multiplied and the pain flowing off the lion shifter hit me in the face like a bat. "He took Billie?"

"No," Raiden said. "But he wouldn't hear reason. He hated her. I tried to make him understand there was no need for it, but he wouldn't listen."

"So, you killed him?"

"Not intentionally. After Billie disappeared, I came to see him. Mel and I kept him locked up in an abandoned factory on the east end of town ever since he attacked you two on those trails. When I questioned him about Billie's kidnapping, he insisted he knew nothing of it. So, I switched tactics."

"You tried to find out who else hated Billie enough to want her dead," I whispered.

Raiden's shoulders tensed, and he crouched next to the makeshift tombstone, letting a hand rest on the rocks. "He was so damn stubborn, ever since he was a kid. Stubborn and easily influenced. I thought if he told me who put him up to threatening you two, I could get to the bottom of it. But he didn't know. No matter how many times I attempted to beat it out of him."

The shifter sighed and my chest constricted. This was probably the hardest thing Raiden had to do, and he did it to help find Billie. He wasn't a traitor as I assumed. He was a friend. And I had put him in an impossible situation.

Fucking hell.

"What happened next?" I asked, though I didn't really want to know.

"Mel thought she could get to him, get him to trust her, or something. We came here intending to let him go once he talked, but it didn't work. He was so angry. I've never seen him act that way before. He always cared for Mel, respected her, even feared her a little. Not that day. That day he was all fight, and when he made a move for her, I snapped. I didn't want to hurt him. You have to believe me! I only wanted to know who he was acting with. But he kept coming for her, and family or not, Mel is all that matters."

My pulse raced and my ears popped. Everything around me stilled while I struggled to keep my attention on Raiden. This couldn't be it. Damen was my last shot at figuring out who took Billie, and if he was dead, I was lost.

I couldn't accept that.

"It's not your fault," I said, knowing my words meant little to him.

"That will never be true. Not for as long as I live."

Careful not to startle him, I inched toward the shifter

and placed a hand on his shoulder. "You tried to do what's right. If Damen didn't want to betray the cowards he was working with, that's on him."

"You don't get it," he hissed. "It wasn't that he didn't want to say anything, it's that he couldn't. He and his idiot friends didn't do this. Even when he was dying, all he kept saying was nonsense. The guy was innocent, and instead of believing him, I killed him. What kind of person does that make me?"

"The kind that takes care of everyone, despite how difficult the choices are sometimes," I said. "Wait, what kind of nonsense are we talking about here?"

Raiden looked at me over his shoulder. His bushy eyebrows kissed, and confusion settled behind the blues of his eyes. "I don't know. He kept talking about trees or something. None of it made any sense."

Frustration tore through me, and I scanned the wooded area around us. Why was Damen talking about trees? Shadowhurst was full of them and for him to latch onto that in his last breaths made little sense. Something bothered me, gnawing on my thoughts like a dog with a bone. Trees were important somehow.

But how?

My mind raced as I tried to recall anything that might be important enough to relate to Damen's last words. I thought of the forest surrounding the house where Billie was last seen, of the trails Damen and his friends attacked us on, even of the evergreen in my own front yard. Nothing clicked. About to give up, an image flashed before me, and I let my hand drop from Raiden's shoulder.

Holy shit... Trees...

"Where is Daria right now?" I asked Raiden, my teeth

grinding so hard, I could hear it cut the silence of the night around us.

"Not sure, why?"

"Trees, Raiden. Your cousin was trying to tell you who it was before he died but you couldn't see it."

He frowned, still clearly puzzled. "What are you talking about?"

"Daria's tree tattoo, the one she got after they broke up. It has to be her that took Billie, but why would Damen not tell you that in the first place? Unless they were in on it together."

Raiden's shoulder dropped as my words began to make sense. He slumped in a pile of muscle on the ground, digging his hands into the earth and shaking. "Crap!" he shouted, slamming a fist into the dirt. "He was protecting her. The idiot! Damen wouldn't go this far to hurt Billie, not after what happened last time and his best friends died. He must have known Daria was responsible and wouldn't tell me. He still loved her, River. I thought he was over it after all this time, but he wasn't. Damn it! Why would she do this? It makes no sense."

"I don't care why," I bit out. "We have to go. Now!"

Not waiting for him to get up, I pushed through the trees and back to the path that led to the quiet streets of Shadowhurst. My legs pumped as I ran, Raiden close on my tail. Chest burning, I rubbed a hand over my heart, feeling its thumps against my skin. *I'm coming, love. I'm almost there. Just hold on.*

Chapter Thirty-eight

Billie

'm almost there. Just hold on.

River's voice wafted through the air and forced me to open my eyes. My head pounded and the ground beneath me was uneven and cold. I pushed up on my elbows, daring to see where Daria's henchmen dumped me, and as I did, confusion settled in my heart.

I couldn't recognize where I was.

This wasn't the same spot they held me in for so many days. There were no abandoned water bottles, no tunnels to lead out. I couldn't even see the sickening stain of blood left from the bear shifter.

Wherever they brought me, it was entirely new.

"Pieces of shit!" I roared and worked to stand.

Before I could rise, the sole of a boot pressed into my back and pushed me down. My jaw hit the ground and a sharp pain rolled through me. I hissed, clawing at the ground but careful not to move again. Eyes close to the floor, I darted my gaze, landing on a pair of filthy boots near to me.

I wasn't alone.

"She's awake," a deep male voice said over me. "What do you want us to do with her?"

A scuffle sounded at my back, and soon, another pair of shoes were in my sightline. Anger permeated my senses. I'd recognize those disgusting red soles anywhere.

Daria groaned and walked the length of the perimeter. Her steps were light, though I could sense the indecision in them from where I lay. It seemed my escape did not factor in well with her plans, and I wondered if she was trying to decide what to do with me next. Daring to look around, I carefully lifted my head and peered over my shoulder.

The rocky surface of the walls told me I was still in the cavern, and I couldn't help but retch in my mouth. The bile burnt going down as I swallowed it, continuing to weigh my options while Daria paced back and forth in my peripheral vision.

It was darker here, so I knew they carried me deep into the cavern's lair, which would make sense. I doubt they wanted to risk having me that close to the exit. There was a small opening about ten feet away and nothing but deep black behind. As I focused my gaze on the distance, fear pounded at my chest.

The ground ended close to me, giving way to only darkness. It looked to be a pit of some sort and I knew that whatever lay beyond the horizon was going to be my doom if I didn't play this smart.

I glanced back at Daria's feet. "Where did you bring me?"

"Shut up, you bitch!" she howled, kicking a rock with her foot. It hit me straight in the forehead. I closed my eyes to shield them just in time. "Don't get any thoughts about trying to escape again." She crouched and pointed to the pit behind us. "There's only one way out of here for you."

I wanted to tell her to suck it but thought better of it.

Instead, I pressed my palms into the ground and prayed for the Goddess to let me connect to the stone. When nothing happened, I tried again.

"Having some trouble?" Daria bit out.

She reached into her back pocket and pulled something out, dropping it in front of my face. Shards of brilliant crystal bounced off the floor, and tears flooded my eyes when I realized what I was looking at. Daria stomped a red sole over my broken ring and laughed. "Not so clever without your little prop, are you?"

Dear Goddess, NO! Was she right? Was the ring the only reason I could connect to the elements before? If that was true, I was screwed beyond recognition.

Time ticked in my ears as I peered from the remnants of the ring to Daria. Her sneer widened and I gasped back sobs as the realization that I was stuck here hit me. I won't lie, it hit me freaking hard. My chest tightened and my neck tensed as sweat rolled off me, hitting the ground and soaking it in my putrid fear. The ring was the answer, and without it, I was as good as dead.

Sobbing, I tried to turn over, but whoever held me down pressed further on my back, flattening me out like a pancake. My hair fell in dirty tresses and obscured my vision. Panic flared, and I found it difficult to breathe.

Nononononono!

Chest burning, I reached into my torn shirt and rubbed the skin over my heart. My forehead banged against the stone, and I sobbed as I tried to calm down. Nothing worked. Everything I did so far, all the magic I was able to tap into, was pointless now. This was how I was going to die. I just knew it.

My pulse raced and the throbbing in my chest deepened. I looked down, eyes wide as beach balls as I watched thin black lines spread over my chest. They thumped a steady beat against my skin while growing over my heart and racing up my neck and stomach.

Just hold on.

The words came out of nowhere and I had to squeeze my eyes shut to keep my grasp on them. River's heady voice penetrated my mind and the burning ache amplified in my chest. Still rubbing at the lines, I looked back to the broken ring, grinding my teeth.

You are nothing but a piece of jewelry. A gift from a man I never knew. You don't define me.

I repeated the words over and over, each time forcing myself to believe them. Daria thought she could beat my magic out of me, that she could break the ring and break my spirit with it. She was so damn wrong.

I wasn't just a witch.

I was something else, something she should have feared. And if River was coming for me, I sure as hell was going to fight until he got here.

The boot on my back pressed down again, and I bit the inside of my cheek, struggling under the shifter's weight. My body shook, and when I slammed my fists into the stone, I didn't let doubt play me for a fool. Closing my eyes, I reached for the element of the earth around me, twisting my greedy fingers over its energy.

It was so weak, I feared I wouldn't be able to grasp it, but

I didn't let that stop me. Shadows swarmed over my arms, and I forced my shaking knees to buckle down. Little by little, I pushed up, fighting against the man that thought he could keep me still.

Somewhere near to me, Daria shouted, and I heard heavy footfalls rush my way. Before they could reach me, I gave one last push, shoving the shifter off my back and sending him flying away from me. My arms shot out and shadows swarmed from my fingers toward the surrounding walls. The cavern shook and I snapped my eyes open to face Daria.

It was impossible to see through the shadows, and I could barely make out the expression on her face. With calculated steps, I inched toward her, dragging the shadows alongside me and sending rocks to fall from the ceiling at her feet. She shrieked, avoiding the boulders that rained down upon her.

As I moved in on her, my lips curled upward and my fingers danced, pulling on every element I could latch on to. My gaze trained on Daria, and I shot my palms in front of me, imagining a strong wind wrapping around her waist.

Daria's face paled and she clawed at her stomach, slapping away my magic.

I laughed and curled my fingers one by one.

My arms vibrated as I raised them, and shock descended on me when I saw Daria's body follow. Her legs dangled under her, sneaker toes trailing the ground while she rose higher and higher in the air. The power of the magic I held scared me to death, but I didn't stop. Around me, the shadows went batshit crazy, twirling like a tornado through space.

Catching Daria's tear filled eyes, I threw my arms up and

slammed her body into the ceiling. The ring was a safety blanket. I knew that now.

When I let Daria's body go and watched it plummet to the ground again, I smiled.

"You messed with the wrong witch!" I roared seconds before lunging for her.

Chapter Thirty-nine

River

By the time I reached the Crystal Cauldron, I was a sweaty, breathless mess. Behind me, Raiden huffed and puffed like someone held him underwater and stomped on his chest for good measure. I couldn't blame him, we just ran across town without breaks, and despite both of us being in decent shape, I regretted not taking Savannah up on her offer to pick us up.

One of these days, I really had to stop acting like an idiot.

We burst through the frosted-glass door and the welcome bell screeched over our heads as we rushed to meet the others at the front counter. Something fell to the floor, and I looped around to see Raiden stand over shards of glass with a blue liquid surrounding them.

He hugged his arms in to avoid breaking anything else in the store, shrugging his shoulders in apology. The guy was freakishly large for the tight space, and under any other circumstances, I would have laughed. Raiden gave the term bull in a China shop a whole new meaning.

Shaking my head, I twirled around and rushed to the counter.

Ms. Broussard and Victoria stood side by side, their noses buried in a pile of books. On the opposite end, Logan, Savannah, and Mel were deep in conversation, but it was Peyton who ran up to meet me. Dark streaks of mascara ran down her face and her nose was so red, she looked like she'd been out in the cold for hours.

"Did you get a hold of her?"

"No one has seen Daria," she answered, "in a while."

"DAMN IT!" I yelled, slamming a fist into the counter. At the edge, a small jewelry stand shook and Logan caught it before it went flying off. "It was her! I know it! I don't know who she was working with or why her and her idiot friends got involved, but it's the only thing that makes sense."

"We believe you, River," Mel said. "Now, calm down and get over here. We found something."

Still fuming, I walked around to stand near Victoria and peered over her shoulder at the book in her hands. It was none other than the Book of Shadows. The way the witch stared at it gave me pause. I leaned in, drawing my gaze over the sketch that entranced her, and my heart dropped to my feet.

"Is that..." I whispered, unable to finish the sentence.

The sketch was rough, made in a hurry, but it was clear enough to make out the tiny figure with ease. I ran my eyes over the face of the child that glared back at me, absolutely baffled. The girl was about five years old, and judging by her stark face, she wasn't human. A bright glow was drawn over her eyes and her hair spread over her shoulders in thick waves. Behind her, tall cliffs rose to the sky, overlooking a shoreline.

"The kid that led Billie away," Peyton said, confirming my suspicions. "Morgan said this is her. No doubt about it."

"How is that possible?" I asked. "This book is ancient."

"Yeah, about that," Victoria interjected. "You know when I said I was going to look for Billie's fae family line in this thing? Well, I did, and we tracked down the Graves name to the original coven."

"That was the name Billie's family had before someone remarried and changed their name to Stonewall. You know, every time a woman does that, a small part of my soul dies."

"Not the time, Peyton," Ms. Broussard scolded.

"Ugh, fine, whatever. But it's still annoying."

I rubbed my eyes, trying not to yell at her. It was the most difficult thing I ever had to do.

Sensing my agitation, Victoria tapped the drawing to get my attention off Peyton. "As I was saying, I knew the fae thing had to lead us somewhere, but I seriously didn't expect it to be this. This is mind boggling. Like crazy weird shit."

My nostrils flared, urging her to get on with it.

"The witch that wrote this grimoire is Graves. It belongs to Billie's ancestor."

What in the sweet hell? My thoughts jumbled when I tried to put the pieces together. The grimoire was written by someone in Billie's family tree, but it still didn't explain the picture of the girl that dragged Billie away from the party being in the grimoire. The party that happened in our freaking century. None of this made any sense.

I ran a finger over the sketch, tracing the girl's brilliant eyes. "This is why Morgan thought it was a shifter. The eyes. But shifters didn't exist back then, right? Or am I missing something?"

"No, that's true," Mel said. "Our kind didn't come about until much later."

"So, who's the kid, then?"

"That's where it gets interesting," Victoria said. "I couldn't think of any creature that could live long enough to still be around today, except..."

Her voice trailed off, and she stared at the book like it was made of pure gold.

"Except who, Victoria?"

"Except for the fae."

My mouth snapped shut and my hands glued to the counter. "Say what now?"

"The fae. The girl in the picture, the girl Billie followed into the woods, has to be fae. It's the only explanation."

"How is that the only explanation?" I shouted. "Billie said the fae are not even real!"

"Everything is real," Logan whispered behind me. The tone in his voice gave me pause, and I wearily turned to look at the mind reaper.

"Care to explain?"

He shrugged. "Bloody hell, mate. You're in an occult shop in the middle of the night with a witch, a mind reaper, a soul sucker, and two shifters. Everything can be real, even the fae."

The guy had a point. Cocky prick.

"Okay, so if the fae are real, how come everyone acts like they're a fairy tale?"

"Exactly!" Victoria shot a finger into the air. "Why *is* everyone acting that way? That's what I kept thinking too. If the fae still exist today, you'd think the High Coven would be all over that. They're the reason we're even here today and their power is astronomical. Something like that would not go unnoticed by the high priestesses. Unless—"

"Unless they knew and kept it quiet," I finished for her.

"Bingo!"

I rubbed my neck, easing some tension that settled there. "If the high priestesses are keeping this information from the rest of you, there has to be a reason for it. More importantly, how does that help us find Billie?"

"See that?" Victoria pointed to the cliffs in the sketch. "After the witches separated from the fae, we were told they just disappeared, right? But I kept thinking, people don't simply vanish, at least not super powerful magical creatures. They had to go somewhere, and the only explanation was they went back to wherever they came from."

"...Okay."

"You're not following, are you?"

I looked around the rest of the group. "No. Is anyone?"

My friends exchanged a few glances, and I rolled my eyes. *I guess just me then.*

"The fae didn't appear from thin air the same way they didn't disappear into it. They must have a place where they are hiding out, a fae world, or something. I know it sounds crazy, but weirder shit has happened."

"Yep," Logan added, not helping at all.

Ignoring him, I focused on Victoria. "So, you think that's where Billie is? This fae world."

"Yes and no."

Very helpful. Stellar job, sister. "Then what? I'm getting whiplash listening to you."

"I think that wherever this world of theirs is, there has to be an entrance. A portal or something." She took a breath in and lowered her gaze to the sketch again. "When I realized that the grimoire belonged to Billie's family, I asked Ms. Broussard what she knew about the Graves family. I'm sure you already know this, but after the humans discovered the witches in this town, they banished them, at least before they tried to burn them all. Thanks for that, by the way. Anyway, the Graves family moved to Carriage Hill with the other witches. When I heard that, a lightbulb went off."

Beside her, Ms. Broussard patted Victoria's hand and cleared her throat. "If the fae existed, the witches would want to stay close to them. It was fae power that fueled their magic, after all."

"Yep, yep, yep," Victoria said, nodding. "So, with the witches being in Carriage Hill, it stands to reason they must have had a way to communicate with the fae there."

"The portal..." I whispered.

"It's in Carriage Hill. Right there in those cliffs, actually."

She tapped the book and my attention drifted to the shoreline beneath the rocky landscape. "The water. That's where the water I heard came from!"

"And he's back!" Savannah teased, avoiding the nasty look I shot her way. "The girl, the water, it's too coincidental. Plus, you said it was dark when you saw Billie wherever she was, right? These cliffs were condemned years ago because people kept getting lost in the caves and the town deemed it too dangerous for public use. Caves are dark."

"Holy. Shit. This is it! That's where she is!"

Tearing the book from the counter, I slammed it shut and tucked it under my arm. Inside, my wolf scraped at my heart and let out wild, desperate whimpers. *I know, buddy. I'm excited too.* My feet pummeled the floor as I ran past my friends and straight for the front door. Pulse racing, I burst into the night air and jerked my gaze from side to side.

"You're not gonna run all the way to Carriage Hill, are you?" Savannah said behind me.

Whirling on my heels, I turned to face her, eyes swaying to follow the key ring she dangled in front of me.

"Come on," my best friend said. "I'm parked down the street, we can be there in half an hour max. Let's go save our Rapunzel."

Chapter Forty

Billie

Daria cried out.

I laughed, throwing my hands up to blast her with another gust of wind. The current wrapped around her neck and I raised my arms to carry her with me. Watching Daria choke under my hold was both the best and worst thing I've ever felt. Days of torture and trauma, all by her hand, left me devoid of sympathy, yet something still ruffled in my heart's core as the blood drained from her sorry face.

This new magic, it scared me.

Shadows swarmed the cavern around us, and I flicked a finger, sending Daria flying to the opposite wall. Her shoulder bounced off the stone and she dropped with an agonizing shriek. My hair clumped around my face as I surrounded myself with the winds I was controlling, a smile spreading on my face.

Someone's hand wrapped over my throat to tug me back, and the hold I had on the magic dropped momentarily. My eyes bulged and muscles twitched in my jaw. Kicking my foot back, I crashed it into my attacker's knee and a loud pop sounded behind me.

I turned, watching the male shifter cradle his broken leg. Screaming.

His wails tore through me, and I cringed as his horrific bellowing surged on. Behind me, footsteps hurried across the ground. Spinning on my heels, I faced the remaining three of Daria's crew diving my way.

They moved fast, which didn't surprise me one bit. Shifters were notorious for their speed, and if I didn't act quickly, the bastards would be on me in seconds. Instinct kicked in and I reached for my dagger, forgetting that it wasn't there. The assholes thought they stripped me bare of my tools, but they didn't count on one thing. I was all the magic I needed.

My arms jerked upward and in one swift move, I brought the cavern's ceiling down upon us.

Dust exploded, stinging my eyes and making me drop to my knees. I buried my face in the crook of my shirt to cough out the debris that settled deep in my throat. Spit gathered in my mouth, and I sucked in a breath like a broken vacuum, sputtering with each gulp of air. When the dust cleared, I dared to look up.

A couch-sized boulder lay before me, crushing one shifter down his center. His eyes were milky, and trickles of blood spewed from his lips while he took his last breath.

I should have felt something. Remorse, disgust, anything but what I was feeling.

Pure, unadulterated contempt filled me, and I couldn't help but shake with joy as I watched the shifter's head loll to the side.

Despite my success in taking him down, victory was not

in sight. Behind the boulder, the other two shook off dirt and trained their burning eyes my way. Their teeth snapped and out of the corner of my eyes, I saw Daria limp to join them.

It's on, bitches!

Drawing in on the elements, I drove their power into me. My magic clasped hold over bursts of energy and I readied to throw another hit at the shifters that wanted me dead. Before I could strike, seven shadowy figures rushed into the cavern.

My eyes blinked fast, and my vision betrayed me. The scene unfolded like a black and white film, shivering as each frame passed.

Are they real? My pulse jackhammered and my attention split between the shifters and the people tearing into the cavern. My friends. Raiden and Mel led the way, shifting into their animal forms mid-stride. Their massive paws hit the ground and their growls filled the cavern with thundering blows. Behind them, Savannah emerged with a mind reaper I vaguely recognized at her side. The hunter's hair was tied into a tight top bun, and she held two curved knives in each of her hands. Her eyes met mine and I breathed out in relief. I never thought I'd see the day when I'd be glad to see Savannah Michaels, but here we were.

I couldn't be freaking happier.

When Peyton walked through the small entrance, I nearly dropped to my knees.

My best friend scanned the cavern, spotting me instantly, and her widening smile brought tears to my eyes. She winked, stepping aside to let the last person enter, and my entire body vibrated with excitement.

River was a sight for sore eyes. His disheveled hair fell in oily locks over his forehead, and he looked slimmer than I remembered, as though he hasn't eaten in days. Sweat covered his blue shirt and beaded off his neck and down his heaving chest. My gaze traveled over him, landing on the glowing green eyes that locked me in place. Peridot. Shifter eyes.

"Billie!" he screamed, pushing past our friends to run toward me.

Not waiting, I broke into a dead sprint to meet him halfway, blasting shadows into Daria and her shifters as I ran. One by one, my magic hit them, pushing them against the rocky wall to my right. My legs pumped and I leaped into River's open arms without a second thought.

Our bodies collided. His fingers clawed at my skin, pulling through my hair and down my back. River's gaze was wild as he inspected me from head to toe, his face darkening with each bruise that caught his attention. He cupped my cheeks, pulling me away from him to scan every inch of my face like he couldn't believe I was real.

I felt much the same.

"You—" I choked out, "I can't believe you're here."

River brushed the matted tresses off my face. "You're okay," he said breathlessly. "You're okay. You're okay."

Tears I could no longer hold back fell down my face and neck in waterfalls. My knees buckled and I fell into him, his solid chest breaking my fall. Rubbing my cheek against the stumble on his face, I hugged him closer, pressing his body against me until every beat of his speeding heart bounced off my skin. "I'm fine," I whispered into his hair.

A gust of air breezed by us, and we both pivoted to see the glistening silver of a rune-covered dagger fly by. Agony-filled screams sounded, and I turned to see the hilt of the dagger protruding from a shifter's chest. My eyes widened, looking past River's shoulders to a face I didn't believe I'd see again.

"Maybe save that for later!" Victoria shouted, fire blazing in the palm of her hands. "Still got work to do here."

The shock of seeing Vic in the cavern slowly wore off and I wavered in River's arms. Hesitantly, I pulled away from him and turned to Daria. "Didn't factor them in, did you?"

She scowled and rounded the boulder to near us, the last two shifters at her sides.

"You'll die for what you did to her!" River yelled.

Behind him, roars enveloped me as Raiden and Mel leaped to flank us. Their vengeful eyes brightened the cavern, and I could see alarm spread over Daria. Shaking it off, she dropped to all fours, shedding her human form. Next to her, the males followed suit and in mere moments, three ragged foxes stood in their place.

The idiots still thought they stood a chance.

They didn't.

Raiden and Mel readied to attack, but I held a hand up to stop them. My chest puffed out and my legs stood ramrod straight as I raised my hands, cocking my head to the side to give the bastards one last chance to back out.

When they didn't, I summoned my magic and let it engulf me.

This time, I had no hesitation, and when I reached for the elemental power around me, I didn't feel the need to fight against it. This was who I had become, whoever it was. I was the energy that filled this cavern, and I was stronger than anyone could have known. Stronger than Beatrix, stronger than the coven, stronger than my own damn self. I was magic and I was anger. More than that, I was finally me.

In the distance, I thought I saw a shadow move but chose to ignore it.

A shoulder brushed against mine, and I peeled my gaze off Daria's trembling form to look at River. The features on his face spoke words I didn't understand. "Babe, your eyes..."

Puzzled, I brought my hands to my face as one would a mirror. My jaw slacked and as my eyes grew wider. A gasp crept to the surface. My hands were flashing a brilliant white. Reflecting the lantern-like light my eyes projected.

Chapter Forty-one

Billie

The larger of the three foxes made a move and I threw my arm out, picking up a rock from the ground to catapult its way. It hit the fox in the side, chucking its filthy body aside. Whimpering, the fox scrambled and rebound quickly.

"Well, this is new," River said at my side.

Our other friends whipped their heads my way and froze me solid. I gulped. "Lots of things are new, it seems."

Before I could explain, the foxes rounded on us, and heated breath burst from their ugly mouths as they galloped forward. Savannah's knives tore the air, missing the beasts by inches. She cursed under her breath and motioned for the mind reaper to join her. I really needed to remember what his name was, but now was not the time for that. The two of them charged for the shifters, not a care in the world. The foxes were quick, bounding off the ground while leaping around my friends and landing closer to the deathly pit that spread behind them.

"Watch out!" I yelled, staring in horror as Savannah skidded to a stop just at the edge.

My friend's feet tripped over a loose rock, and she went flying, right into the pit. I screamed and heard Peyton follow suit. To my relief, the mind reaper threw an arm out around Savannah's stomach and pulled her back before she could plummet to her death.

That was the first time I saw Savannah Michaels fumble.

Blood drained from her face, and she clutched the reaper's arm with every polished nail digging in. I could see him grimace from the pain, but he let her continue, tugging her lightly away from the edge. Behind them, the foxes closed in.

"Raiden! Mel! They're trying to push them over!" I yelled.

The lion and lioness jumped into action, and as they neared the foxes, I forced a strong wind to shove Daria and her beasts out of the way. Their paws scurried over the rocky ground, and they clawed to fight against my current. Teeth snapping, they growled and hissed, but I kept them away long enough for Raiden and Mel to get there. My friends took on a fox each, pinning them down with enormous paws.

When the lions exposed large teeth and sunk them into their furs, I didn't look away.

Cries ripped through the cavern and death soon followed.

I cringed before turning my focus to the last one standing. Daria. My anger knew no bounds, and I pulled on every inch of my magic, planting my feet into the ground and readying to end the bitch that brought me so much pain and suffering. My fingers spread as I pulled on the energy that built up in me and my lighthouse eyes brightened to lead the way.

A sturdy hand gripped my shoulder, twisting me sideways.

"She's mine," River hissed.

I wanted to fight him on this, mostly because I knew he didn't stand a chance against Daria. She may have been smaller than him in her current form, but I remembered how well Daria could fight. She was going to tear River into pieces if he didn't let me finish her off.

Before I could argue, River crouched at my feet and a sound I never wanted to hear again filled my ears. His body contorted and bones snapped and cracked as he arched his back, letting a loud howl tear from his throat. River's clothes ripped to shreds, falling to the ground in pieces while my jaw hit the floor. "Holy mother of..."

Baffled, I watched as River—my River—shifted before my eyes. Taut, inhuman muscle bulged through his skin, and gray fur sprouted from every inch of him. His mouth shot outward, forming into a long snout. When he curled one side of his lips, sharp fang-like canines dripping with saliva protruded.

Lots and lots and lots of things are new.

The wolf shook his fur next to me and cast a longing glance in my direction. Even in this state, I knew it was River. I could feel his heart beating in my own chest. *This is insane.*

River pushed back on his hind legs and cleared the air. His fur ruffled as he barreled to Daria, landing a foot in front of her. The vapid fox had the nerve not to back down and instead, pulled a lip back to match his sneer. I had only a chance to blink once before River lunged for her. Massive talons protruded from his paws, and he dug them into her side, forcing her to the ground. Daria twisted under his weight, but he kept her steady, arching his snout to the ceiling and letting out a bellowing howl.

Goddess, he's beautiful.

I wanted to run my fingers through his fur and almost inched toward them. *What the hell are you doing, moron? Don't touch the angry wolf. This isn't a petting zoo.*

River's mouth flung open and he brought his sharp teeth to Daria's neck. This time, I looked down. Somehow, I knew that seeing River tear the fox apart was not something I could unsee, and as much as I wanted to watch Daria suffer, I couldn't draw myself to raise my head. Growls and whimpers blasted toward me. I pressed my hands to my ears to block the sounds. Someone's thin arms wrapped around my shoulders, turning me away from the killing.

As Peyton held me buried in her chest, a mixture of joy and regret flooded my system and I breathed against her while River finished the job. Bones cracked, and when the cavern was silent again, I dared myself to look up.

Slowly, my vision regained focus and I was staring at a very naked River leaning over Daria's frail, blood-covered body. Her chest rose and I fought back nausea when I realized she was still alive. Breaking free of Peyton's hold, I ran to them.

My fingers wrapped around River's, and I tried not to think of all his parts hanging out for the world to see. We were seriously going to need to talk about shifter etiquette when we got out of here.

Daria gasped in air, and I choked back a sob. "This is torture, we have to finish it."

She deserved to be left here to die, but I couldn't let

myself do that. No matter what Daria put me through, I would not be like her. If we didn't ease her pain, I would never survive the guilt. Kneeling beside her, I rested a hand on her shoulder, the only part not covered in blood.

"You deserve so much worse than this, I hope you know that."

To my shock, she forced a weak smile. "They're not done with you," she breathed out, blood dripping from her lips as each word formed. "This was just the beginning."

What the heck?

"Who? Who told you to bring me here?" I shouted. I gripped her other shoulder and shook her violently.

Daria's eyes rolled back, and her head slumped.

"WHO?" I roared.

With one last breath, Daria raised her head and looked at me. "The fae. They're coming for you. You will never escape them."

Chapter Forty-two

Billie

"You ready for tomorrow?"

River rearranged his arm under his head and spun to lie facing me. We had spent the last twenty-four hours in my room, coming out only once to welcome the Chandlers home from their trip. Pretending that everything was normal was a tougher task than I imagined considering that I spent the last week trapped and tortured in a dirty magical cavern getting ready to die. Luckily, my newly discovered fast healing took care of all the bruises and wounds, so I at least looked like I had a good break while Thomas and Imala were away.

How I felt was a stark opposite to my appearance.

"You mean school?" I asked, running a finger across his arm. "After this week, I think I can handle algebra classes like a champ."

"You clearly haven't met Mr. Hollows, your dictator math teacher," River joked.

I tried to laugh, but nothing came out.

"Hey," he whispered, tipping my head to face him. "It's going to be fine. I promise."

"Yeah, I don't know if that's true, but sure. Fine. Totally fine."

River flashed a row of teeth—his human teeth—and leaned over, pressing his lips to my forehead. His warm breath flowed over my skin, sending familiar shivers down the back of my legs, and I relaxed into him. After everything, it was amazing to know the time I spent in the cavern hadn't killed my mojo. One small win for team Billie. I was a damn mess.

"I still can't believe Daria did all that," River said. "And that we couldn't figure it out for so long."

Smiling, I ran my fingers through his messy hair. "Don't be too hard on yourself. She was a tricky bitch, even I trusted her before all this happened. Mostly, I just feel bad for Raiden. That stuff with Damen was dark. I hope he's handling it okay."

"Yeah," River whispered. "I guess Daria had everyone fooled except Damen. It sucks he was still hung up on her or we would have figured it all out earlier."

"Love makes you do crazy things. Even protect someone when they're making the worst decisions. Damen cared about her. It wasn't his fault. If I was in his situation, I don't think I would have handled things differently. Not making excuses for him, but you know, I kind of get it." My hand pressed to River's chest, feeling for the thumping of his heart. "So, how does it feel to be a big bad wolf?"

He cringed.

"That awful, huh?"

"Not awful, just weird. I'm still not sure how I feel about it, but I have to admit, I'm getting used to living with the annoying bastard inside me. It's like having a younger brother, but furry. And really angry all the time." He swallowed hard. "It's weird, I guess."

"It'll take time," I said. "Raiden and Mel said you're handling it well and that the other wolves are coming around. That's a big step."

"I don't think I'll ever want to be around those guys, but sure, it's a step."

"Come on!" I exclaimed, punching his shoulder. "You're telling me you have no interest in being the alpha of a bunch of scary-looking wolves with attitude problems? That's right up your alley!"

He let out a chuckled and turned to lie on his back. His chest rose with heavy breaths, and I rolled over to rest my head atop it, tracing idle circles over his bare bronze skin. "You've had plenty of practice handling Savannah, so I'm sure the wolves won't be an issue."

"HA!" River bellowed. "She was pretty cool throughout this week, you know. Helped me keep my shit together. I was a disaster."

His words broke my heart and I blinked away the tears that threatened to fall. River and I were back together and that should have made me happy. Still, thinking about everything that took place in the cavern, all the lies those damn visions showed me, I couldn't help but be back in that place every time we spoke of it. I knew it would take time to heal, for both of us, but Goddess how I wished to forget the entire ordeal already.

"I'm sorry you had to go through that alone," I whispered into his chest.

"I wasn't alone," he said. "But not having you there was awful. That first shift, I thought I was going to die. And when I realized you were gone, well, let's just say, other people thought they were going to die too. I was out of control. Billie, if I lost you..."

His words trailed off and darkness gathered in his green eyes. "You didn't lose me. I'm right here," I insisted. "The whole time I was in that place, I knew you'd come for me. Even when the cavern told me otherwise, I could feel you somehow."

"Yeah, about that..."

He turned over again, sliding me off him so our eyes could meet. "We still haven't talked about the lines we both saw on our chests and what they could mean."

"We'll figure it out," I said. "I know what we both want it to mean, but at this point, I have no clue what's going on with my body. Those lines could be anything."

"So, you don't care if it's not the mate bond?"

The hurt on his face was so intense, I wanted to hug the stupid idiot until he got over it. Placing my hand on his cheek, I rubbed my thumb over his bottom lip. "Of course, that's what I want it to be. All I'm saying is that even if it isn't, I don't need a mate bond to tell me what to feel. Almost dying in that cavern taught what's important and you, hunter, are it."

"I don't think we can call me that anymore."

"Then what are we going with here? Fuzzball? Oh! How about White Fang? That's a good one!"

River pushed me over, laughing. "No nicknames. I'm putting my foot down."

My eyebrow arched and I bit my lower lip, curling myself into him. The air between us heated and when I wrapped my leg around his waist, River pulled me tighter. His lips brushed mine and I closed my eyes, reveling in being close to him again. After so much time away, nothing felt as good as this. When River pulled away from me, I almost growled in frustration. Correction, that was exactly what I did. It wasn't my finest moment.

"As much as I want to stay here forever," he said, rising off the bed. "If we don't get down to Peyton's place soon, she's going to kill me for monopolizing your time."

Rolling my eyes, I straightened my shirt and followed him out the door. Now that I was back, River and I had all the time in the world. At least I hoped we did.

We barely made it to the Ling's front door when Peyton hopped on me like a freaking monkey. Her leather jacket clung to my skin and the red streaks of her hair covered my entire face. I blew them off, giggling while I twirled my tiny friend around like a hula hoop. Laughing, Peyton crawled off when we came to a stop and punched a hard fist into my shoulder.

"Don't ever do that again! I'll kill you myself, B! I meant it!"

I shook my head. "Wasn't really my choice, but okay."

"Come on, everyone's in the backyard. They're dying to see you again."

Peyton led us around the house to her insanely big backyard. Despite the cool weather, there were a few people in the pool, though it didn't surprise me to see Raiden and Mel swimming. The two splashed water at each other, laughing hysterically when one of them got drenched. When they saw me, they rushed to jump out and flew in my direction. If I thought having Peyton on me was bad, having two wet, half-naked shifters took the cake.

"Ew! Gross, guys!" I shrieked and brushed water from my hair. "Towel off before you do that to someone."

"It's good to have you back," Mel said, nodding appreciatively. "Wasn't the same without you."

Raiden ruffled a humongous hand in my hair while I frowned. "Glad you didn't die. We need you here to deal with this one." He pointed a thumb over his shoulder at River and wiggled his bushy eyebrows. "He's a pain in the ass, I don't know how you do it."

"He has his moments," I teased.

When the shifters backed away from my personal space, I got a chance to scan the other people in the yard. All of our friends gathered at the long deck table and every set of eyes was on me. Savannah peered from around the mind reaper, Logan, that helped save me and waved us over. On her other side, Tyler, Abigail, and Jayden grinned from ear to ear as we neared, each one screaming at the top of their lungs when I approached.

Cheers and excited chatter broke out around the table, and questions fired off my way. I had half the mind to turn tail and get the heck out of there, but River's chest against my back kept me locked in place. It was as if he knew I would bolt the second all the attention was on me. Clever bastard.

My gaze traveled past the hunters to Ms. Broussard whose warm smile relaxed my nerves, but it was Victoria's inky glare that caught my attention most and I held her gaze for a few long moments before daring to breathe again. I still couldn't believe Vic switched sides for me. It was such a badass move that I wished I was there to see Sebyl's face when it happened. It must have been epic. From what River told me, she saved the entire resistance from the witches, and I loved my friend for having the guts to do that. Giving the High Coven the middle finger was not easy to do, something I was familiar with, and I would forever be grateful to Vic for going through with it.

"Hey, fae princess," Vic said. "How's it hanging?"

I knew she was only teasing, but I still winced at the joke. So much has transpired in the cavern, and it only raised more questions that I didn't have answers to. We still had no idea how I could control elements without the use of magical items and if my fae background had anything to do with it. If it did, it scared me half to death, and I dreaded the day we got to find out what it could all mean. Vic's revelation that she believed the fae were real and still very much alive today didn't help matters one bit. Not to mention that if she was right, then what Daria said before she died could be true.

The fae wanted something from me, and I kept thinking a lot of it had to do with what the shadow man said in the cavern. Could that freak seriously be my father? I didn't know, and I had no desire to find out.

Vic, on the other hand, was insatiable.

Finding out that the witch who wrote the Book of Darkness was a long-lost ancestor of mine lit a fire under her ass like I've never seen before. She was gung-ho on finding out everything she could on my fae background, and while I understood her motive, it still made the hair on my neck stand at attention.

The more I uncovered about my sordid family past, the more I craved to hide under a rock and never come out. *Thanks a lot, Beatrix. Way to screw me up for good with all your lies.*

It seemed everywhere I turned, someone was gunning for me, and I was growing tired of constantly looking over my shoulder. The High Coven would not let any of this slide, and Vic was sure they would come for us sooner rather than later. The fae were possibly hiding out somewhere, and they too wanted a piece of me. To top it all off, I still had no idea why they wanted the Book of Darkness in the first place. Something was in there that was important to them, something the witches knew that they didn't, and it drove me wild not knowing what it could be.

I loved Shadowhurst, yet a part of me wished I never came here. Granted, one look at River, and I knew how foolish that thought was.

Whatever danger loomed in the shadows, we were going to get through it. Together. River, me, and all the people at this table. All of my friends.

I looked at their cheerful faces, scanning each one so intently I could draw them with my eyes closed. These were my people, my family, and we would continue to kick ass for as long as we all breathed. My eyes narrowed as I studied the group, realizing someone was missing.

"Hey, guys?" I asked, looking around. "Where's Morgan?"

Behind me, River's shoulders tensed, and a questioning eyebrow met me when I turned to look at him. He stared at me like I had grown a second head, his mouth opening and closing without a sound.

"Seriously, where is she?" I asked again.

"Uh, B?" Peyton asked, concern in her voice. "Who's Morgan?"

My head shot from one person to the next, registering the same confusion on their faces. Abigail and Tyler exchanged awkward looks, and Jayden shrugged in my direction. Even Savannah seemed troubled, which was a huge first for her.

Knots formed in my stomach and my breath quickened as shock ran through my system.

For the love of the Goddess, what was Shadowhurst up to now?

What is Shadowhurst up to this time? People are disappearing and Billie Stonewall is the only one that still remembers them. Not to mention, with her magic acting up, the group is in for a whirlwind of danger. Will Billie be able to save everyone before she forgets them too? Find out in Book Four of the Shadowhurst Mysteries: **Town of Illusions**. CLICK HERE to read **Town of Illusions** now!

You can also check out the cover and description for the Town of Illusions below.

People I love are vanishing one by one... and so are my memories of them.

Every day here at Shadowhurst is a dream, but not the kind you think.

In this Goddess-forsaken town, things come to die. But as the only one who can remember those who've disappeared, I should do something. That would be a lot easier if my magic wasn't on the fritz.

If I don't at least try, it will be bye-bye for everyone in Shadowhurst.

With absolutely no plan and more fear than I'll ever admit to having, I'm diving in the deep end. Hold on tight, it's going to be a bumpy ride...

CLICK HERE to start reading the **Town of Illusions** now!

Haven't read the beginning of the story and wondering what's going on? **Witch of Shadows** will catch you right up! Read the first book of the Shadowhurst Mysteries here:

READ THE BOOK NOW!

Interested in finding out what happened to Beatrix Stonewall? Read the prequel novella Coven of Deception for FREE!

READ COVEN OF DECEPTION

Magic is real and it's coming for you.
Did you know all those fairytales you heard as a kid

about witches weren't fairytales at all? Well, neither did I. Imagine my surprise when I found out that not only did I possess magic, but that an entire secret coven of witches lurked right under my nose my whole life.

When my powers first manifested, I wanted nothing to do with them, but as I discovered more of the women welcoming me into their fold, I couldn't get enough! Unfortunately, life has a tendency of knowing when you're happy and jumps at the chance to throw a wrench in all your plans.

That's exactly what happened to me. One minute I'm starting a new life and minding my own business, and the next, I'm barreling face first into trouble. Oh, did I mention the mysterious, alluring stranger that won't leave me alone no matter how much I push him away?

So, yeah. I think it's safe to say I'm in for quite the ride. Care to join me?

Just kidding. Stay away if you know what's good for you.

Start reading Coven of Deception by CLICKING HERE.

ACKNOWLEDGMENTS

Another book in the Shadowhurst Mysteries is finished and I simply cannot believe it. This series is beginning to have a life of its own and I couldn't be happier to follow the rabbit hole it leads me on. If you're new to this series, you might want to hang on, there are twists aplenty coming up!

Thank you to everyone in my family and friend circle that helped me keep going when I hit blocks. Brainstorming with you is always the most brilliant time, and I am so grateful to have you all in my life.

As always, a huge and tremendous thank you to my beta readers and critique partners. Giving your book baby away to be judged is a scary thing but your advice has made this book so much better! Thank you!

And of course, the biggest thanks of all goes out to you, my reader. Without you, this series would not have existed, and I hope to make you proud with this book and the next to come. I am truly blessed to have you in my life.

Stay magical!

ABOUT THE AUTHOR

A.N. Sage has spent most of her life waiting to meet a witch, vampire, or at least get haunted by a ghost. In between failed seances and many questionable outfit choices, she has developed a keen eye for the extra-ordinary.

Since chasing the supernatural does not pay the bills, she dabbled in creative entrepreneurship, marketing and retail management. A.N. spends her free time reading and binge-watching television shows in her pajamas.

Currently, she resides in Toronto, Canada with her husband who is not a creature of the night.

A.N. Sage is a Scorpio and a massive advocate of leggings for pants.

For more books and updates:

www.ansage.ca

Connect on social media:

Facebook Group:

facebook.com/groups/945090619339423/

Instagram:

instagram.com/a.n.sage/

Twitter:

twitter.com/ANsageWrites

Facebook:

facebook.com/ansagewrites

Pinterest:

pinterest.ca/ansagewrites

Goodreads:

goodreads.com/author/show/18901100.Alexis_N_Sage

Amazon:

amazon.com/author/a.n.sage

www.ingramcontent.com/pod-product-compliance
Lightning Source LLC
Chambersburg PA
CBHW020910060726

47591CB00004B/1174